Mel Bay Presents

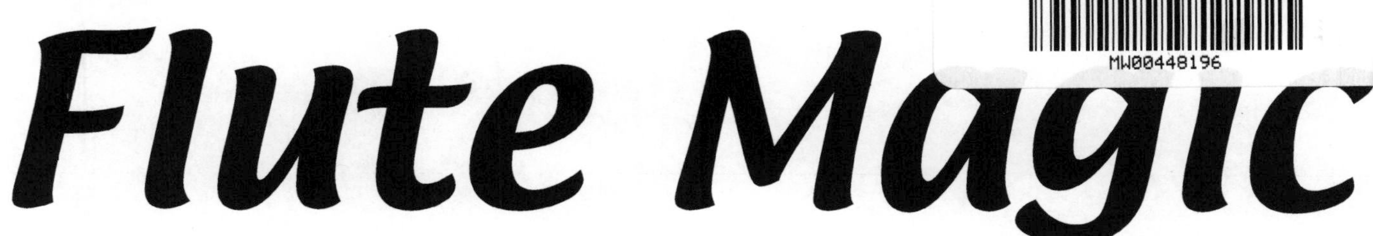

Flute Magic

An Introduction to the Native American Flute

Third Edition

by Tim R. Crawford

with Dr. Kathleen Joyce-Grendahl, Editor

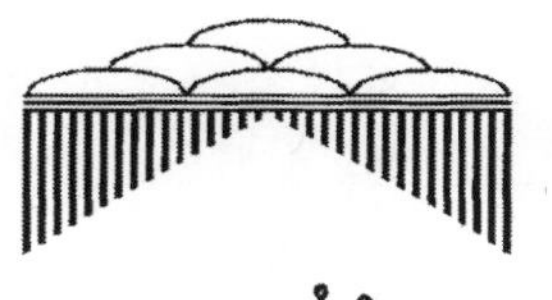

RainDance Publications™
Suffolk ~ Virginia

2 3 4 5 6 7 8 9 0

Visit us on the Web at www.melbay.com — E-mail us at email@melbay.com

Third Edition

Book Design, Text, and Graphics by Dr. Kathleen Joyce-Grendahl
Text and Music by Tim R. Crawford

Manufactured in the United States of America

Library of Congress Control Number: 2003091186

Table of Contents

Introduction 1
Origins, Designs, and Decoration 3
Playing the Native American Flute 19
Flute Care 29
Elementary Music Fundamentals 35
Instrument Key 43
Native Flute Construction Based Upon Body Measurements 47
TABlature for Trained Musicians 49
TABlature for Non-Trained Musicians 53
Introduction to the TABlature Exercises: Five-Hole Flute 61
Introduction to the TABlature Exercises: Six-Hole Flute 79
Early Flute Music of the Indigenous Peoples 97
About the Music 107
Note to Educators 108
Additional TABlature and Finger Chart Sources 110
References 111
Additional Resources 115
Music for the Four-Hole Native American Flute (TAB) 118
Music for the Five-Hole Native American Flute (TAB) 122
Music for the Six-Hole Native American Flute (TAB) 136
Song Writing 171
Appendix A: Bull Roarers 173
Appendix B: Eagle Bone Whistle TAB and Information 175
Appendix C: Music, Healing, Wellness and the Native American Flute 177
Appendix D: Using the Native American Flute to Imitate a Loon's Call 179
Appendix E: Organizations for the Native American Flute 181
Appendix F: Building Your Own Native American Flute 186
Appendix G: Flute Builders 187
Appendix H: Early Windway Design of the Native American Flute 195

Introduction

The single greatest beauty and enduring quality of this lovely instrument is that an individual really does not need to know anything technical about music, nor does he or she require sheet music or lessons to learn to play the Native American flute. All that one really needs to do in order to learn the Native American flute is to venture out in nature, find a stump, sit down, and then blow through the pointy end. That is the real magic of this musical instrument!

> "As a flute maker, I've watched the evolution of the interest in the Native American flute among non-Indian people. At first, most of the people who were attracted to the Native American flute were people who had no previous musical background or who had bad past musical experiences. The haunting sound of the flute intrigued and attracted them. Many had been inhibited by the idea that only 'musicians' could perform and play musical instruments and who also felt that they were not capable of learning to play one themselves.
>
> Now, my grandfather knew that everyone had music in them and that they just needed a way to express it. He knew it was a need as important as the need for the warmth of another human fire. So, these people who couldn't get away from the sound of the flute would set aside their fears and give it a try. All I do with these people is spend a little time with them, showing them the basic scale and giving them a few tips about breath control. Then, I turn them loose and watch the amazement on their faces as they make their own music for the first time.
>
> It is always an absolutely incredible joy for me to see a need fulfill itself. These people did not know what notes they were playing. I'm sure that they weren't concerned about whether or not they were playing in a minor scale or a major scale. It seemed to be just a joy for them to hear themselves making the music that they did not believe themselves able to create. Being able to see this is one of my motivations to make flutes."
>
> ~ Hawk LittleJohn [Cherokee] ~

This book has two central purposes: [1] to serve as an introductory text for beginning Native American flute players and to aid in the learning of necessary techniques that will enable the flutist to explore the capability of the instrument, as well as learning a TABlature system through simple lesson exercises combined with some old traditional songs, and [2] to present both intermediate and advanced students of the Native American flute with a variety of music for both the four-hole [limited], five-hole, and six-hole Native American flute, as presented in TABlature form, together with the "tools" necessary to learn and understand the TABlature system.

While intermediate and advanced students might choose to skip the chapter on playing the Native American flute, it is imperative that the chapters discussing key, TABlature, and TABlature exercises be examined carefully. Beginning students may prefer to go directly to the chapter on playing the Native American flute before attempting to digest the other information.

This book is not intended to be a primer on the technicalities involved in reading sheet music; there are other texts better suited for this purpose and I encourage the purchase of such items from a local music or book store. Regardless, I feel that what is presented here will enable the beginning music-reading student to master the TABlature system and the music contained within this book.

While the two central purpose of this book remains, for the most part, unchanged from previous editions, it should be noted that there is a significant addition of textual material in the third edition. This new edition will benefit any reader who has an interest in the Native American flute and its history, regardless of whether or not the desire to learn to read music or the TABlature system is present.

From an old German opera house comes the following:

"BACH gave us God's word,
MOZART gave us God's laughter,
BEETHOVEN gave us God's fire,
GOD gave us MUSIC that we might pray without words."

~ Author Unknown ~

I believe that Mother Earth gave us a gift of the ideal instrument to make that music - the Native American flute. There exists a connectivity between ourselves and our Mother Earth. Unfortunately, few among us ever have the opportunity to truly experience this emotional and energized communication. The link is there, simply waiting. If an individual believes, and if he or she will allow, it will reveal itself. I hope that some part of my music will enable that connection to develop. It is truly a wondrous experience. At the very least, I hope that this text and sheet music will provide you, the flutist, with enough stimulation to create your own music.

The radiance of one flute
shines healing warmth
upon the hearts and souls of many.

The songs from one flute
caress the inner minds and bodies
of all Nations.

The melodic prisms from one flute
pour forth in abundance,
inebriating those who are thirsty
for the life-giving drink of harmony.

~ Dr. Kathleen Joyce-Grendahl ~

Play and the music will come!

~ Tim "WindWalker" Crawford ~

Origins, Designs, and Decoration

Origins

The origins of the Native American flute are currently lost to the past, as is much of the rest of the world's antiquity. The indigenous peoples of North America did not maintain written chronicles of their music practices, as far as is known. However, they did bequeath to us the knowledge of several intact prehistoric flutes, as well as some historical documentation about them, through the use of images carved into or painted upon rocks [petroglyphs and pictographs], as did many other ancient peoples in various parts of the world. Examples of rock art are particularly predominant in the southwestern United States.

Rock art discovered in the American Southwest, dating from around 500 A.D., shows an individual playing what appears to be a vertically-held flute. It is believed that these images were created by the Anasazi whose culture encompassed the four-corner area of Utah, Colorado, Arizona, and New Mexico. Rock art dating from around 1,000 A.D. and on depicts the flute player as being somewhat of a humpbacked individual. The Hopi name for this "second" generation flute player is Kokopelli, a name that is generally used to describe all of the rock art images of flute players throughout the southwestern United States (Slifer and Duffield).

In 1931, five whole prehistoric flutes were discovered in Broken Flute Cave in the Prayer Rock District of northeastern Arizona - present-day Apache country (Morris, 1980). These Anasazi flutes have been dated to 620-630 A.D. and are the oldest intact flutes ever discovered. These flutes are currently on display at the Arizona State Museum [University of Arizona] in Tucson.

History for Native Americans was, and still is to a large extent, dependent upon the oral transmission of events from generation to generation. While this oral tradition appears to have enriched us all, with a number of legends and mythological depictions regarding the origins of the flute, it has not apparently been beneficial in recording much in the way of actual "historical" references. An exception manifests in that it has been noted that the flute was used as a courting instrument in some cultures, as well as a ceremonial instrument in other Native American communities. Additionally, as far as I am aware, there is no definitive text that discusses musical instruments utilized in the Americas, so research is limited to basically incidental references from the journals of early travelers, as well as short discourses in various texts on either indigenous peoples of the Americas and/or musical instruments.

Several early ethnomusicologists, such as Frances Densmore [1867-1957] and Natalie Curtis [1875-1921], spent time among various tribal cultures gathering and recording information about their music and their musical instruments. Curtis' *The Indians' Book* [1968], comprised of 584 pages and originally published in 1907, covers the music and musical instruments of some 14 various cultures; yet, this book's index lists only a few short references to the flute, with information totaling only a few paragraphs.

Frances Densmore produced the largest body of written and recorded information about the music and musical instruments of many different tribal cultures. My personal collection of 16 separate publications by her, which is not a complete collection, references more than 18 different tribal cultures that she studied. Yet, like the Curtis publication, the Densmore publications' references to the Native American flute are somewhat limited. For example, two volumes devoted to Chippewa music, totaling 556 pages, published in 1910 [volume 1] and 1913 [volume 2] contain only three short references to the Native American flute.

The lack of discussion of the flute in ethnomusicological and anthropological research either suggests that the instrument was never ubiquitous or possibly that the use of the instrument in many tribal cultures had undergone a substantial decline, which is certainly within the realm of possibility given the trauma of the many uprootings and changes being forced upon these cultures through the reservation system and its forced relocations.

Francis Densmore, who spent time with the Seminole people from 1931 through 1933, commented:

> "The use of a flute among the Seminole is traditional, but difficulty was experienced in finding anyone who remembered it definitely. Jim Gopher, a Cow Creek Seminole living near Dania, remembered hearing a flute but could not make one... Concerning the use of a flute by the Seminole, Bartram says [that] 'on this instrument they perform badly, and at best it is rather a hideous melancholy discord than harmony. It is only young fellows who amuse themselves on this howling instrument' [Bartram, 1793, pp. 502-503]. This observation by a man who heard the instrument played at an early day is exceedingly valuable. It would probably be impossible to find any Seminole at present who could play the cane flute." (Densmore, 1956)

In fact, when Natalie Curtis began her research of the indigenous peoples of the United States [circa 1900], the residents of the various reservations were strictly forbidden from the practice or the use of their culture's music within any government schools. She states that "on one reservation she was warned by a friendly scientist that if she wished to record the Indians' songs she must do so secretly, for if the government office should hear of it she would be expelled from the reservation" (Curtis, 1968).

It should be noted that, as a result of Natalie Curtis' appeal to President Theodore Roosevelt, he endorsed her recording of tribal songs on the reservations and further used his influence to alter many of the Bureau of Indian Affairs' practices. So, among the many reforms adopted was one that not only officially permitted the singing of tribal songs within the government schools on the reservations, but also encouraged the practice (Curtis, 1968).

One modern day ethnomusicologist noted that:

> "Courting flute making was one of the Sioux tribal arts that was not continued and developed in the 20th century by succeeding generations, which was probably due to the acculturation and assimilation process. The reservation system almost destroyed their entire traditional culture..." (Wapp)

While some very serious musical research and gathering of the indigenous peoples' music, predominantly vocal, was accomplished by several early ethnomusicologists, including Alice C. Fletcher [1838-1923], Frances Densmore, and Natalie Curtis, as far as I am aware there does not exist any "early" definitive text that discusses only the musical instruments utilized in the Americas, and certainly none devoted to the Native American flute. The task of collating many of the incidental references, study and measurement of original examples [mostly in museum collections], the gathering of various oral histories, and the organization of early ethnological studies that covered specific geographical locations and cultures has basically been left to a group of five "present-day" ethnomusicologists who used their research efforts to create a college thesis/dissertation for either a master's or doctoral degree. Listed in chronological order, they are as follows: "The Flute and Flute Music of the North American Indians" by Judy Epstein Buss [1977]; "Instrumental and Vocal Love Songs of the North American Indians" by Mary F. Riemer [1978]; "The Flute of the Canadian Amerindian: An Analysis of the Vertical Whistle Flute With External Block and Its Music" by Paula Conlon [1983]; "The Sioux Courting Flute: Its Tradition, Construction, and Music" by Edward R. Wapp [1984]; and "The Native American Flute in the Southwestern United States: Past and Present" by Kathleen Joyce [1996].

The earliest known written record of the Native American flute comes to us from the journals of Coronado, the Spanish explorer, who traversed the American Southwest in the 1540s. In a letter written by one member of the expedition, from an area that is now New Mexico, on April 17, 1540, the following appears:

> "The Indians hold their dances and songs with the aid of some flutes which have holes for the fingers. They make many tunes, singing jointly with those who play. Those who sing clap their hands in the same manner as we do. I saw one of the Indians, who accompanied the Negro Esteban and who was a captive there, play, since they had taught him how to do it there.

> Others were singing, as I said, although not very harmoniously. They say that five or six get together to play, and that the flutes are of different sizes." (Hammond and Rey)

At Drummond's Island, Minn., in 1826, upon hearing the notes of a Native American flute being played by an Ottawa [a local section of the Ojibwa], Thomas L. McKenney wrote:

> "It rose - that chanted mournful strain,
> Like some lone spirits, o'er the Plain;
> 'Twas musical but sadly sweet,
> Such as when winds and harp strings meet
> And take a long unmeasured tone."

McKenney continued by stating:

> "Nothing can be more mournful in its tones. It was night, and a calm rested on everything; It was moonlight, all which added to its effect. We saw the Indian who was playing it, sitting on a rock... We afterwards learned that this Indian was in love, and that he would sit there all night indulging in this sentimental method of softening the heart of his mistress, whose lodge he took care should be opposite his place of melody and within reach of his monotonous but pensive strains." (Winchell)

While there are a number of myths and legends that have survived by oral tradition, although they differ by geography and culture, most all of them seem to have a common thread in that the flute was basically a gift from the "Great Spirit" or the "Creator." One notable exception comes from the Mandan and Hidatsa cultures and is a lengthy description of how the flute was given to the people by the Old Woman Who Never Dies. In the story, the Old Woman Who Never Dies is a mythical character associated with agricultural beliefs (Densmore, 1923).

The Cheyenne also have a legend concerning the flute. It is as follows:

> " 'Many years ago before the white man came,' begins the story of how the flute was given to the natives of this land. As the legend goes, it begins with a young Indian boy who was lost, wandering aimlessly alone in the forest.
>
> It was there, deep in the forest, that the Great Spirit saw him. Having pity on one so young, He decided to give to him a gift so that he would not be alone.
>
> From the heavens He sent a small bird to sit upon a hollow branch of a large tree. Underneath the shade of the tree sat the young Indian boy. As the brisk northern wind blew through the hollow branch, it produced a sound which he had never heard before. Looking up he saw a bird perched high in the tree. Soon the bird began to peck holes into the branch and with each hole that the bird made, it changed the pitch of each note as the wind continued to blow. The young boy realized that the beautiful sound came from the hollow branch and that it was a gift to him from the Great Spirit. He carefully climbed the tree to reach the branch and gently broke off the branch. He blew into it, imitating the northern wind, thereby making the beautiful sound. Later he would find his people and tell them about his wonderful gift.
>
> This is how the first flute was brought to us by the Great Spirit, and also why the small bird sits atop each flute." (Bushy)

One study, *Native American Music* by Marcia Herndon, shows the distribution of Native American flutes to have primarily occurred throughout North America from the Great Lakes into Central America. This study did not document the existence of any flutes east of a line drawn from approximately Chicago, Ill. to Charleston, S.C. A collation of several distribution studies of the flute (Riemer) basically agrees with the conclusions except that additional western locations were identified, as well as at least one further east in New York.

Dennis Slifer and James Duffield, writing in *Flute Player Images In Rock Art - Kokopelli*, suggest that..."The flute player's origin is lost in time, but some believe the tradition may have come north from ancient Mexico or South America..." Mary F. Riemer, writing in her thesis entitled "Instrumental and Vocal Love Songs of the North American Indians," wrote: "The inclusion of [pre-Columbian Mexico] to this list [distribution] should be noted since it has been suggested... that the flageolet [Native American flute] originated in Mexico and subsequently spread northward."

Ancient artifacts have been discovered in a Hopewell mound at Mount Vernon, Ohio, that show a possible link between the musical explorations of the indigenous peoples of North America with those of Central and South America. These artifacts are three panpipes, each consisting of three tubes made of wood. Two of the specimens had tubes covered with silver, while the third was covered with copper. These instruments were analyzed as being instrumental examples dating from between 1 A.D. and 500 A.D. (Tomak)

Many brief articles regarding Native American flutes have inaccurately referred to them as being strictly courting instruments. While it is very true that they served that purpose in the majority of cultures, there is significant evidence suggesting that they were also used for ceremonial and other purposes. For example, one source states that the flute was utilized in the Hopi Flute Ceremony which is held in alternate years for the purpose of bringing forth rain (Curtis).

Some time in 1769, while traveling with the first expedition of the Spaniards to Monterey, Captain Don Pedro Fages wrote in his diary upon observation of a Chumash dance/ceremony:

> "Finally that nothing may be omitted in the narrative, I will tell (the customs) which these Indians observe in their dances. The women go to them well painted, and dressed as has been described (short antelope hide skirts, colored or white), carrying in both hands bundles of feathers of various colors. The men go entirely naked, but very much painted. Only two pairs from each sex are chosen to perform the dance, and only two musicians who play their flutes. Nearly all the others who are present increase the noise with their rattles made of cane, dried and split, while at the same time singing, very displeasingly for us who are not accustomed to distressing the ear with this kind of composition." (Fages)

The very lengthy Hopi Flute Ceremony is more fully described in a recent work, a doctoral dissertation, entitled "The Native American Flute in the Southwestern United States: Past and Present." It also describes how the Zuni associated the flute with both crop productivity and the fertility of the people. Furthermore, it includes a description of an elaborate day-long flute dance ceremony performed by the Jemez, a branch of the Pueblo Indians of the Southwest. Here, the flute plays a part in ensuring the fertility of the land. In addition, other ceremonial uses of the flute by the ancient peoples of the Southwest are described (Joyce).

There are several descriptions of the Native American flute as simply being used for enjoyment and musical relaxation. One such description is of Sioux flutes occasionally being used for enjoyment of the player and friends, using love songs to reminisce. Another description reports that Iroquois flutes were used only for musical relaxation (Conlon). [See the extensive culture listing for identified uses of the Native American flute at the end of this chapter.]

Designs

In researching this subject, it soon becomes obvious that early ethnomusicologists and other researchers used considerable latitude when referencing flutes, flute a becs, flageolets, fipple flutes, and whistles, with regard to their utilization in various Native American cultures. This latitude can sometimes be confusing to modern-day researchers. The confusion seems to stem directly from the fact that the evolved design [by the early 1800s] of the Native American flute was unique and without previous musical reference, thereby leaving the authors to use European musical instrument descriptions and terms for their references to the Native American flute. To a lesser degree, the fact that North American cultures used both flutes and whistles, which sometimes had similar appearances, also contributed to the confusion.

The word "flute" is a general name for a very large and varied family of wind instruments, each consisting of a hollow body and sounded by an "edge-tone in which the player blows and directs a stream of air against the sharp edge of an opening." The sharp edge or lip puts the air in motion causing it to vibrate in the body of the instrument, thereby creating a sound. Flutes have existed since very ancient times, have been found on every continent, and exist in many forms, shapes, and sizes (Bennett).

The hollowed-out Anasazi flutes [circa 620 A.D.] were actually a straight-bore flute that required an embouchure to produce sound, whereas the contemporary Native American flutes do not require any specific shaping of the mouth to produce a tone. "Music was played by directing a stream of air against and across the half of the proximal end farthest from the player. In effect, this directed the stream of air into the barrel of the flute through a restricted aperture, serving a function similar to the mouthpiece of modern instruments of this general type [i.e. the silver flute]" (Morris, 1959). Straight-bore flute usage has been documented as late as the 1800s. They were used by the Yuma of Arizona. These were actually played in a transverse manner by blowing across the end (Densmore, 1927). The straight-bore flute was generally prevalent in ancient cultures all over the globe.

The next evolution in flutes that occurred in many cultures is the v-shaped notch or u-shaped notch flute. Here, a "v" or a "u" shape was cut into the rim of the mouth end of the flute. The flute was then held directly against the mouth, in a vertical manner, and the performer used an embouchure to split the air stream across the v-shaped or u-shaped notch. This is the same principle used for the shakuhachi of Japan and the quena of South America. Interestingly, in his book *The Hopi Flute Ceremony*, Richard W. Payne comments: "Recent models of flutes used by the Hopi, usually made of cane in various lengths, show six tone holes... a notched edge is seen on some of these instruments, similar to the shakuhachi, facilitating sound production yet retaining sound qualities of the traditional flute" (Payne, 1993). This information seems to indicate that, in addition to a possible relationship to the shakuhachi, the straight-bore flute of North America actually survived into the 1900s.

The idea of partially plugging up a portion of the upper part of the flute was well known to both the ancient Greeks and the Hindu. Also, in Europe this technique evolved into a number of different instruments including the flute a bec, flageolet, recorder, and the tin whistle. These European instruments shared a common design feature in that the initial portion of the mouth piece formed a duct or air channel created by the insertion of a block into the lower and major portion of this area of the flute, thereby leaving a small duct area above the block to channel the air to the open splitting edge called the lip. This mouth piece block is called a fipple. These types of flutes are also referred to as "duct flutes" (Randel). I have on occasion noticed several modern discussions incorrectly referring to the fipple as being the "splitting edge" of the Native American flute, or the Native American flute itself being a fipple flute, which it is not.

Keeping in perspective that early organ pipes were made of wood, it is intriguing that the flute pipes of those early organs had a "principal" design that used an internal block, called a languid, separating the pipe into two chambers, with the upper lip [the splitting edge] being close to the same location as that of the later Native American flutes. The two chambers in this early organ design were roughly the same proportions as that of the flute. This particular design actually has the flue [air channel, windway] interior to the pipe, as opposed to the external air channel of the Native American flute. Another point of interest is that 19th century French organ makers created flute pipes to provide what is referred to as an undulating sound (Randel). This effect is much the same as that of the warble produced by some Native American flute, a concept which is discussed later in this book.

The singular, and apparently unique, contribution of the early Native Americans to the design of the flute, in the absence of any research to the contrary, was the introduction of a vertical block. This actually created two separate chambers in the previously open bore of the flute and added an external air channel to connect the two chambers together. This, together with the aid of an external "block," directs the air to a splitting edge from one chamber to the other chamber. While it remains to me a mystery as to the exact chronological manifestation of this development, at least three different designs of the Native American flute have been documented from the mid to late 1800s, with the design shown in figure one having been dated to 1832 [See Appendix H]. This line drawing was made by George Catlin.

Today, Native American flutes are styled after all three of these original designs, based upon the same principle of a cylindrical tube with two separate chambers, four to six finger holes, and either constructed by the hollowing out of two separate halves which are then glued together or by the boring out of a single piece of wood.

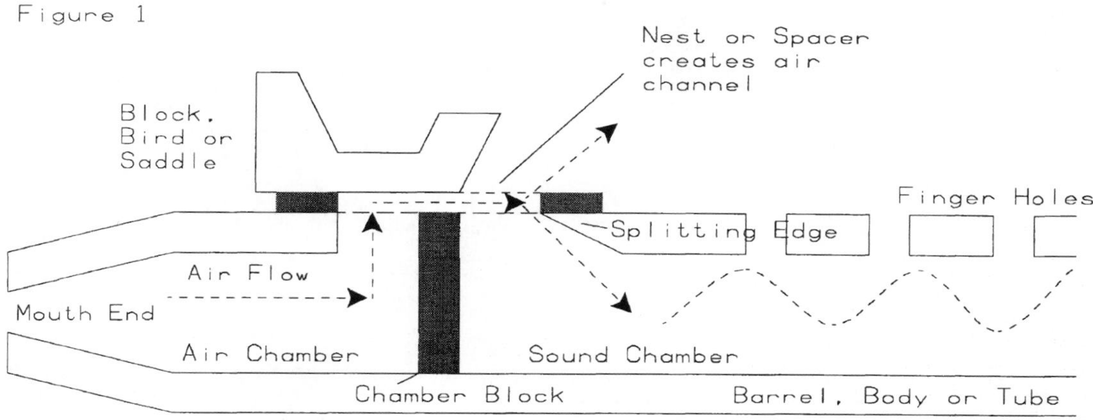

The Air Channel Is Formed Within The Nest Or Spacer

In Figure 1, the air is moved from the air chamber to the sound chamber by means of a nest or spacer, thereby forming an open rectangular frame which sits on the flute and creates a channel for the air to cross from, and two access holes cut in the top of the flute on either side of the chamber's separating block. The mouth-end air chamber is proportionately shorter in length than the sound channel length. On top of the nest or spacer resides what is referred to as a bird, block, or saddle. An excellent description of this was provided by one ethnomusicologist:

> "Small square holes were cut into each chamber just above and below the partition. The surface around these holes was then made smooth and flat and a thin wooden or metal plate laid over it. This plate had a rectangular hole cut into it which fit exactly over the two holes in the cylinder. Finally, a wooden block, flat on the underside and carved according to the maker's fancy or tradition on top, was tied or glued over this plate. Air blown into the end of the shorter chamber flattens into a thin stream as it passes between the partition and the plate. At the entrance to the longer chamber the air stream impinges on the sharp edge or 'lip' of the plate and sets the column of air in vibration." (Riemer)

Figure 2

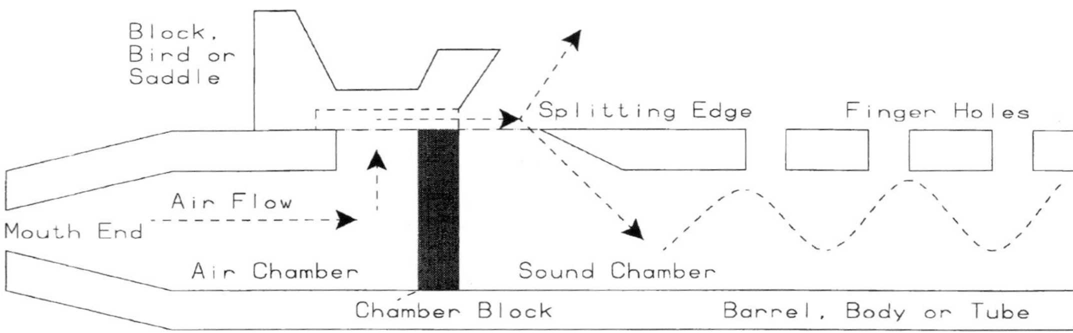

The Air Channel Is Cut Into The Block, Bird or Saddle

In Figure 2, the air is moved as in Figure 1 except that there is an absence of a nest or plate. Instead, in this diagram, the thin air channel or windway is cut directly into the bottom of the bird, block, or saddle.

Figure 3

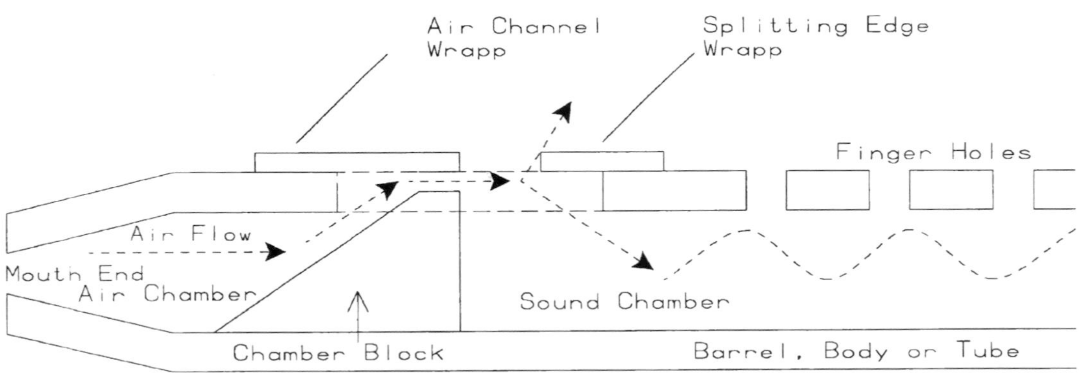

The Air Channel Is Cut Into The Body Of The Flute while the leading edge of chamber block typically slopes upward

Figure 3 displays the cutting of the air channel directly into the body of the flute. Mr. E. H. Hawley, at one time the curator of musical instruments for the United States National Museum [now known simply as the Smithsonian], described the design of a specimen from southern Arizona:

> "... A section of cane forming two tubes separated by a joint or internal block. Two holes were made from the outside into the cavity with the unbroken septum of the joint between them. A groove is made on the outside from one hole to the other. Covering the upper hole and the groove with a bandage and blowing in the upper tube, the bandage directs the wind from the upper hole against the lower edge of the lower hole, thereby producing a sound like a whistle. The lower tube has three finger holes." (Densmore, 1927)

Frances Densmore described and photographed an interesting variation of this version that shows the Papago player using the index finger of his left hand over the channel cut into the body of the flute in order to direct the air from one chamber to the other. The index, middle, and ring fingers of the right hand were used to play the three holes of the instrument (Densmore, 1929).

Regarding all three aforementioned designs, according to Lew Paxton Price during a personal correspondence with the author in 1998:

> "The splitting edge directs the airflow up and down once the flute is played for a cycle or two [a few hundredths of a second], rather than splitting it. There is very little compression in the entry chamber if the flute is designed correctly. The chamber is designed for letting the airflow relieve itself of turbulence in a well-designed flute. The pitch is not caused by the distance the air travels within the sound chamber. It is caused essentially by the distance of the wave movement of the air within the sound chamber. Precisely, it is the distance the wave movement travels within the theoretical length of the sound chamber."

Flute size varied from somewhere between 1 and 3 feet in length, with diameters ranging from just over one-half inch to almost 2 inches. There are a number of references suggesting that the size of the flute was in accordance with various measurements of a maker's body parts. "The finger holes are placed in a manner convenient to the player's hand, not by any fixed rule... The length of a typical Indian flute varies with the stature of the player, a desirable length being from the inside of the elbow to the end of the middle-finger" (Densmore, 1936). "...a young Kiowa Indian, in Washington a few years ago, showed the writer (Wead) how the holes on a flute on which he played were located by measuring three finger-breadths from the lower end to the lower hole, and then taking shorter but equal spaces for the succeeding holes" (Wead, 1902).

In reference to the Hidatsa Indians, "The length [of the flute] was from the inside of a man's elbow to the end of his little finger" (Hamilton). Richard W. Payne states the following:

> "The older Plains flutes were frequently constructed according to the dimensions of the maker. Using body measurements, the length of the flute was measured from armpit to fingertips, and the fipple edge was marked at the bend of the elbow. The top tone hole was placed a hand's breadth below the last tone hole... the bore of the flute was sized according to the diameter of the index finger" (1988)

The Native American flute had several types of mouth end designs. [See the chapter on playing the Native American flute.] One researcher who studied some 97 different flutes, mostly on display in museums, noted that of the 97 examined 27 percent had a blunt end, 39 percent had a tapered end, and 34 percent had a tubular projection. It was also observed that the shape of the end did not appear to be a specific characteristic of an area or culture, but rather simply varied from maker to maker (Conlon).

Wood seems to have been the most common material used for flute construction, although cane and clay are also much in evidence (Herndon). Woods used include: alder, ash, box elder, basswood, cedar, cottonwood, elderberry, juniper, maple, pine, redwood, and sumac (Conlon). Other woods used were chokecherry, fir, osage, orange, and walnut. Some less common woods that were used include the sunflower stalk and the dry reed of wild parsnip (Buss). I suspect that most likely, at one time or another, flutes were constructed out of most of the woods found in North America, with the various cultures using whatever was locally available.

In addition, flutes made out of copper were also created (Boulton), as well as some built out of catlinite (Wapp). Some of the wood flutes were covered with animal skin (Jeancon) and even occasionally made completely from an animal bone (Densmore, 1956).

In her thesis entitled "The Flute of the Canadian Amerindian," Paula Conlon lists extensive metrical measurements of 25 museum flutes representing eight different cultures. These measurements are so detailed that even the spacing between each finger hole is presented, as well as the diameter of the finger holes.

Edward Wapp made accurate measurements of a number of original Sioux flutes, and his thesis is also highly recommended to those students who have a serious interest in this subject area. The thesis is entitled "The Sioux Courting Flute: Its Tradition, Construction, and Music."

Richard W. Payne, in his book entitled *The Native American Plains Flute*, offers extensive measurements of numerous "original" Plains flutes which were discovered in various museums and libraries. He also includes in this book a very detailed AutoCad drawing with measurements of his own "toubat" F# flute which he designed (Payne, 1999).

Lew Paxton Price has written many small books on contemporary measurements of the Native American flute, as well as instructions on how to build the instrument. Additionally, Harry Brown has an excellent article on making the American Indian flute in the *Woodwind Quarterly* 7 (1994).

Contemporary Native American flutes are primarily made out of wood. While many are made out of cedar, there are examples of flutes built from pine, birch, maple, aspen, cherry, fir, Sitka spruce, walnut, and cane. Each wood provides the flute with a different timbre or tone quality.

The fundamental key or lowest note of a flute occurs when all finger holes are covered. The actual fundamental pitch is determined by the length of the flute and its diameter. The different pitches or notes of a Native American flute are created by opening and closing the finger holes. The quantity and spacing of those holes determine the availability of pitches.

The number of finger holes present on the early Native American flutes varied anywhere from zero to seven. While the number of finger holes on some flutes seem to have possibly been culture specific, other cultures used multiple finger holes on their flutes. The Cheyenne, for example, have been documented as using five, six, and seven finger holes on their flutes. [See the extensive culture listing for identified number of holes of the Native American flute at the end of this chapter.] An additional comment regarding finger holes: "It is further noted that the edges of the finger holes are beveled. This is unusual and permits a tight sealing by the finger, stopping the hole completely. The finger holes were burned with an iron and the beveling done with a knife" (Densmore, 1956). In the book *Thurlow Lieurance Indian Flutes* (1990), Betty Austin Hensley noted that a number of "original" flutes in Thurlow's personal collection had finger holes that were beveled, with indications that the holes were formed by being burned. Contemporary Native American flutes are mostly five-hole or six-hole, with a few makers producing four-hole and seven-hole flutes.

Because of a lack of suitable tooling for boring, it would appear that the majority of recent [1800s] Native American flutes were made in two halves and then glued or wrapped together. A major exception manifests with those woods that could be hollowed out by the removal of soft fibers, such as the removal of pith from box elder and cane, although cane required the removal of all but one of the joint septums.

Many contemporary makers of Native American flutes continue this tradition of making the flute from two pieces, having separate air chambers "scooped" out of each half which are then glued together. However, some of these makers will clean the bore entirely and insert a separate block to separate the chambers, rather than leaving a thin bridge of wood in place between each chamber. However, because of the availability of modern tooling, other builders prefer to bore the body from a single piece of wood.

In designs using a separate nest or spacer to create the air channel or airway, the nest may be made of leather, wood, metal, or even cardboard. "A Chippewa flute had a piece of birch bark with a rectangular opening over the sound hole and a bit of silk across the opening, which furnished a sharp, thin lip on which the current of air impinged" (Densmore, 1927). The height of the nest or spacer, or the depth of the air channel or windway cut directly into the bird, block, or saddle is very critical to the process and typically ranges any where from .015 to .050 inches. The bird, block, or saddle that sits on the body is usually tied on with a thong of leather, thereby permitting some adjustment in relationship to the air chamber block or partition, which has some effect on the volume and the quality of tone.

Decoration

Two of the five ancient Anasazi flutes from the Broken Flute Cave [circa 620 A.D.] had a variety of colorful bird feathers - stellar jay, pinion jay, red-naped sapsucker crowns, and red shafted flicker heads - tied with yucca plant fiber string to the barrel of the flute near the mouth end. The feathers were actually laid out lengthwise on the body of the flute, not hanging down from it, with the tips of the feathers pointing in the direction of the mouth end (Morris, 1959). "It was interesting to note that the bird feathers were ruffled by the breath of the player, adding a visual counterpart to the music itself" (Morris, 1959).

Many of the Native American flutes were also decorated with either carvings, incised and painted designs, or attachments such as a small medicine bundle. Sometimes the designs and carvings had specific meanings, while other times they seemed to be simply decorative, or possibly had a hidden meaning known only to the maker (Wapp). Some examples of ornamental and ceremonial devices used on flutes are: "beads, shells, feathers, glass, and chips of metal" (Buss). Other ornamental devices include "feathers, animal and human hair, paint, crayon, pendants, beads, animal tails and claws, quills, shells, pieces of leather and ribbons..." (Conlon). Elizabeth Ann Morris, in an article in *American Antiquity*, commented while discussing the early Anasazi flutes from the Broken Flute Cave that a flute discovered in a burial site nearby was "encrusted with white beads set in pitch" (Morris, 1959). In addition, flutes were generally wrapped with leather thongs or cordage made of sinew or other material. Whether these wrappings were ornamental or just a structural addition to help hold two halves together, it is not absolutely known. Most likely, it is a combination of both.

Probably the most obvious and common decorative feature was the carving of the bird, block, or saddle into effigies of either animals or birds. Flutes with carved blocks represented 29 percent of the Native American flutes of the 97 studied in museums by Paula Conlon. In addition, about 80 percent of those with the carved blocks depicted the face of an animal or a bird effigy facing the player. Conlon speculates that the feature of the effigy facing the player may signify some type of communication with a spirit by the player (Conlon). Interestingly, of the contemporary flutes that I have with carved blocks by five different makers, only one maker has chosen to have the effigy facing the mouth end of the flute. "The custom of pointing towards the player may have been lost or considered unimportant to contemporary flute makers" (Conlon).

Decorative holes near the base of the flute were another very common feature and appeared on 19 percent of the flutes studied by Conlon. Four holes appear to be the most common. I should point out that wherever on the flute body the decorative holes appear, this defines the actual length of the sound chamber.

The open end of the flute was also carved on a number of flutes. Birds appear to represent the majority of the carvings of the open end, rather than animals. One study shows the percentage of flutes with carved open ends to be around 11 percent. However, this study has a Plains bias in that 55 of the 97 flutes studied were Plains flutes which had carved ends on 10 of the 55 flutes (Conlon).

While not a common feature of most contemporary Native American flutes, colors were also an important decoration for the indigenous peoples. Yellow and red have connotations of love, green of life, white of clouds, and blue of the water and sky (Conlon). "Some colors such as red, pink, black, yellow, and green are particularly widespread. Colors are applied to the flutes either by staining or drawing specific symbolic figurations such as arrowheads, zigzags [depicting lightning], the horned water serpent, and stars. Each color may be linked with certain aspects of life and the universe" (Buss). "One Kiowa myth directs the player to put the rouge which he uses on his face on the end of the flute to personalize it" (Conlon).

I would suggest to owners of contemporary Native American flutes who would like to have more decorations on their flutes that they consider adding decorations to reflect their personal tastes and experiences, or commission a flute builder to build one that matches a personal vision.

A Beautifully Decorated Flute and Its Story

I own a flute with the fundamental of middle C that is approximately 31 inches in length, with a bore diameter of 1-3/16 inches. The flute has a carved buffalo block, painted white, which is tied to the body with white leather lacing. The body of the flute is mostly painted white, except for several green, black, red, and yellow painted stripes. In addition, in a number of places, the natural wood appears in either a stripe or a saw tooth design within the white painted area. Toward the open end of the flute there is a large wrapping of white leather with a lot of fringe hanging below the bottom of the flute. On top of the flute, in the center of this white leather wrapping, is a circle cut into the leather. The two strips of leather left within the circle create four separate quadrants within the circle [the four directions] and each individual quadrant is painted green. This white leather wrapping is also accented with a stripe of red on either side. There are also four decorative holes near the open bore.

During the first weekend of October, 1994, I was camping with a large group of muzzle loading friends and enthusiasts at Tok, Alaska, near the border crossing of the Alaska Highway into Canada. That Sunday night presented us with the most spectacular display of the Northern Lights that I have ever had the pleasure of observing, either before or since. Keep in mind that the Northern Lights are a fairly common occurrence here in south-central and northern Alaska, especially during the fall months. The Northern Lights stretched across the sky from horizon to horizon in all directions. Reds, blues, greens, and whites were all brilliantly displayed in many changing shapes and patterns. Amazingly, our group just happened to be standing and watching a particular quadrant of the sky when a magnificent giant silhouette of a white buffalo appeared and seemed to linger. It took our breath away! The head, shoulders, hump, back, and legs all appeared to be accurately depicted - no imagination was required to interpret the image.

During the time that I was captivated with the buffalo image and listening to the comments of the others watching, a close friend was jumping up and down to my right and tugging on my sleeve and hitting my shoulder to try and get my attention to turn in the direction that he was viewing. Finally he yelled, "Crawford, it's Kokopelli!" That got my attention, but by the time I turned to take a look at the Kokopelli image it was just starting to dissolve. However, I did see enough of it to be certain that it was in fact a white image of Kokopelli.

I was aware that Scott Loomis had previously created several flutes with painted designs when I called him in 1998 about the possibility of making me a flute. Scott informed me that, at the time, he was not really doing that kind of work because the individual he used to decorate his finished flutes was not available to him anymore. After I explained to Scott the story of the Northern Lights and the images that we saw, he agreed that the vision should be celebrated and preserved with a flute and that he would undertake the project, which ultimately resulted in the beautifully decorated flute described at the beginning of this story. At one time, Scott had this flute displayed on his Web site, but I am not certain that it will still be there when this is published. I suspect that many readers will question the credibility of the images that we observed. I could describe even more strange images that we observed that night, but I suspect that to do so would weaken what credibility remains with those that accept this description. I have since often wondered why we were "chosen" to observe this phenomenon. I guess the answer is that we were not really chosen but simply at the right place at the right time. Furthermore, there are still many mysteries about the universe that we do not fully comprehend. I know that, as a result of this personal experience, I tend to be more receptive to the stories of others describing their own strange and mysterious experiences, for I now know for certain that they can and do happen.

"THE EARTH HAS MUSIC

FOR THOSE WHO LISTEN"

~ William Shakespeare ~

Cultures Known to Use the Native American Flute

Culture	Holes	Uses	Location[15]
Achomawi[22]		CT	CA
Acoma[9]	5[20], 6	CR	NM
Alabama[1]			AL, FL, LA
Algonkin[3]	6	C T	ON, PQ
Anasazi[13]	5, 6		AZ
Apache[1]	3[22], 6	CT[6], SA[6]	AZ, CO, MX, NM, OK, TX
Arapaho[1]	6[36]		CO, KS, MN, MT, ND, NE, OK, SD WY
Arikara/Rees[3]	4[36]		MT, ND, NE, SD
Assiniboine[3]	5[36]	C T	MB, MT, ND, SK
Atsugewi[27]	6		CA
Bannock[1]		CT[31]	CO, ID, MT, OK, UT WY
Blackfoot[3]	4[6], 6	CT,SA	AB, MT, SK
Caddo[20]	6		AR, LA, TX
Cahuilla[27]			CA
Cayuga[3]	6		NY
Cherokee[16]	0[20], 5, 6	S A	AL, AR, GA, KS, NC, OK, SC, TN, VA
Cheyenne[1]	5[7] ,6[8], 7	CT[3], SA[3]	CO, KS, MN, MT, ND, NE, OK, SD, WY
Chickasaw[20]	3		AL, AR, TN, GA, KY, SC, OK
Chilcotin[28]			BC
Chimariko[27]		CT	CA
Choctaw[20]	2	CR[22]	AL, LA, AR, TX, OK
Cocopa[9]	4		AZ, MX
Coeur d'Alene[1]			ID

Cultures Known to Use the Native American Flute

Culture	Holes	Uses	Location[15]
Comanche[3]	6[37]	CT, S, SG	CO, KS, NE, NM, OK, TX, WY
Costano[27]			CA
Cree[1]			MN, ON, PQ, SK
Creek[20]	6[36]		AL, FL, GA, LA, OK, TN, TX
Crow[20]	6	CT[1], S[3]	MT, WY
Chumash[27]		CA	CA
Delaware[3]	6[37]		DE, IN,KS, MS, NJ, NY, OH, PA
Flathead[1]	6	CT	ID, MT
Fox[2]		S	IA, IL, KS, MI, MN, MO, NE, OK, WI
Haida[3]	6[36]	CR	BC, AK
Hidatsa[3]	7	S	ND, MT
Hopi[19]	4[23], 5, 7[22]	CR[6]	AZ
Hualapai[26]			AZ
Huba[27]		SA, CT	CA
Huron[3]	6		ON, PQ
Iroquois[3]	6, 7	CR, CT, SA	IN, KS, NY, OH, OK ON, PA, PQ, WI
Jemez[4]	4	CR[6]	NM
Kalispel[1]		CT[32]	ID, MT, WA
Kamia[27]	4		CA
Kansa[33]	6		KS, NB, OK
Karok[25]			CA
Kato[27]	4		CA
Kawaiisu[31]	6		CA
Kickapoo[3]			IL, IN, KS, MI, MO, MX, OK, OH, WI
Kiowa[1]	6, 7[7]	CT[3], S[3]	CO, KS, NM, TX
Kitksan[22]		CT	BC
Konomihu[25]		CR	CA
Kutenai/Kootenay[1]	7[32]	CT[32], CR[22]	AB, ID, MT, WA
Lassik[27]	3, 4, 5, 6		CA

Cultures Known to Use the Native American Flute

Culture	Holes	Uses	Location[15]
Lipan[1]			NM, OK, TX
Luiseno[27]			CA
Maidu[27]		CA	CA
Maliseet[34]			ME, NB
Mandan[1]	6[36]		ND
Mattole[27]	3, 4, 5, 6		CA
Menomonee	6	CT[3]	MI, WI
MicMac[17]			NB, NS, PE, NF
Mojave[14]	3, 4		AZ, CA
Navajo[26]			AZ, CO, NM, UT
Nez Perce[3]	6	CT, SG	ID, OR, WA
Nongatl[27]	3, 4, 5, 6		CA
Ojibway[1]	6	CT[3], SG[3]	IA, IL, IN, MB, MI, MN, MT, ND, OH, ON, SK, WI
Okanagan[3]	6	CT, SG	BC, WA
Omaha[1]	6	CT[3]	IA, MN, MO, NE, SD
Oneida[3]			NY
Onondaga[3]	6		NY
Osage[20]	6		KS, AR, OK
Ottawa[10]	4	CT	IA, IL, IN, KS, MI, MN, OH, OK, ON, WI
Paiute[3]	6	SA[31]	AZ, CA, NV, UT
Palouse[32]	6		WA, ID
Papago[9]	3		AZ, MX
Patwin[23]	4	SA	CA
Pawnee[20]	6	CT[3]	KS, NE, OK
Pima[4]	3		AZ, MX
Pomo[20]	4		CA
Potawatomi[3]	6[36]		IA, IL, IN, KS, MI, MO, OH, OK, WI
Quapaw[20]	6		AR, KS, LA, MS, OK, TX
Salina[27]			CA
Sanpoil[1]	0[22]	CT[22]	WA
Sauk[3]	6[36]		IA, IL, KS, MI, MN, MO, OK, WI

Cultures Known to Use the Native American Flute

Culture	Holes	Uses	Location[15]
Seminole[9]	4		FL
Seneca[3]	6	CR	IN, OH, OK, ON, PA, WI
Seri[30]			MX
Shasta[27]			CA
Shawnee[24]	8	CT, SA	OH, IN, PA, TN, MO, KS, KY, VA, AL, GA, MD, DC, SC, IL, TX
Shoshoni[4]	4, 6[7]	CT[2]	CA, ID, MT, NV, UT, WY
Sinkyone[27]	3, 4, 5, 6		CA
Sioux (Lakota/Dakota)[5]	5, 6, 7[21]	CT, CA[3]	IA, MN, MT, MO, ND, NE, SD, WI, WY
Taos[20]	4		NM
Tarahumara[30]			MX
Tenino[1]			OR
Tewa[7]	4[29], 6	CR[2]	NM
Thompson[3]	6	CT, SG	BC, WA
Tubatulabal[27]		SA	CA
Umatilla[1]	6[36]	CT[33]	OR, WA
Ute[1]	6	CT[31]	CO, NM, NV, UT, WY
Wailaki[27]	3, 4, 5, 6		CA
Wappo[27]			CA
Wichita[3]	6[37]		KS, OK, TX
Winnebago[20]	5[36], 6, 7[11]	CT[12],CR[3],SG[3]	IA, IL, MN, SD, WI
Wintun[27]		SA, CT	CA
Yahi[27]			CA
Yakima[32]			WA
Yana[27]			CA
Yaqui[6]		CR	MX
Yaquina[30]		CA	AZ
Yokuts[27]			CA
Yuchi[1]	6	CT[3], SG[18]	GA, FL, SC, TN
Yuma[9]	3, 4[20]	CT[6]	AZ, CA
Zuni[20]	4	CR[6]	AZ, NM

Uses Codes

CR = Ceremonial SA = Self-Amusement CT = Courting SG = Signaling S = Spiritual

In some respects, with the possible exception of self-amusement, all of the uses are very similar in nature in that the belief was that by playing the flute some power would be evoked that would create some benefit to either the player or the culture. Self-amusement includes individual playing and meditation, as well as group playing.

References

1. Riemer
2. Buss
3. Conlon
4. Crawford
5. Wapp
6. Joyce
7. Hensley
8. Bushy
9. Densmore
10. Winchell
11. Boulton
12. Curtis
13. Morris
14. Cunningham-Summerfield
15. Waldman
16. LittleJohn
17. Diamond, et al.
18. Speck
19. Gilman
20. Payne
21. Wead
22. Seder
23. Lieurance
24. Voegelin
25. Gray and Schupman
26. Tschopik
27. Sturtevant (1978 - California)
28. Sturtevant (1981)
29. Sturtevant (1979)
30. Sturtevant (1983)
31. Sturtevant (1986)
32. Sturtevant (1998)
33. Sturtevant (2001)
34. Sturtevant (1978 - Northeast)
35. Jones
36. Wolf, DMC
37. Wolf, SI

Note: The reader should be aware that no attempt has been made, herein, to differentiate between open-bore flutes and those with an external windway, an apparent 19th century design. While some sources do make this distinction, there are so many sources not known to me that an additional column was not added for this type of flute distinction. In the future, this subject will be revisited so that this omission may be partially resolved. As a broad generalization based upon limited information, the open-bore flutes tended to be more prominent than the external windway flutes in the Southwest and along the western coast of the United States.

"I need only listen to the sounds of the earth traveling to my heart and then transmitted through my fingers and breath into haunting musical structures to have my soul transported to a higher ground wherein I may dwell, even if only briefly, in tranquil harmony with my being."

~ Tim "WindWalker" Crawford ~

Playing the Native American Flute

[Beginning Students]

Fingering

The lower three holes are covered by the right hand, while the upper two [five-hole flute] or three [six-hole flute] are covered by the left hand. Use only the index, middle, and ring fingers of each hand to cover the holes on the flute.

While not shown, the four-hole Native American flute would use only the index and middle finger of each hand.

Positioning

Rest the body of the instrument on the thumbs of both hands, with the open holes facing outward. Next, position the fingers as described above. The flute is stabilized, a necessity when playing all holes open, either by pinching the flute slightly between the thumb and the index finger of the right hand or by using the little finger of the right hand in a downward pressure against the upward pressure of the thumbs.

Basically, the head should be parallel with the body. It should be neither overtly tilted forward nor backward. Above all else, the player needs to be comfortable and enjoy playing; therefore, just do what seems natural and comfortable.

Hole Covering

It is very important that you use the pads of your fingertips to cover the holes on the flute, as opposed to the tips themselves. The finger pads must completely seal the hole to avoid fuzzy and squeaky notes. As you practice playing, the importance of technique will be readily noticeable.

Embouchure (Mouth Formation)

The following is an illustration of four possible Native American flute mouth piece designs. When we whistle, we form a type of "O" with our lips and they slightly protrude forward. For the Native American flute, the lips need to be pulled slightly back as if blowing softly without forming an extreme "O." Then, place the mouth piece against the lips. Although there is no "correct" design in terms of mouth pieces, they are somewhat unique in how the lips are positioned for blowing. For example, style D and B require that the lips not be wrapped around the mouth piece but rather placed against the mouth piece, sealing it against the lips. On the other hand, style C requires that your lips partially wrap around the very tip of the mouth piece, but be sure not to over do this. Finally, style A depends upon the size of your lips and the size of the mouth piece projection. Depending upon how everything sizes together, this flute can be blown into with either of the previously-described techniques. Personally, I find that with my embouchure, the upper lip seals while the bottom of the flute's mouth piece slightly rests upon my lower lip. In the final analysis, there is no exactly right or wrong mouth position for playing the Native American flute. Use the above as a guide and do what works best and what is most comfortable/productive for you.

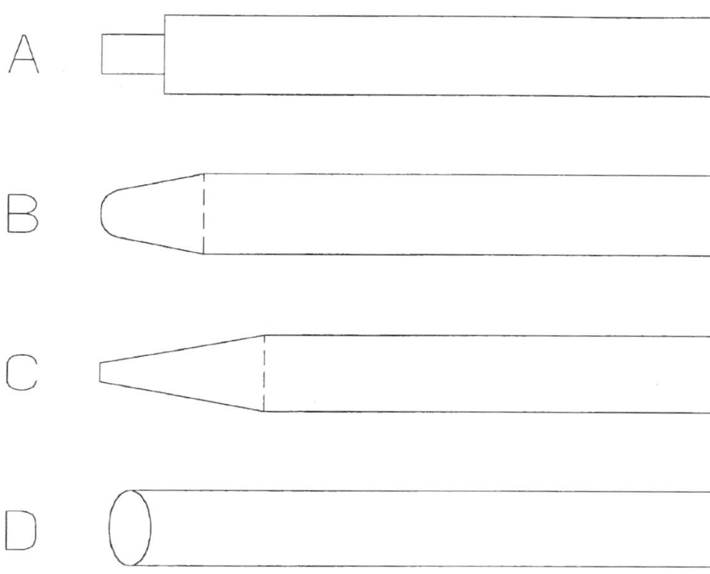

An important fact about playing the Native American flute is that a large volume of air is not required and will generally be counter productive to the quality and success of your initial efforts. The lower frequency notes [i.e. few holes uncovered] will require less air than the higher frequency notes [i.e. all holes open]. I sometimes suggest to students who are applying too much air, causing an overblow [a raising of the pitch], to cover all of the holes and then blow just a bit more air than they would use if blowing into a baby's ear. If that is not enough air velocity then increase the air speed gradually until the fundamental note is clear. With practice, you will automatically apply the correct volume of air for the various finger combinations without any conscious effort.

I recommend to all beginning students that their initial sounds be with all of the holes covered and perhaps the first hole uncovered. Then, begin raising the fingers furthermost from the mouth, one at a time, while listening carefully to the sounds that are produced. This will aid in learning the appropriate volume of air required for the higher frequencies. Once all of the holes are uncovered, proceed slowly back down the scale, one finger at a time.

As you gain confidence, experiment with different finger combinations. When you are fairly comfortable with your sound and the movement of the fingers, up and down, then go to the TABlature practice exercises in this book and begin the exercises after you have read the "Introduction to the TABlature Exercises" chapter. Just play the instrument and play it often, but only when you are motivated to do so. While you will most likely be comfortable with the traditional songs provided within this book because the songs are familiar, if you are not familiar with musical notation symbols and the duration of specific notes then it will be necessary for you to study the

"Elementary Music Fundamentals" chapter before attempting to play any of the music included within this book. When you do begin attempting to play the included music, I would suggest something somewhat simple such as "Friends" for the five-hole flute and "Mountain Sunrise" for the six-hole flute.

My latest CD, *In Remembrance*, contains the following songs from this book: "Broken Heart," "Come to Me," "Friends," "Hear My Heart," "Horizons," "Longing," "Moon's Light," "Mountain Sunrise," and "Reaching Out." My CD *Voices* contains the following songs from this book: "Alone," "Cloud Watcher," "Coals," "Destiny," "Eagle Flight," "Embers," "Leaves," "Old Ways," "Passages," "Reflections," "Story Circle," and "Watching You." CDs are $15.95 each, postpaid by check or cash. Please send funds to: WindWalker, P.O. Box 946, Cannon Beach, OR 97110-0946. Sorry, credit cards are not accepted.

Adjustments

It is important that the block [also called the bird or saddle] be correctly aligned, in order for a good sound to be produced. It should be parallel with the openings on either side of the air channel and not be off-center in any way. The leading front edge of the block should be about flush with the front edge of the air chamber block [a vertical piece which separates the two chambers of the flute].

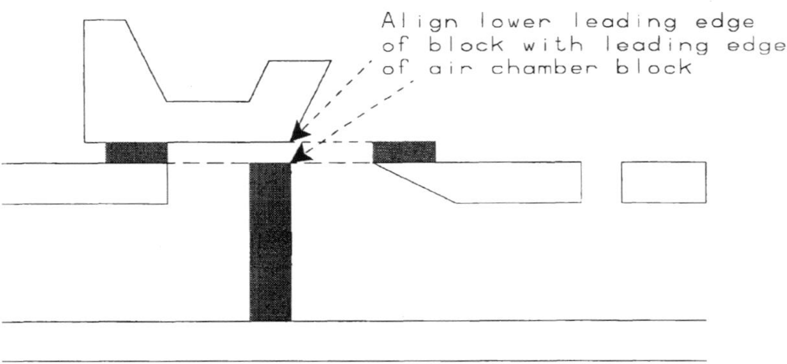

Through experimentation it will be discovered that the pitch, volume, and "quality" of the flute's sound can be varied by moving the block slightly forward or backward.

Intermediate Students

Embellishment Techniques

The following are explanations of various embellishment techniques that are utilized by many performers of the Native American flute:

Over Blowing: This is a technique used to raise a given fingering combination an approximate octave. An *octave*, eight steps, is a musical term that is used to label the distance between two notes. For example, the distance from a low G to a high G is an octave (g-A-B-C-D-E-F-G). An octave is, simply stated, the exact same note, but higher in range. Each flute will typically only have two or three finger combinations that permit this technique.

Most flutes will allow for an "over blow" to occur with all of the holes covered. To try this technique, first develop a clear fundamental note [all holes covered]. Then, increase the air volume until the note jumps an octave in range. Practice this and experiment with various finger combinations to learn the capabilities of your flute.

Lift Off: This is a frequently used technique which allows for the creation of a sudden and sharp upward "pop" at the end of a note, particularly at the conclusion of a musical phrase. When listening to the music of various well-known performers of the Native American flute, this embellishment technique is often utilized.

Accomplishing this technique requires a quick burst of air at the end of a note, while suddenly and simultaneously lifting all, or just a few, of the fingers from the covered holes. The inside of the mouth is also involved in this process. To produce the "pop," the inside of the mouth must stop the flow of air immediately following the rapid lifting of the fingers. To do this, the oral cavity will form the word "WHAT." Notice the placement of the tongue at the end of the word "WHAT." The tongue is at the roof of the mouth and air is cut off. This must be done to achieve the characteristic "pop" that is heard so frequently in Native American flute music. This embellishment technique is musically notated as follows:

Vibrato: This is the sound effect that singers use on sustained notes that causes the note to vibrate, pulsate, or waiver. As with a singer's voice, this effect will considerably enhance the quality of the sound that is created while playing, especially upon sustained notes.

This embellishment technique does require considerable practice. The muscle involved in producing vibrato is called the diaphragm and is located beneath the rib cage. This is an involuntary muscle that is charged with the duty of inflating and deflating the lungs [i.e. breathing]. To feel how this muscle works, and how you can manipulate it to work for you, place a hand on your stomach. Next, simulate laughter by saying "HA, HA, HA." The muscle that is pushing the air out is the diaphragm.

The diaphragm can be controlled to create vibrato on a sustained note, whether one is singing or playing the flute. A suggested practice would be to try creating a vibrato with your own voice while sustaining a pitch; the vibrato really should come all the way from the diaphragm. Even so, some of it will be produced in the throat, although total throat vibrato is not desired because it constricts the throat muscles and often yields unwanted throat sounds while playing. If a vibrato can be produced using the voice, then vibrato upon the flute should be accessible. Just pulsate on the air stream while blowing into the flute.

Vibrato can also be accomplished by a pulsation of the lips, or even a rapid puffing of the cheeks. These are alternative methods, but not the preferred method.

For those of you who have difficulty with vibrato production, I would suggest that you consider mechanically "shaking" the flute in a gentle manner against the lips with your hands. With minimal practice, this can provide an excellent vibrato, although, here again, this is not the preferred method.

Trill: This technique is accomplished by raising and lowering a finger in a series of even, rapid movements. For example, cover all of the holes on the flute with your fingers. Now, take the ring finger of your right hand and rapidly lift and replace it in even, regular movements. The resulting sound is what is called a *trill*. Experiment with different notes on your flute and see what trills will result. A trill is indicated in music as follows:

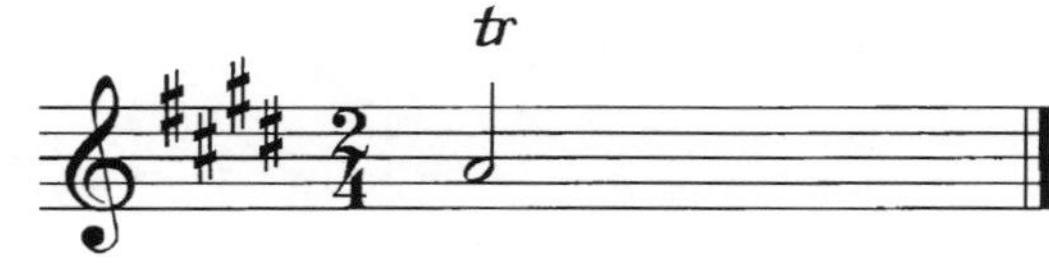

Mordent: This technique calls for a single, quick alternation of the written note with the note immediately above it. As used with the Native American flute, it means to rapidly lift a finger off and then back on to a hole. It is depicted in music as follows:

Flutter Tonguing: This effect is achieved by a rapid "fluttering" of the tongue, which is achieved by rolling the tongue against the roof of the mouth while blowing through the flute. This is the same technique that is used when one rolls an "R" with the tongue as in the Spanish language, or in the simulation of a machine gun. Practice rolling the "R" and making the sound before using the effect with your flute. It is musically notated as follows:

Double Tonguing: This technique is utilized when the notes are to be performed at a velocity which exceeds the tongue's natural ability to articulate. In singular tonguing, "ta-ta-ta-ta," only the tip of the tongue is used. This can be slow for some people. But, in double tonguing both the front and the back of the tongue are utilized, theoretically doubling the articulation speed. To achieve double tonguing, a syllable aid is used. The performer uses the syllables with regard to tongue and mouth formation only - the voice is not used. To double tongue, the following syllable formations can be used: ta-ka-ta-ka; da-ga-da-ga; du-gu-du-gu; or tu-ku-tu-ku. There is no notation that indicates to the performer that he or she should double tongue. It is purely up to the performer. When the music goes too fast to articulate by using single tonguing, then switch into double tonguing. However, there is a symbol in music that indicates to the performer to rhythmically divide the quarter note into four sixteenth notes. When the performer sees two slash marks through the stem of a quarter note, then the performer should play four sixteenth notes on that pitch instead of just playing a quarter note. These slashes do not, however, mean that the performer is to double tongue. Only double tongue if the notes are too fast to single tongue. See the example below:

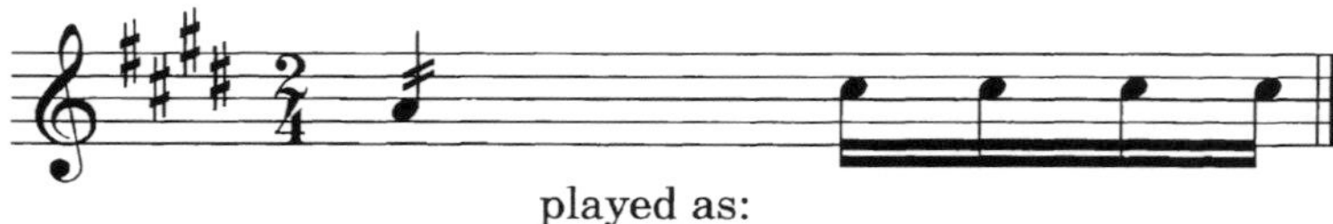

Bending or Sliding: By allowing the finger or fingers to gradually and slowly raise or lower upon the hole or holes of the flute, the result is a bending of the note or a sliding into or out of a pitch/note. The first example indicates a slide into a note from below. Here, play the first note and slowly lift the fingers to produce the second note. In the second example, the note is to be slid into from above.

It is important that the bending or sliding be a smooth transition. This technique requires practice in order to master the specific finger velocity necessary to achieve the smooth transition between pitches, which, by the way, can vary from flute to flute.

Lowering the Fundamental: By positioning the end of the flute close to your leg or some other object, you will discover that, on many flutes, you can lower the fundamental pitch up to a full half-step. This extends the range of the flute. [The fundamental pitch of each flute is the tone that is sounded with all fingers down.]

Additional Note Regarding Embellishments

I would strongly suggest that if you have difficulties with any of these techniques, or do not grasp their fundamentals, that you seek out any wind instrument player and ask for a bit of help. If you do not know any wind instrument players then stop at a few music stores and ask for some help. The person behind the counter may very well be a wind instrument player. If not, then they will know to whom to direct you. Some individuals are simply rather bashful about asking for help or are even slightly embarrassed. Do not be afraid to ask for help!

Regarding performer embellishments, Mary Riemer states the following:

> "Finally, there are a number of ornamental features which together create an idiomatic flute style. The most characteristic of these is the intense vibrato with which the tonic of the melody is played. Grace notes, an octave above the tonic... Grace notes within the melodic line, turns, mordents, and trills are commonly used, as are downward glissandi and rising releases at phrase endings."

I do not rely upon the written music to direct me to add many of these embellishments, but rather add them as I see fit and where I feel that they are appropriate within the song. I believe that these techniques should be left, as much as is possible, to the whims of each of us as individual flute players to use or not use.

Final Advice - Beginner and Intermediate Students

Please do not take any of this book too seriously. Playing the Native American flute should be a purely pleasurable experience. When it gets to be a struggle, then stop. It is not necessary that you learn any of what you have read, or will read. As stated in the introduction: the single greatest beauty and enduring quality of this lovely instrument is that you really do not need to know anything about music, nor do you need any sheet music or music lessons to play the flute. Be patient and play at your own pace. At all cost, avoid paralysis through analysis. Just keep blowing through the pointy end and take pleasure in the maturation of your own sounds that come from your heart.

> "Don't make a science out of the flute - it won't work. The flute is not about science and it is not about 'music.' The flute is about the heart and spiritual connection. Listen to the flute - it will teach you all that you really need to know about it. The flute will teach you patience, too. Learn to listen with your heart and not your mind so much. The 'longest distance' is 18 inches - the distance from your head to your heart. Don't spend so much time trying to make such a big deal out of the stuff that isn't as important."

~ Stephen McMahan, flute maker ~

The Warble - Advanced Students

The warble is a "natural vibrato" effect occurring in some flutes when the fundamental is played. Some people find this to be a pleasing attribute, while others do not. Many have read about this effect, but not many people have actually heard the warble since few Native American flutes exhibit this effect.

Betty Austin Hensley, in her book covering the early 20th century flutist Thurlow Lieurance and his flute collection, referred to this effect as a "bubble" and indicates that approximately 10 percent of his flutes produced a good bubble (Hensley).

Educator Edward Wapp Wahpeconiah [Comanche/Sauk and Fox] wrote that:

> "There were three main characteristics of the flute that were preferred by both makers and players and are yet important to players. The two most important were a pleasing tone and a usable arrangement of scale tones; otherwise, the flute was discarded and never played. The third characteristic, which is not found on many flutes, was a warbling sound on the lower pitch of the scale. The warble, in actuality, is a rapid alternation between two different pitches [acoustical beats] and was probably incorporated into the instrument's design to imitate vocal pulsation that is characteristic of Indian singing. This sound was and is yet preferred by flute players and achieved by only a few makers." (Wapp, 1984)

Later, Ed Wapp wrote the following to Tim Crawford in a personal letter:

> "One thing helps to explain another. The flute used the vocal love song as source material. In singing the vocal love song, the singer tried to disguise the voice. As well, an aspect of vocal performance practice of the love song, a vocal pulsation was sung on the fundamental. The warble imitates the vocal ornamentation. My grandfather's flute has the warble. Doc Tate Nevaquaya really liked the flute. I remember Dr. Payne when he was trying to figure out the warble. Several makers around Anadarko claimed that they knew how to put it in a flute. Basically, and it takes precision to do it, the nick on the lip [splitting edge] causes [it]… I had to laugh. The flutes that we use at the Institute of American Indian Arts [IAIA] in Santa Fe, New Mexico, have the warble, and they are made from PVC pipe. One of the female students got one with a strong warble. When she played it, it frightened her."

So far, the warble has been commented upon the most by Richard Payne. In 1988, Dr. Payne wrote:

> "Using a properly constructed Plains flute with all tone holes covered, diaphragmatic air will produce the tonic pitch F sharp in warm vibrato. This accentuated vibrato, known as the 'warble,' is an important feature of traditional Plains Indian flute playing. It is accentuated by directing the air blade slightly high over the fipple edge and further enhanced by added support of the air column slightly compressed in the pressure chamber of the flute. Tone frequency of the vibrato can be increased by as much as a half-step by pushing cold air to produce a multiphonic warble, the tempo and tonality of which can be controlled in an effective manner. This warble, scrupulously avoided by organ pipe builders who term it "burble," is a prized attribute of the Plains flute which can be driven with considerable variation in air pressure, in contrast to the organ pipe." (Payne, 1988)

Then in 1999, Dr. Richard Payne wrote:

> "The 'toubat flute' [this is the name that he gives a specific flute of his own design] requires particular skills in playing technique. In the old style of Plains flute playing, the vigorous multiphonic 'warble' on the fundamental note was highly regarded. This requires careful alignment of the block, nest, and roost so that the air stream is directed slightly high on the fipple edge [splitting edge]. Breath control is critical to execution of the oscillating warble; this is accomplished with warm diaphragmatic breathing dynamics.

> Air compressibility is also aided by providing slight impediment to the air stream, resulting from a slightly narrowed embouchure hole and air vent." (Payne, 1999)

From trial and error observations, it appears that the warble is generally best achieved with the bird/block's leading edge being just forward of the chamber separating block. In addition to the position of the block, an increase in air pressure, thereby creating a higher compression of the air in the air chamber, appears to be a general requirement for the production of this "natural" vibrato.

Excluding double bore Native American flutes, I have five principal flutes that I use to demonstrate the warble: a D# flute by Ken Light; an E flute by James Gilliland; an F# flute by Dr. Richard Payne (a.k.a. the "toubat" flute); a G flute by Timothy Nevaquaya; and a G flute by Dr. Oliver Jones, Jr. Each flute seems to have an observable difference in the velocity of the oscillation. Ken Light's is by far the fastest, while Timothy Nevaquaya's is the slowest. Dr. Jones' flute appears to be in the middle with regard to oscillation speed and has one of the more stable and consistent warbles. The Ken Light flute and the Dr. Payne flute both have a metal nest. The Dr. Jones flute has a wood nest. The James Gilliland flute has the air channel cut into the body of the flute, while the Timothy Nevaquaya flute has the air channel cut into the bird/block.

Dr. Payne was of the tentative opinion that a narrow mouthpiece end might possibly be a perquisite for warble production; however, the James Gilliland flute, being constructed of river cane, has a totally open air chamber and, interestingly enough, appears to be one of the easiest with which to demonstrate this effect. The point that Dr. Payne was most concerned about making was that an increase in compression within the air chamber is required, whether by the player blowing harder or possibly by windway design.

In preparation for a presentation on this topic at the first INAFA convention, I took a dial micrometer and set about to measure every possible and conceivable flute attribute that would cause the warble. After taking a variety of measurements on four of the flutes that warble, as well as on flutes that do not warble, it was concluded that there was not any single characteristic or combination of characteristics that could be identified as being physically responsible for this effect.

As far as is known, of my five warbling flutes, Dr. Payne, Sonny and Timothy Nevaquaya, and Dr. Jones are the only builders that specifically set out to create flutes that will exhibit a natural warble. In a conversation with the author on this topic in April of 2001, Dr. Payne confessed that not all the flutes that he builds exhibit this effect; those that do not, he destroys. While on this subject, Dr. Payne is not in the business of building flutes to sell. He only builds a few each year (Payne, 2001). However, Jeff Calavan of Laughing Mallard Flutes informed me in February of 2002 that Dr. Payne had granted him a license to build the warbling toubat flute. Jeff will be building them to order.

Dr. Jones of Wild Horse Mountain Flutes in La Jolla, Calif., does build warbling flutes for sale. In a conversation with the author on February 7, 2002, Dr. Jones stated that he has yet to discover with certainty what physical characteristics or attributes are required to produce a warble; however, he has discovered that for his flutes there are two very specific criteria necessary in their construction for them to have the warble characteristic. The first is that the air column spacing under the block has to be very thin - 1/64 of an inch. Second, the distance from the block [bird, saddle] across to the beveled splitting edge must be 10/32 of an inch.

Flute builder Michael "Searching Bear" Smallridge of Searching Bear Flutes in Ravenna, Ohio, stated that he is now achieving consistency with building warbling flutes:

> "Every flute I make now I am able to find where it will warble without even blowing on it. At least with my flutes and the way I make them, it's all in where the totem is positioned in relation to the 'bottom' of the window. I tend to burn my windows at a slight slanted angle. I have also found that just because it warbles does not mean this is the best totem position for the rest of the notes on the flute." (Smallridge, 2002)

In a phone conversation with Lew Paxton Price, he stated that, while he personally is not attracted to this effect, it is a result of a flute's tendency to over blow. To increase the tendency of a flute to over blow, given equal diameters, a change in the ratio of the length of the air chamber to the sound chamber can contribute to this tendency. This is best accomplished by lengthening the air chamber. In addition to an increase in the length of the air chamber, the next important variable is the angle of the bird/block chimney and the shape of that chimney. The bird/block variables are open to experimentation, with the important objective being that of reducing the induction of outside air into the air stream as it crosses over to the lip or edge (Price, 2001).

R. Carlos Nakai sent the following in response to an inquiry on the warble:

> "In actuality, the warble sound which is sounded at the all-closed position only on all five- and six-hole flutes is, to my experience, merely an indicator that the sound-producing mechanism is well made and is correctly positioned for optimum air flow from the the air chamber over the block and directed by the saddle/bird mechanism against the distal edge of the body tube hole. The oscillations of air movement coincidence with the Coreolis effect and the standing sine wave in the body tube helps to make this effect possible. That's all. There's no mystery, as my 1985 air pressure smoke tests have shown! As an effect, if one only played the flute's tonic pitch then the warble effect would be a useful embellishment for modulating that singular pitch. The variations of air intensity in effecting a more or less pronounced and sometimes faster or slower warble is also an indicator of effective use of embouchural air control by the flutist and adds to the quality of the resolving pitch.
>
> In more cases than not, the subsequent quavers/vibratos that are performed at various stages of one's performance are matched to the warble. So, upon returning to the resolving pitch, if it is the lowest one, it will be the use of the warble rather than the vibrator. It's simple, but difficult in practice!" (2002)

I have two drone flutes and both of these flutes exhibit a warble. Only one of these flutes is constructed in such a manner that I can blow down either bore, individually, as well as both together. On this drone flute, neither bore will produce a warble individually.; yet, a warble is created when playing both bores on the fundamental. The drone warble then appears to be the result of an oscillation between the tones produced in each bore, created because neither bore is precisely tuned to the other. When a tuner was put to this particular drone flute, what was revealed was that there is a difference of about 30 cents between each bore of the drone.

What is clearly happening with the drone warble is termed a "beat frequency" which results

> "... from the interference between two sound waves of slightly different frequencies. The frequency of the beats will be equal to the difference between the frequencies of the sound waves. Since the beats will disappear if the two frequencies are made identical, the phenomenon is useful in the tuning of musical instruments. Beats can occur between the fundamental of one pitch and a higher harmonic of another, as well as between the two fundamentals." (Randel)

This same explanation may also hold true for all single bore flutes, and it helps to further explain the differences in the warble speed described in different flutes. This means that the warble in single bore flutes is a result of the differences in the frequencies of the secondary tone being produced. However, an understanding of the beat frequency concept being a physical explanation for the warble still leaves the mystery of how this effect can be induced by flute builders themselves.

Two of my warbling flutes have noticeable nicks at the splitting edge, when viewed with magnification. Timothy Nevaquaya's and Dr Oliver Jones' flutes have this characteristic, as well. Dr. Jones' flutes also show the splitting edge to be slightly angled across the opening. While I do not know if this is the sole reason for these flutes to warble, it does cause me to speculate that there might possibly be several different and correct explanations as to how to cause a flute to warble.

The drone effect has led me to conclusions about the single-bore flutes that warble. I believe that something must be happening at the splitting edge to create, in effect, a balance of some type between the fundamental note and an overblown note, whether another fundamental note of a different pitch or simply some higher harmonic. Whether this is due to a part of the air stream being delayed, which could occur by the splitting edge being angled or possibly compressed, or angled windows, or by the splitting edge possibly being nicked (or angled) somewhat, the definitive answer is unknown to me. It is hoped that some future researcher will be able to resolve this issue with clarity. Quite possibly, Nakai's explanation already has solved the mystery.

A final observation of interest concerns a 19th century French craftsman who, when building organ flue pipes, found it to be important to have certain pipes constructed in two ranks, with one turned slightly sharp to create what was referred to as an undulating sound, also know as a beat frequency and/or warble (Randel).

Note: For those interested in hearing some earlier recording that exhibit a flute warble, there is a tape that accompanies the thesis, entitled "Instrumental and Vocal Love Songs of the North American Indians." On this tape are three recordings that exhibit the warble effect: "Meskwaki Melody" by Wilson Roberts [1956] and "Winnebago Melody" [1964] and a "Kiowa Melody" by Everett Cozad [1964] (Riemer, 1978).

In addition, on the tape that accompanies the thesis "The Flute of the Canadian Amerindian" by Paula Conlon there are eight recordings which exhibit the warble: "Kiowa Flute Song by Belo Cozad [1954]; "Meskawaki, Love Song for the Flute" by Wilson Roberts [1956]; "Winnebago Love Song" [1964]; "I Saw an Eagle Fly" by Doc Tate Nevaquaya, Comanche [1964]; "First love Song for Flute" by Ed Wapp, Potawatomi [1982]; "Second Love Song for Flute" by Ed Wapp, Potawatomi [1982]; "I Saw an Eagle Fly" by Ed Wapp [1982]; and "Comanche Modern Courting Song" by Ed Wapp [1982]. Two of the songs on this recording appear to be the same as two selections on the Riemer recording.

Flute Care

No process, procedure, or chemical product is recommended or endorsed in this book. The reader should consider what is presented herein as the personal experience, observations, and opinions of a number of individuals, and use it as background information that may or may not be accurate or appropriate. The reader is further advised to proceed with caution before using any named product or quoted procedure. Use personal due diligence and research all literature and warnings that accompany any specific product and/or chemical.

Most importantly, the best advice about the care of your flute are the instructions provided by the builder of your instrument. Flute owners should read the literature that may have come with the flute and/or contact the flute builder directly for detailed instructions.

Wetting Out

While it is dependent upon the relative humidity of the air, as well as the temperature, sooner or later there will be a problem with the flute losing its tone due to an excess retention of moisture, especially within the very narrow space or air channel underneath the block or bird. This moisture build-up is common to wind instruments and is caused by the warm breath condensing upon the colder surface of the interior of the flute. This moisture is not saliva, and the cooler the interior of your flute is then the greater the amount of moisture that will accumulate, especially in the air channel under the block. This results in a loss of tone.

At the workshops hosted each year by R. Carlos Nakai and Ken Light at the Feathered Pipe Ranch in Montana, Nakai teaches that there is a "wet breath" and a "dry breath" and that when we play we should try and play with the air coming from the upper part of our lungs, as this is where the dryer air resides. The dryer air will help reduce the accumulation of moisture in the flute.

One method of "prevention" that I find helps with this problem in some flutes, at least softwood flutes and those made of plastic, is to keep the surfaces in the windway or air channel well waxed. This seems to me to slow down the adhesion of moisture drops in this very critical area. I would suggest checking with your flute builder as to what type of wax might be appropriate.

While somewhat contradictory in content to my own method of waxing, a novel approach that should be considered for "prevention" was suggested by Joel Shaber, a musician from Idaho. In an e-mail dated January 1, 2002, Joel said:

> "The windways of hardwood flutes are often smooth and highly finished, usually with oil-based products. This creates surface tension and encourages droplet formation. Just as water on a waxed automobile finish tends to bead up, moisture on a smooth, oil finished or waxed windway will tend to bead up - exactly what you do not want. There is a product called 'anti-condensation fluid' sold for recorder windways which will greatly reduce the surface tension on windway surfaces and allow moisture to flow away, rather than form droplets. It is essentially a refined detergent. It will not damage the finish, in my opinion, and it works exactly like a rinse agent for glassware - it reduces the surface tension so that the moisture remains flat, in a sheet, and flows away rather than beading up and 'sticking' to windway surfaces. Anti-condensation fluid is available at most good music stores. To use this product, remove the block from the flute, apply a few drops of the solution to the windway floor [on the flute] and the windway ceiling [the underside of the block]. Gently move the solution around with a Q-tip such that it covers all surfaces and bevels of the windway. Allow it to dry on the instrument. Do not wipe it off. Repeat at regular intervals and always after cleaning the windway."

Flute builder, author, and researcher Lew Paxton Price suggests the use of a silicon spray in the windway (Price, 1999).

During performances, I grasp the barrel of the flute with my fingers around the block [to prevent it from flying off] and then vigorously shake the mouth end toward the floor to remove the accumulated moisture. However, try not to send any of the moisture flying in the audience's direction. In addition, I often carry a small can of compressed air and place the tube at the front opening of the air channel, under the bird, and blow back towards the mouth piece to clear the moisture.

There are a number of options that can be used to reduce and prevent moisture accumulation, as well as for dealing with it once it does begin. I have correspondences from a flute builder and two performers regarding this issue. Study all of their suggestions, as they are all useful and informative.

> "The cooler the surfaces of the flute, the more condensation, hence the increased tendency for 'watering out' of the PF-Series flutes as the ABS is denser with more cool thermal mass than cedar; however, some of the dense, exotic tropical and domestic hardwood flutes that folks are making are probably just as problematic in this regard. Okay, now what to do with the moisture? The only way to ameliorate the formation of the water is a warm flute in a warm, dry place. All portions of the cedar flutes that I build are finished so that the water beads up and can be dealt with in any number of ways. Use a thin [and I mean thin!] coating of a paste-type furniture wax on the bottom of the block and the top of the wall. Many individuals believe that bee's wax, especially the liquid variety, works quite well for this purpose. The wax lessens the ability of the condensed water droplets to stick to the surfaces of the interior flute where they can accumulate, come together, and ultimately form the large drops that occlude the air channel. Because they cannot stick as well, these droplets are more likely to be blown on their way and less likely to come together into the larger drops that cause the problem of occluding the air channel."

~ Ken Light, Amon Olorin Flutes ~

> "After a playing session, or during a long session, I swab out my flutes using shotgun cleaning pads [little soft white squares] attached to the end of a 22-caliber pistol cleaning rod, after removing the block to allow it to dry. Do this carefully so as not to damage the air chamber walls. During a session, I also clear out the air chamber by holding a finger over the hole in front of the block, while simultaneously blowing vigorously into the mouth piece. This blows a lot of moisture straight out of the air chamber. As a precaution, I avoid eating or drinking immediately before playing. Sucking on a lemon has a drying effect on the mouth which might help."

~ Bob West, performer ~

> "I purchased a very porous, thin, soft foam pad and cut it into pieces about the same diameter of the flute and about three-fourths of the length of the air tube. I then eased the foam down through the exit opening from the air tube and made sure that the foam did not get in the way of the bird area and then proceeded to play some songs. Normally, I need to shake out the moisture after about fifteen or twenty minutes, depending on the humidity, etc. Well, the end result after three sessions on alternate days was that I was playing for about one hour at a time and found only very light moisture lines on the bird and air wall crossover area. At the end of each session I removed the bird, eased the foam out of the air chamber, and washed and dried the foam. I should mention that I found no problem blowing my breath through the foam. If you decide to try out my idea you will need to obtain foam that allows unrestricted air flow."

~ John Burns, performer ~

There does exist a consensus among many builders and players that the best way to care for your flute after use is to remove the block and stand the instrument on the air chapter [end you blow through] at an angle, so that moisture can drain out onto a towel. Use a portion of the towel to wipe the bottom of the block off, as well as the top of the external windway and nest if provided.

Caring for the Flute's Finish

As I stated at the start of this chapter, the best advice about the care of your flute, in all cases, is that provided by the builder of your instrument. In fact, failure to follow the builder's care instructions may very well void any warranty that may exist. The proper care of both the exterior and interior surfaces of your specific flute will be very much dependent upon the type of finish used, if any, on the wood. Your builder is the best source for this information!

Presumably, most of the finishes used by builders offer some degree of protection from moisture by creating a vapor barrier, although "barrier" may be a misleading term in as much as the finishes often protect to a matter of degree rather than an absolute. This protection, in some degree or another, helps to reduce the incidence of warping and cracking that can occur when the wood absorbs and/or releases moisture. Incidentally, where and how you store your instrument can have an effect on this issue; hot and/or humid storage conditions between use should be avoided, if at all possible.

Surprisingly, I own a number of flutes in a variety of woods by a builder who never uses any type of finish, inside or out, on his flutes. There have been no adverse reactions, although I have waxed the exterior of some of these instruments over the years. This same builder did recommend the use of mineral oil in the air chamber, as well as on the sound-chamber face of the block that separates the two chambers.

About once a year, I take each of my finished flutes and remove the block. With an old t-shirt, I apply an imported German furniture paste wax called Bekos to all of the exterior surfaces, including those of the block. I take a chamois and polish the tube and the block, and then I reassemble the flute. I use Bekos wax, as that is what was suggested to me by builder Ken Light for his flutes. Most flute builders have a wax or oil that they recommend for maintaining the specific finish of their flutes. Therefore, it is important to check with your builder for specifics.

Much more infrequently, and only if necessary, I take a small wooden dowel and wrap a piece of old t-shirt around it and insert it into the open end of the flute. I do this in order to remove the accumulated dust within the sound chamber.

Flute builder Scott Loomis uses an oil finish and recommends using a suitable oil for occasional maintenance on both the inside and outside of his instruments. He has detailed steps on the care of an oil-finished flute on his Web site: www.loomisflute.com. Scott, in an e-mail dated March 12, 2002, wrote: "... the reason that I use an oil finish is because I want to see, feel, and hear the wood and not the finish; this is just part of my philosophical approach to these very special musical instruments. Oil is the most natural form of protection for wood and, in my belief, enhances the beauty of the wood and the tonal quality of the flute over time."

On the other hand, flute builder Dave Fields stated in an e-mail to his Internet group, dated January 5, 2002, that he no longer oils the inside of his flutes, as he believes it changes the tone. Flute builder Jim Adams, in an e-mail dated January 6, 2002, to the same group stated: "I don't suggest the use of oils to clean the inside chambers of your flutes, as some types of oil can actually contribute to bacteria growth and/or weaken whatever protective finish was initially applied to the wood."

After providing flute builder perspectives on the oiling of bores, hearing from a performer on the subject might offer another insight into the subject of oiling. In an e-mail dated January 6, 2002, world flute performer and recording artist Peter Phippen wrote: "Oil is a personal preference!!! I feel that oil protects natural bore bamboo and wooden flutes, and, in my opinion, improves the tone by making them more mellow sounding. Most of you know that I love bamboo. This same debate goes on in the shakuhachi world, as well. Some folks like to oil their flutes and some don't."

Splits and Glued Seams Separation

As with other flute care issues, contact your instrument builder before attempting repairs, especially if you have a split or a separation of a glued seam.

Back in the early 1990s, I purchased a bamboo flute in Phoenix, Ariz., while visiting friends. It was a very inexpensive flute, but to my ears it had a very sweet sound. Up to that point, it was the most interesting bamboo flute that I had ever played. Oh, how I loved this instrument! Quite foolishly one winter afternoon, a few years later while on my way to a "gig," I slipped on the ice and the flute landed on the ice and broke part of my fall. My round flute was flattened. I did not have the heart to toss the instrument, so I kept it in its sorry condition for several more years.

After they opened an Eagle Hardware Store in Anchorage, Alaska, I approached one of their clerks and stated that I needed some help with a major gluing project. The clerk said, "One moment, sir. I will get for you one of our adhesive experts." About 3 minutes later the clerk comes back with the youngest looking employee that I have ever seen working in a retail store. I explained my problem with the flattened, splintered bamboo to the young man and he quickly replied that I should follow him, as he was sure he had the correct solution. After showing me a small bottle of white Elmer's wood glue, I questioned him on whether or not it would dry clear as I did not want the glue to show on the outside. He replied that he had a great deal of personal experience using this particular adhesive and that it would dry clear.

I reluctantly purchased this adhesive and figured that I had nothing to lose. As best as I could, I very patiently worked the glue around the circumference of the tube into each split and crack and clamped it up. Surprise! The glue worked and did not show. The instrument even played. Unfortunately, it lost its very sweet sound.

Flute builder Terry Austin, in an e-mail dated May 6, 2000, suggested the following for repair of a crack, other than a glued seam failure:

> A solution to this problem would be to use two-part clear epoxy. The disadvantage to this approach lies in the viscosity of the adhesive. It may be hard to get it inside the split without a high-pressure syringe. If you can do so without widening the split, you might gently level the split open to assist in completely coating the edges.
>
> Following either of these approaches, you will want to clamp the seam shut. With a finished flute, especially one with thin walls, this may be difficult to do without further damaging the flute. The best way to apply this pressure will be with rubber tubing or rubber bands. Following this gluing/clamping procedure, you will need to sand the area. Of course, at this point, you will need to renew the finish on the flute as well."

In an e-mail dated May 27, 1999, regarding the failure of a player's flute at the glued seam, Terry Austin offered this advice:

> "You can try to patch it. Try this test first, without glue. If you have clamps available [C-clamp, squeeze-grip clamps, etc.], try padding the flute with leather or a few layers of cloth and clamping the flute to see if you can squeeze the gap back together. Be careful not to apply too much pressure or you may crack the wood with clamp pressure. If you do not have access to clamps, you might try rubber bands or a rubber strip cut from a bicycle inner tube. Just wrap it tightly. This rubber strap puts a nice even pressure on the flute.
>
> If you find that you can force the split together, you can then try to glue it. Remove the clamp and the padding, and inject a waterproof glue. If possible, use a syringe with a fine tip so you can get as cleanly into the gap as possible. Once the glue is injected, re-clamp the flute. If you use a polyurethane glue, be aware that it foams as it dries and will expand out onto the outer surface. This may require light sanding to remove. You may need to refinish this spot on the flute after sanding. Polyurethane glues are moisture catalyzed and work much better if you add a bit of moisture to the joint before applying the glue. You can do this by running a wet [as opposed to damp] paper towel over the joint a few times before injecting the glue. The splitting is probably caused by the moisture of your breath and is the primary reason that most flute makers use a waterproof glue."

Another tip for this problem is to, once you are able to get the split closed, wrap it with a thin cordage similar to that used to bind the eyes on a fishing pole and also used by some flute builders on their flutes. The flute will be bound and less inclined to reopen. I purchase cordage for this purpose from a local leather supply house which they stock in a variety of colors; the ends must be secured underneath the wraps to be most effective. Where practical, try to treat any such wraps with either a varnish or by rubbing glue into the wrap, anything that will be effective in securing the wrap and not be distracting to the appearance of the flute. Monty H. Levenson of Tai Hei Shakuhachi Flutes has an excellent presentation entitled, "Binding to Repair Cracks in Bamboo," on his Web site that shows how to secure the ends of the wraps: www.shakuhachi.com/Y-BindingRepair.html

Transportation and Storage

When I fell and smashed my first bamboo flute, there were not many casing options readily available from builders. Now, many flute builders offer some form of a soft case to go with the flute purchase made either of cloth or leather, whether included or separately priced. The soft cases will help to keep the flute from being scratched and soiled, but they will not prevent crushing and denting which should be an equal, if not greater, concern.

Today, many flute builders offer hard cases as an accessory item. Some of these cases are identical to those manufactured for take-down fishing poles, being a cloth covered plastic tube with a zippered closure. Other builders offer customized cases of plastic pipe and covered with blanketing material, also with a zippered closure.

I have also heard from some folks who have gone to their local hardware store and purchased plastic "utility" pipes, glued one end shut and then screwed the other end closed with an access cover, not unlike a plumbing clean out. For carrying some of my longer flutes, I have an aluminum case made for shotguns that works quite well. Gun cases come in a variety of materials and sizes, and many of them are quite practical for flute protection. In today's atmosphere, however, they probably are not the best option for air travel.

Flute performers who travel on air planes must either purchase something quite strong for freight handling or have something custom made that will dimensionally fit within the standards imposed upon carry-on luggage. My main metal carrying case was custom manufactured, from aluminum, to meet the airline standard in effect at the time.

Regardless of your choice, I cannot emphasize enough how important it is to provide crush protection for your flutes when transporting them.

Flute Hygiene

Some flute players are uncomfortable about sharing their instruments with other players, or with picking up a flute from a sale table to try. I am unaware of any specific "studies" that have been completed or undertaken by "knowledgeable" individuals that could offer adequate guidance in this area regarding the sharing of wooden musical instruments .

My original draft for this section was several pages in length, and it described the pros and cons of various approaches used and suggested by a number of players and builders. However, upon reflection, I have reached the conclusion that this topic is still too controversial and "unresolved." I am not comfortable presenting those pros and cons of specific approaches, especially as I have no medical expertise.

For those readers who do have concerns, the best advice that I can offer is to discuss this with your family physician. Always respect the flutes of others. Do not play another's flute unless given permission to do so. Even then, follow the advice of your physician with regard to precautions.

Note: As a general caution, the reader should be aware that all or some individual woods, finishes, and PVC products can potentially have some negative health impact, depending upon manufacture and use. Flutists are encouraged to discuss their concerns with their health care provider and/or other qualified professionals.

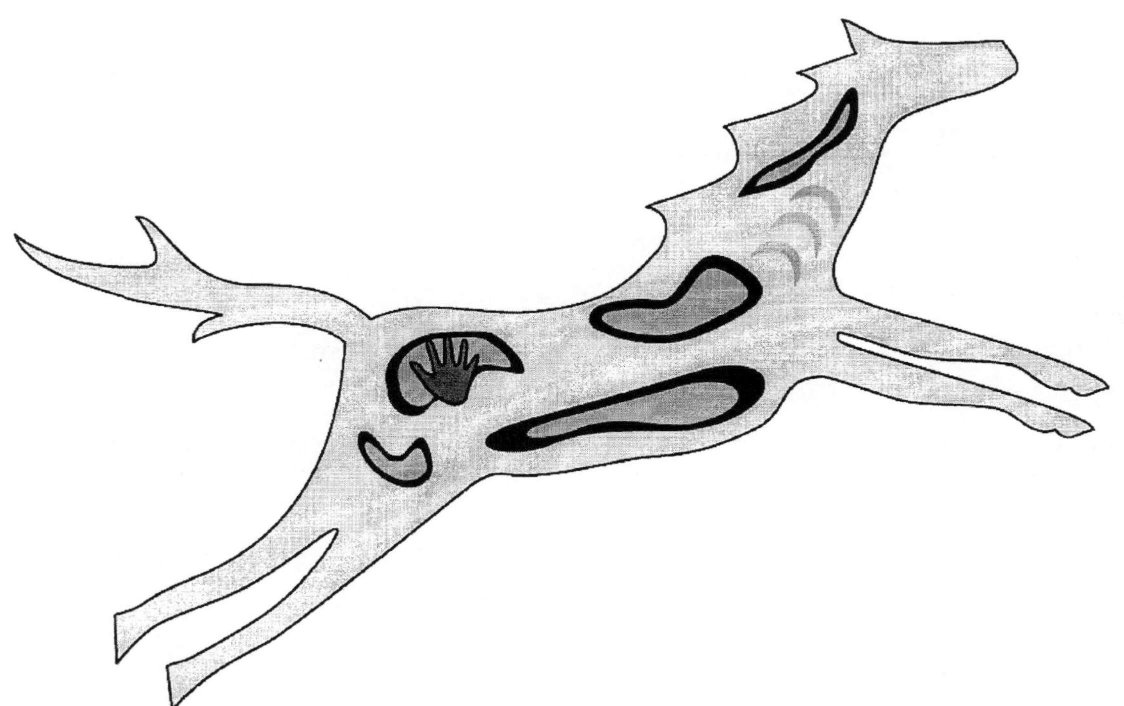

Elementary Music Fundamentals

As it was mentioned previously in the "Introduction," this book is not intended to be a primer on how to read sheet music; there are other texts better suited to that purpose, and I encourage you to purchase one at your local music or book store, if this ability needs to be addressed. Nevertheless, I feel that what is presented here will enable the beginning student to read the TABlature music contained within this book.

Essentials

Staff: 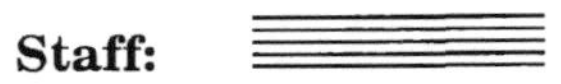

A *staff* is comprised of five horizontal lines called *staff lines*. The position of the notes on the staff determine the note's name or its relative pitch [frequency]. Every staff has five lines and four spaces, and each possesses a name that identifies a note.

Clef: This is a clef symbol and it is used on the left hand side of the staff to denote the pitch and range of the notes. This particular clef sign is called a *treble clef* or *G clef.*

Measure and Bar Lines: A *measure* is the area between two bar lines and contains various note durations. Musicians often use the term *bar* interchangeably with the term *measure*, that is three *bars* of music means the same thing as three *measures* of music.

Note and Rest Durations:

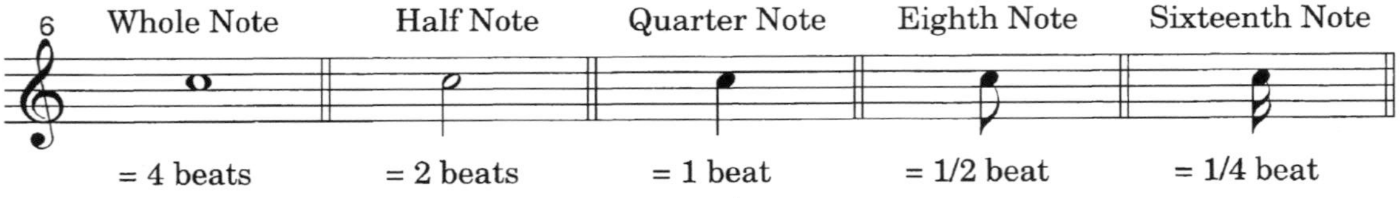

As an example, if the beat or tempo of a song was indicated as 60 beats per minute, then the whole note would be 4 seconds long, the half note would be 2 seconds long, the quarter note would be 1 second long, the eighth note would be one-half of a second long, and the sixteenth note would be one-fourth of a second in duration. It should be noted that 60 beats per minute is considered to be a slow tempo, while 120 beats per minute is a moderately fast tempo.

Many students find it easier to grasp rhythm and note durations by learning to relate everything to the quarter note, which is equal to one beat. When we tap our foot to the beat of a song, we are usually tapping out quarter notes. Quarter notes are easy to count - one, two, three, four. Tap your foot and think about the count - one, two, three, four. Repeat this several times. Try varying the rate or tempo at which you tap your foot, while still counting to yourself - one, two, three, four, etc.

The idea is to start training yourself to think of a quarter note as a single beat, with the length of that beat being determined by the tempo of the music. All the other notes are either multiples of the quarter note [i.e. the half note and the whole note] or fractions of the quarter note [i.e. the eighth note and the sixteenth note].

Once you are comfortable with the quarter note, then you can begin working on the eighth note. The eighth note is half as long as the quarter note; therefore, there are two eighth notes for each quarter note duration. As you tap your foot, the first eighth note occurs as the foot hits the ground while the second eighth note is articulated as the foot comes up. The count now changes slightly. It is now: one-and, two-and, three-and, four-and. An eighth note appears on the number and an eighth note occurs on the "and." Try this a number of times. It is rather awkward at first, but keep trying and you will catch on.

The half note is easier because it is simply twice as long as the quarter note. When you see the symbol for a half note, hold the note for two taps of your foot.

There are four sixteenth notes in each quarter note. Therefore, every eighth note has two sixteenth notes. The syllables used in counting sixteenth notes are as follows: 1 e & a, 2 e & a, 3 e & a, 4 e & a. A note occurs on each syllable. The foot comes down on the number and up on the "&." The sixteenth notes must be counted in an even manner. Until you are really comfortable with the previously explained durations, I would not get overly concerned with the sixteenth notes. Now would be a good time to start this section over to review the basic quarter note concept.

Please keep in mind that, with the Native American flute, precision of note durations is not that critical. Obviously, the duration of notes is important for individuals in an ensemble, otherwise chaos would ensue; however, you are playing your own instrument for your own enjoyment. So, relax and enjoy it, and do not get hung up on note duration precision.

As with notes, *rests* [durations of silence] have a defined length.

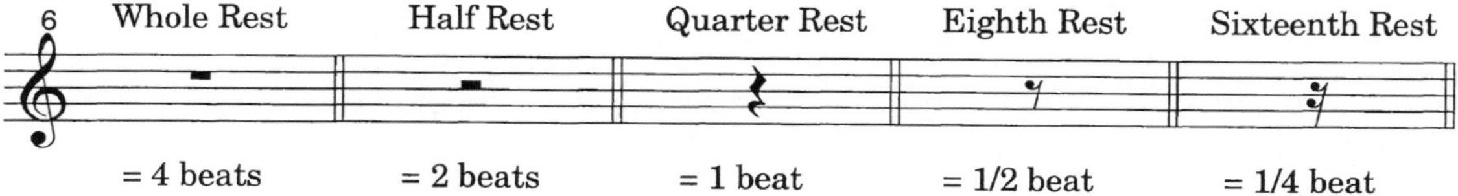

Additional duration symbols and notation are shown below:

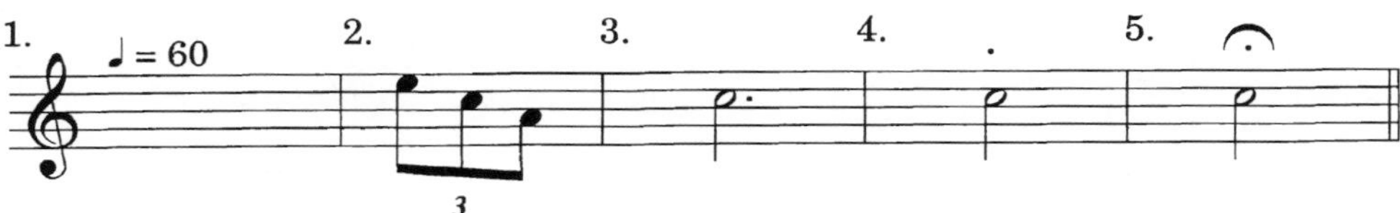

The first measure in the second illustration shows the tempo symbol, in this case 60 beats per minute. Often, especially with Native American flute music, the actual beat is not listed but rather suggested through some informational comment such as "*Slowly, With Feeling*." This type of indication is not defined, therefore leaving the tempo decision up to the performer's personal taste.

The second measure of the second illustration reveals what is called a *triplet*. This rhythmic indication requires that the three eighth notes shown be played in one beat. Thus, one beat must be divided evenly into three portions. The number three will always appear if the group of notes is to be played as a triplet. Syllables that will help to divide the beat evenly into three parts are as follows: straw-ber-ry. Thus, when your foot taps the floor, begin to say the divided-up word "straw-ber-ry." Say the word slowly across one beat. You should only begin the word again when your foot taps the floor.

The third measure in the second example shows a dotted half note. Notes and rests which have a dot to the right are to be held for half as long as the original written note/rest duration. In measure three, the note is to be held for three beats. This is because the written note is a half note and the dot adds one beat because that is half the duration of a half note, the original duration indicated.

The fourth measure shows a dot over the head of a note. This *staccato* marking means to play the note separated and detached, instead of its full duration. The beat or tempo does not change, only the character and aural duration of the note sound different. In technical terms, the note that is indicated to be performed in a staccato manner should be played exactly half the length of the note's actual duration. For example, if a half note is marked to be played staccato, the performer should hold it for only one beat with an entire beat of silence manifesting before starting the next note.

The fifth measure shows a symbol called a *fermata*. In this context, it means to extend the note longer than is indicated, generally twice the typical value of the note.

Ties, Grace Notes, and the Caesura:

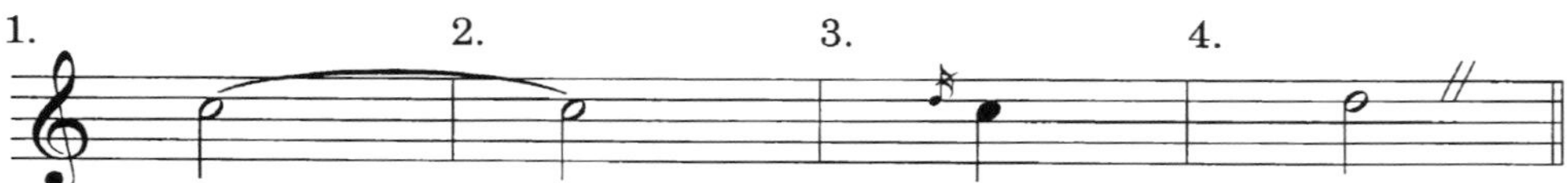

The first and second measures illustrate two notes tied together. The arc that connects two notes of the same pitch is called a *tie*. When notes are tied together across a measure or within the same measure, they have the duration of their combined values.

The third measure shows a small note just in front and above a regularly sized note. This is called a *grace note*. This ornamental note has no rhythmic importance. It is not to be figured into the counting of the measure. It is to be played very rapidly prior to the performance of the important, written note. [Note: In the sheet music contained within this book, the grace notes do not necessarily have the TABlature pitch indicated. Instead, the grace notes are simply any note of a higher pitch of the note that they precede. It is left up to the discretion of the performer.] One of the easiest ways to play a grace note is to raise a finger off of any covered hole toward the mouthpiece, and then rapidly recover the hole again. This will almost always provide a suitable grace note of a higher pitch value. The best advice is to experiment.

The fourth measure shows two slashes [i.e. //] across the top staff line. This is called a *caesura* and indicates a complete stopping point of an uneven duration. The duration of the pause is subject to the whim of the performer.

Time Signature:

Musical compositions are comprised of a sequence of differing note durations and pitches. These are arranged into measures. Each measure is separated by a vertical line on the staff called a bar line. The *time signature* of a song determines the number of beats within each measure, as well as their organization.

The most common time signature in music is that of 4/4 time, also called *common time*. This is illustrated in the first measure of the above example. This means that each measure contains four beats [top number], with the quarter note getting the beat [bottom number].

In the second measure, the time signature of 3/4 is shown. This means that each measure contains three beats [top number], with the quarter note again getting the beat [bottom number].

The last measure of the previous music example shows 6/8 time. This means that each measure contains six eighth notes or the equivalent [2 beats] in a measure, with the eighth note [bottom number] equaling one-third of the beat. In 6/8 time, there are two beats per measure, with each beat being divided into three eighth note - the subdivision of the beat.

Important Symbols:

Measure one of the above illustration shows a single measure repeat symbol which simply means to repeat the preceding measure of music.

Measure two shows an *ottava* symbol. When one encounters this indication, all of the notes falling within the range of the dotted bracket should be performed an octave above what is written. [See the discussion of over blowing in the chapter entitled "Playing the Native American Flute."]

Measure three shows the *turn* symbol over the note C. Measure four illustrates the progression to be played when encountering a *turn*. The note immediately above is played first, followed by a return to the written note, then the note below is played, with the conclusion of the turn on the original note. However, this must take place within the given note duration.

Measures five and six show a curved line under all of the notes. This is called a *slur* and requires that the notes all be performed together in one smooth flow, without any individual emphasis or break. More specifically, only the first note that is at the beginning of the slur is to be started with the tongue.

Also, measure six shows the *lift-off* symbol [♩ ⁄] as I use it. Please see page 22 for a description of the lift-off. With one or two exceptions, I do not use this symbol too often as the technique is up to the individual performer to use when he or she feels that it is appropriate.

Dynamic Markings:

Dynamic markings are utilized to indicate changes in volume. This is notated in the music either by use of a standard set of specific letters or by symbols. This is illustrated below:

pp = pianissimo = very soft
p = piano = soft
mp = mezzo piano = medium soft
mf = mezzo forte = medium loud
f = forte = loud
ff = fortissimo = very loud

Dynamics are important in music. They provide variety and coloration to a performance. In addition, the use of dynamics enhances the expressiveness of a musical composition. With the Native American flute, as with any instrument, it takes time and practice to learn the dynamic capabilities of your particular instrument, as well as the technique and control necessary to carry out the varying degrees of loudness and softness.

Other symbols used in music to indicate dynamic change are illustrated in the example below:

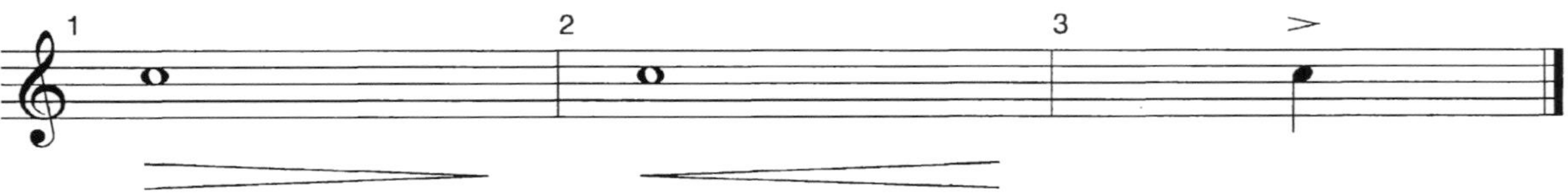

Measure one in the above musical example shows a *decrescendo* symbol which means to gradually decrease the volume of the note[s]. Measure two illustrates a *crescendo* symbol which means to gradually increase the volume of the note[s]. Sometimes, the dynamic changes are expressed with the words themselves, or their abbreviations, rather than the symbols.

Measure three shows an *accent* mark. This symbol means that the note[s] should be emphasized. The achievement of this can be done through a harder attack of the note with the tongue, accompanied by an increased burst of air.

Repeat Symbols:

The repeat symbols used in the sheet music within this book are as follows:

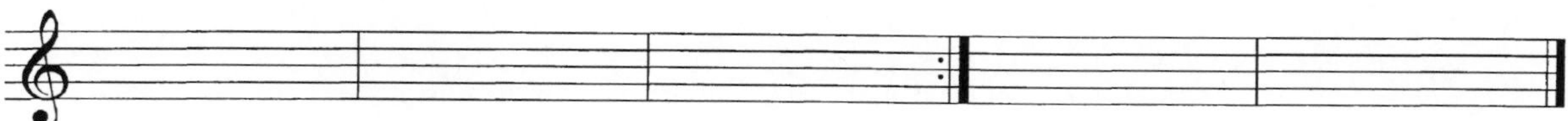

The above example indicates to play to the repeat sign, then go back to the beginning and play to the end.

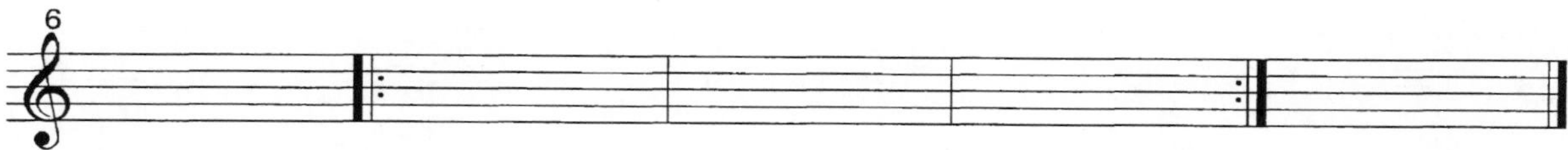

The above example indicates to play to the right-facing repeat sign [the second sign] and then go back to the left-facing repeat sign [the first sign], and only repeat that section. After repeating that section, play to the end.

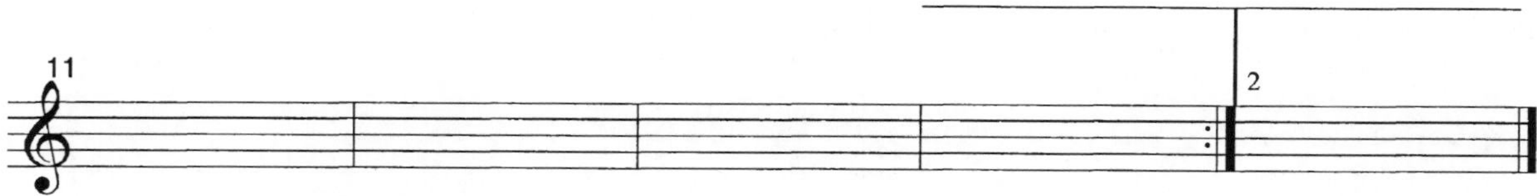

The above example indicates to play from the beginning to the repeat sign, and then go back to the beginning. When the first ending is encountered, do not play it. Instead, skip to the second ending.

In the above example, the *D.C. al Coda* means to repeat from the beginning until you reach the first *coda* sign, and then skip to the second *coda* sign and play until the end.

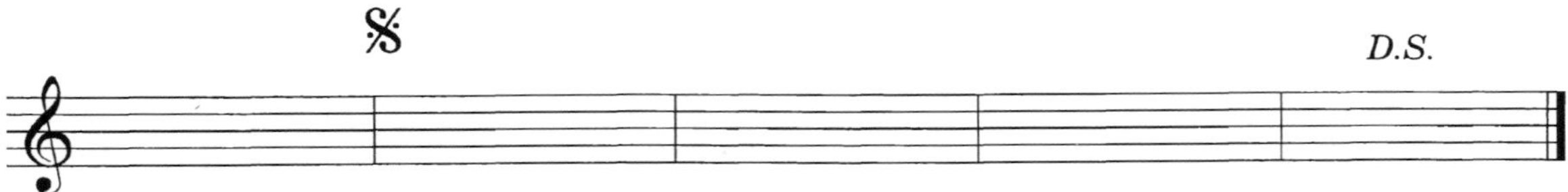

In the above example, the *D.S. al Segno* means to go back to the *sign* and repeat the section.

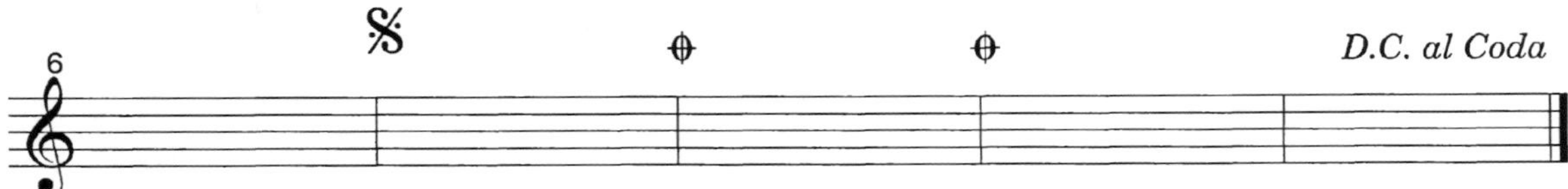

In the above example, the *D.S. al Coda* means to repeat from the *segno* sign to the *coda* symbol, then skip to the next *coda* sign.

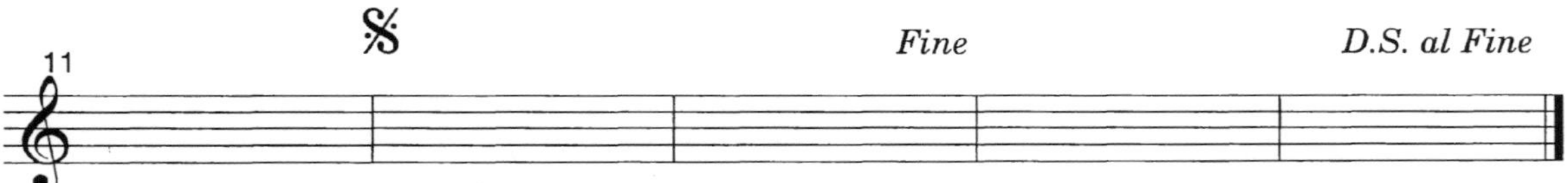

In the above example, the *D.S. al Fine* means to go back to the *segno* sign and end at the word "*fine*."

Instrument Key

Given that the Native American flute is rarely chromatic in that it is not usually capable of producing all 12 pitches within an octave and only sometimes diatonic, meaning that it does not naturally play the familiar pattern of Do-Re-Mi-Fa-Sol-La-Ti-Do. However, all Native American flutes have a key. This is true regardless of whether or not the flute is of "traditional" or contemporary tuning. The "key," or fundamental frequency, of the Native American flute is determined by covering all of the holes and blowing the note this fingering provides. This note will be the lowest note capable of being produced by the instrument and establishes the key of the instrument.

The keys on a large piano contain eight octaves. Specifically, an octave is comprised of the twelve pitches between two notes of the same name, such as all of the black and white piano keys from C^1 to C^2: C^1 , C#, D, D#, E, F, F#, G, G#, A, A#, B, and C^2. These pitches are all half-steps.

To place pitches in their proper octave, it must be noted that the octaves are numbered as C^1 through C^8. Middle C on the keyboard is noted as C^4 and is the C immediately below the treble clef staff. The C on the third space of the treble clef staff is C^5. This notation then allows us to relate the key of a flute to its specific range. A flute with a key of F^4 would then have the same beginning range as the F on the first space of the treble clef staff or the first white F key to the right of middle C on the piano. A flute with a key of F^5 would have the same pitch as the F note on the top line of the treble clef staff. Please also realize that, in this discussion, I am talking about actual pitches, not the TABlature designation.

Paula Conlon studied 25 early Native American flutes from approximately 14 different cultures and determined the fundamental [or key] of each flute. She showed the following distribution of keys in this limited but valuable study. I have put the range indication next to the fundamental note indication provided by Conlon:

Pitch	Qty	Pitch	Qty
D^4	1	$G\#^4$	2
$D\#^4$	1	A^4	4
E^4	3	$A\#^4$	2
F^4	1	B^4	3
$F\#^4$	1	C^5	2
G^4	4	$C\#^5$	1

Interestingly, Morris reported that one of the ancient Anasazi flutes from the Broken Flute Cave had a key and range of $A\#^4$ (Morris, 1959).

In another limited study of 10 "original" flutes of Thurlow Lieurance believed to represent up to seven different cultures (Hensley), the following distribution was noted, with the range indications being inserted by myself:

Pitch	Qty
F^4	1
$F\#^4$	1
G^4	2
$G\#^4$	1
A^4	4
$A\#^4$	1

Generally, the lower the pitch then the larger the length and diameter of the flute, while the higher the pitch the shorter the length and the smaller the diameter of the flute.

In my personal collection of contemporary Native American flutes, the largest is in the key and range of A^3. This instrument is 33 inches in length and is 2 inches in diameter. The smallest flute is in the key and range of E^6 and measures 14-3/4 inches in length, with an overall diameter of one-half inch. The following is a list of the flute keys and their corresponding ranges that I have in my personal collection. The 18 flutes examined represent the efforts of 10 different contemporary builders. Six are five-hole flutes and 12 are six-hole flutes:

Pitch	Qty	Pitch	Qty
C^4	1	$G\#^4$	1
$D\#^4$	1	A^4	3
E^4	2	$A\#^4$	1
F^4	1	D^5	1
$F\#^4$	3	$D\#^5$	1
G^4	3		

My observation of various flute students leads me to believe that the two most popular contemporary keys are $F\#^4$ and G^4, followed by A^4. Please keep in mind that there is no such thing as a "correct" key. It is quite conceivable that the $F\#^4$ and the G^4 flutes are the most popular because these are the keys and ranges which the builders tend to create the most. It is difficult to say whether that is in response to a specific demand or the demand responded to what is readily available. Most builders offer flutes in several different keys, while some offer them in a very wide variety of keys. Do not be afraid to ask for what you are seeking.

Random Tuning Observations

I am highly skeptical that there ever existed any such concept as a uniform traditional tuning for the Native American flute among the various indigenous cultures of North America. What little documentation that does address the issue of construction suggests that the instruments were built to body part measurements, specifically the arm, hand, and fingers of the individual builder. To help place the issue of original tunings in perspective, I have included some random observations on this subject by three early researchers and one contemporary researcher.

> "I cannot find that there is ever any attempt to place the finger holes scientifically, and the result is that the instruments are ludicrously out of tune and no two are ever alike in fundamental pitch, or scale... it has a soft, rather melancholy tone that would be agreeable if the intervals were in accordance with any recognized scale." (Burton, 1909)

> "No. 91, a flageolet piece which I transcribed in Nebraska, illustrates somewhat imperfectly the defects of this flageolet as regards the key relationship of tones... The flageolet is evidently built 'by guess' and only remotely approximates the Indian voice in accuracy of intonation... There is apt to be more or less wavering of pitch under any circumstances and this defect is most pronounced in the Indian flageolet, which always gives out its tones in false key-relationship owing to is faulty construction. Therefore the more it is used, the more it accustoms the ear to false intonation... [Filmore]."
> (Fletcher, 1994)

> "What do we mean by 'our scale?' Presumably we mean the major and harmonic or melodic minor. The diatonic scale was not introduced into our musical system until the sixteenth century and is based on the laws of sound, the great underlying law being that of the upper partials of a fundamental tone. If we speak of 'the pentatonic scale' we may refer to either the major or the minor pentatonic which can be played on the black keys of a piano. Helmholtz designated five pentatonic scales in which each of the black keys

Native Flute Construction Based Upon Body Measurements

To reiterate information from the "Origins, Designs, and Decoration" chapter:

> "The finger holes are placed in a manner convenient to the player's hand, not by any fixed rule... The length of a typical Indian flute varies with the stature of the player, a desirable length being from the inside of the elbow to the end of the middle-finger." (Densmore, 1936)

> "... a young Kiowa Indian, in Washington a few years ago, showed the writer (Wead) how the holes on a flute on which he played were located by measuring three finger-breadths from the lower end to the lower hole, and then taking shorter but equal spaces for the succeeding holes." (Wead, 1902)

In reference to the Hidatsa Indians, "The length was from the inside of a man's elbow to the end of the his little finger" (Hamilton).

> "The older Plains flutes were frequently constructed according to the dimensions of the maker. Using bodily measurements, the length of the flute was measured from armpit to fingertips, and the fipple edge was marked at the bend of the elbow. The top tone hole was placed a hand's breadth below the last tone hole... The bore of the flute was sized to the diameter of the index finger." (Payne, 1988)

John Davis, the Chauga River Whittler of Westminster, S.C., offers classes on flute construction using body measurements as a guide. He begins by having each student select his or her own bamboo blank which is cut-to-measure based upon the maker's outside elbow to his or her fingertips, with the bamboo node being at the wrist. The length above the node does not particularly matter and this section could be bit shorter or longer, as desired by the maker. The first tone hole is located one hand width from the sound chamber hole at the node, with a hand width being across the knuckles. Each tone hole thereafter is centered one thumb width apart, until all six holes are placed. John believes in burning all the finger holes and window holes into the instrument. He has a specially sized wood burner [approximately 1/4 of an inch] to do this; the window hole of the air chamber is squared off, with all other holes remaining round.

In a phone conversation on March 3, 2002, John informed me that these particular measurements were given to him a number of years ago by Hawk LittleJohn [Cherokee], who also mentioned that the measurements had been passed to him by his grandfather.

After having constructed a flute in the manner taught by John Davis, I played my flute with a chromatic tuner to measure the scale that my body's measurements produced. The first 12 notes of the TABlature produced the below-listed scale, starting with the fundamental at C^4. The bottom row of numbers represent the cents variation from the actual pitch. If any, there is an interval of 100 cents between each semitone or, put another way, between each key, black or white, on the piano keyboard.

Note:	C	D	D#	E	F	F#	G	G#	A	A#	B	C
Cents:	0	-20	+10	-40	0	-40	-20	-50	0	-30	+10	0

I was somewhat surprised by these results, especially the "on pitch" of the octave from all holes closed to all holes open. I found it to be very intriguing that the first interval was a whole step rather than the typical step and one-half, or occasionally two steps, that my other flutes exhibit.

By way of comparison, I am also including the analysis of two flutes in my collection that I classify as "concert" quality. The first has a fundamental of E^4, while the other flute's fundamental is $F\#^4$.

Note:	E	G	G#	A	A#	B	C	C#	D	D#	E	F
Cents:	-10	-10	+20	0	+40	+10	+30	0	0	0	-40	-40

Note:	F#	A	A#	B	C	C#	D	D#	E	F	F#	G
Cents:	-20	-20	0	-15	0	-30	0	-30	0	0	+20	-40

Playing my own instrument built to my arm/hand measurement and then charting the instrument with the tuner led me to realize that, in my opinion, this approach was more of a practical system to use in the construction of a Native American flute than people realize.

My body-measurement flute is a bit breathy. This is probably related to the thickness of the leather nest/spacer that I did not cut as square and properly sized as could have been done. Nevertheless, I like the flute as is, although I may experiment with a new nest at a later time. While this instrument will not make my "concert" quality list, it will be played as often as the others and it will be one of my main "improvisation" instruments.

Michael Zapf in a December 1, 1999, e-mail to the Montana-based Internet group relayed the following:

> "Let me give you a European example of current folk transverse flute construction: Unit of measurement is one hand's width. The total length of the flute is six units. From top to bottom, the blowhole is after one unit. The first of the six finger holes is exactly in the middle, after three units. The last finger hole is after five units, or at a distance of one unit from the end. The other four holes are spaced equally in between, with slight empirical modifications. The source for this is Sarosi, 1967, page 69, quoted in Heyde, Musikinstrumentenbau. If you build such a flute, knowing not more than what I just cited, you will end up with a fairly decent sounding tenor transverse flute, at a pitch of around D if the hand is a standard male one."

Obviously, using hand/arm measurements to construct a wind instrument is not unique to the indigenous cultures of North America, and the technique was probably used at one time or another by most of the world's cultures that crafted wind instruments belonging to the flute class. Common sense would certainly suggest that hole placement had to be convenient for the players' hands and arms, and, therefore, the use of body parts for measurement almost certainly was a requirement in the construction of early instruments in all the world's cultures.

TABlature for Trained Musicians

While it is true that the TABlature notes are the actual pitches of some of the F# minor flutes built by several different builders, **the notes in the TABlature are not the actual pitches**. Also, the Native American flute, for all practical purposes, is not a transposing instrument like the trumpet, clarinet, or saxophone, as it is not chromatic when played with full fingering and only sometimes will individual instruments accurately be found to be diatonic. [Remember that chromatic instruments are capable of producing the 12 pitches represented by the black and white keys within a given octave of the piano and diatonic instruments are capable of producing the seven pitches represented by the white keys within the octave from C to C on the piano.] Because the pitch interval limitations of this instrument do not allow it to be treated as a transposing instrument, then we have no other "practical" option left to allow us to communicate the music of this instrument except by the generation of a TABlature system, whose indicated pitches are basically arbitrary. I own, play, and write music for a variety of flutes whose fundamental notes represent over a dozen different pitches. Can you begin to imagine the difficulty of trying to remember the correct fingerings for the actual pitches of each of these instruments? Obviously, it is not a practical consideration. With the TABlature system, I need only learn and remember 15 notes, as an example, with their corresponding fingering to read and write music for any of the flutes, regardless of their actual key and the actual pitches of the various fingerings. For this, I am eternally grateful to R. Carlos Nakai for the development and publication of this TABlature system, as it has allowed me to write my music for the Native American flute in a practical manner which, in turn, allows others the opportunity to play it.

Historically, the Native American flute appears to have been primarily used as a solo instrument, although some cultures played them collectively. While many of today's performers utilize the flute in a solo context, there are professional performers who often find themselves performing with players of other instruments in a group context. These performers generally prepare themselves by creating a chart showing the TABlature's arbitrary pitches, together with the actual pitches, for each fingering combination for a specific flute. This is done to minimize harmonic problems. I have included at the end of this chapter two pages for the notating of actual pitches of your five- and six-hole Native American flutes. Make copies of these pages and, with your tuner, determine the actual pitches and write them out.

Additionally, experienced performers learn that some flutes require alternative fingerings for some of the pitches desired and they learn to simply notate these alternative fingerings directly upon the score underneath the TABlature notes. This can be achieved by using very small open and closed circles to represent the alternative fingerings in a small vertical space, so that it can easily be read when playing the piece.

At the beginning, I stated that the flute is not chromatic when played with full fingering and only sometimes will individual instruments accurately labeled as truly diatonic. There is a technique [and one that I do not recommend] which can be employed that will allow some flutes to actually appear to play a chromatic scale and to allow others to appear to be at least diatonic. This technique is called either *half-holing* or *half-fingering*. As an example, I have a G flute that normally goes from the G fundamental to an A# when the first hole is uncovered. However, by just partially raising my ring finger above the sixth hole, the flute will register the pitch A. This takes some practice and requires a tuner to facilitate the exact positioning of the finger off of the hole.

Now, having said this, it has been my own personal experience that the aforementioned technique is not very reliable during a performance. While, with considerable practice, you can come close to achieving the designated pitch when partially lifting a finger off of a hole, I think you will find it almost impossible to manage to accurately hit the desired pitch if the half-holing or half-fingering technique needs to be used with the finger descending towards an open hole on notes of short duration during a performance. I bring this subject up because you will run across it sooner or later. However, as I said previously, I do not recommend use of this technique as it is too unreliable during a performance. If you have to have a chromatic instrument, I would suggest that you purchase a recorder instead and not attempt to make a "sows ear out of a perfectly fine purse," in a manner of speaking.

The TABlature system is explained in some greater detail for trained musicians in the book written by R. Carlos Nakai and James DeMars entitled, *The Art of the Native American Flute.* It is distributed by Ken Light of Amon Olorin Flutes [406-726-3353] and Canyon Records [1-800-268-1141].

At the end of the next chapter there are two identical sheets showing the TABlature fingering systems. Please remove one of the sheets and cut it into three separate small parts. These references can then be placed on your music stand at the bottom of the music with which you are working [or adjacent to], and they can be used when necessary to learn the songs that I have included in this book. For more permanent reference, you will find it highly beneficial to laminate each of the pieces.

Five-Hole Native American Flutes
Actual Pitch

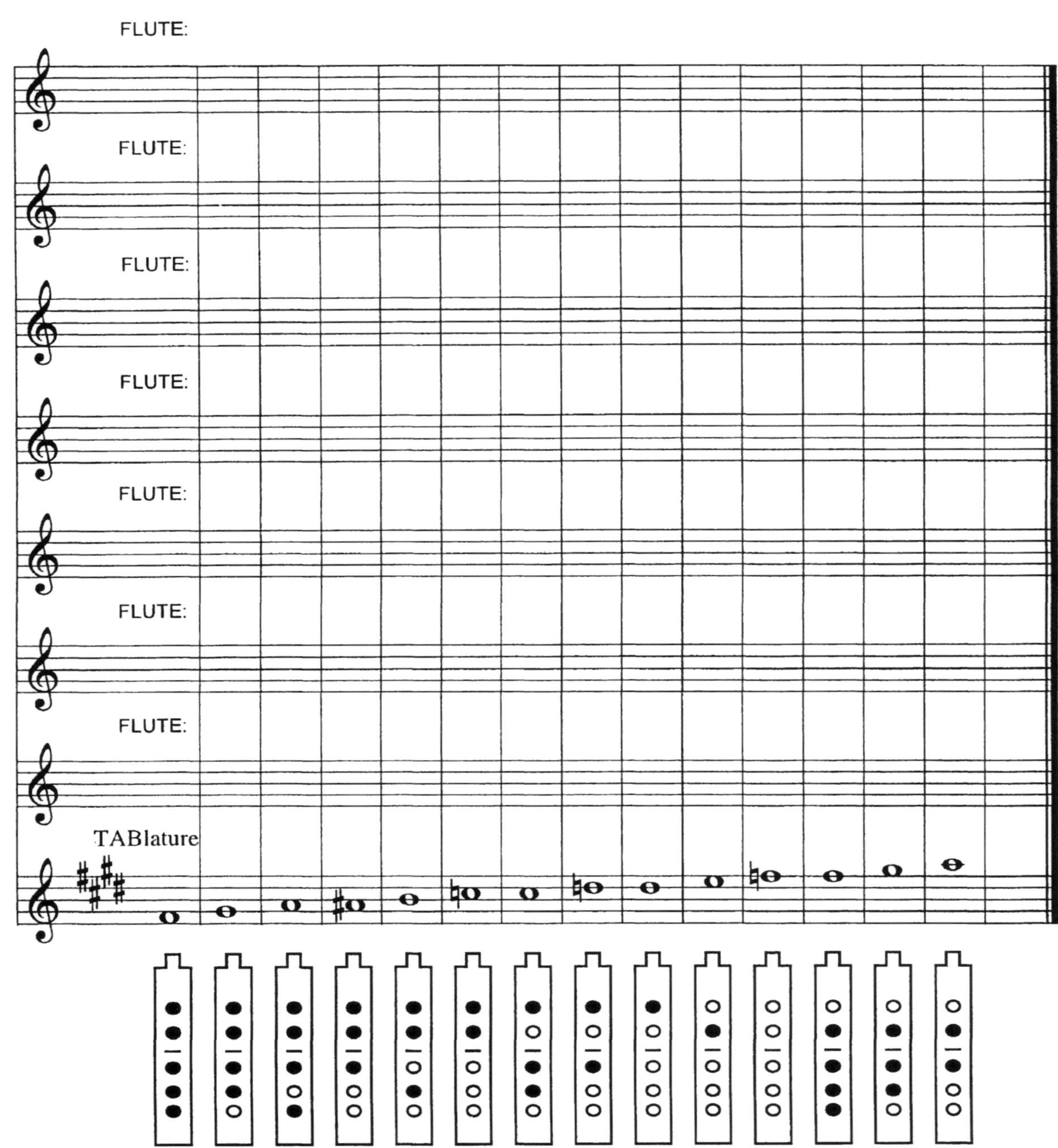

Six-Hole Native American Flutes Actual Pitch

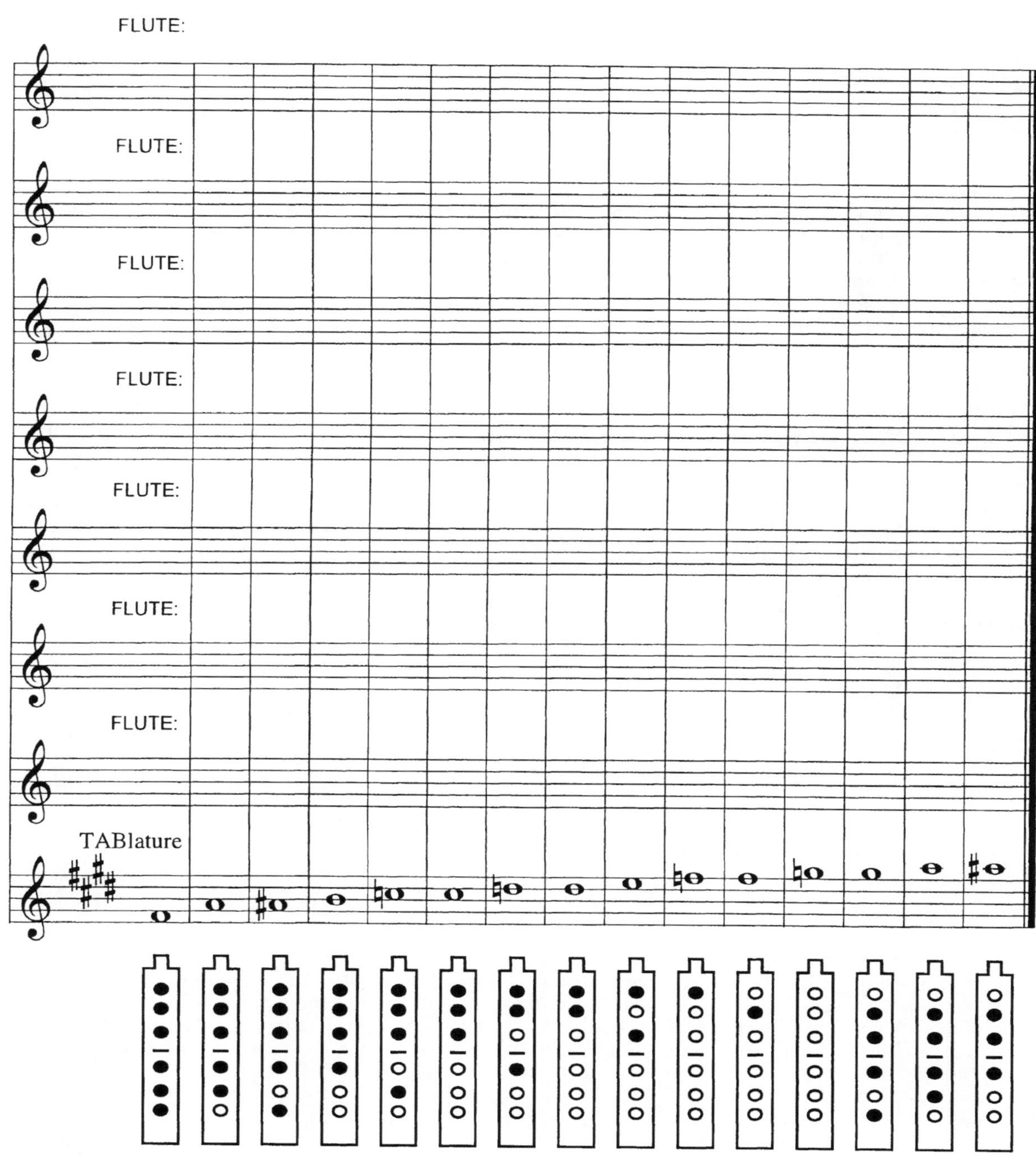

TABlature for Non-Trained Musicians

Range of Notes, in TABlature Notation, for the Native American Flute

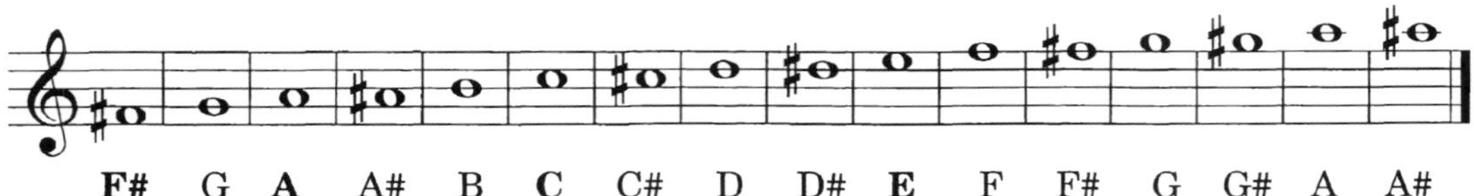

The range of the Native American flute is roughly an octave plus a third. This is represented in the above illustration. Here, we see the addition of accidentals. *Accidentals* are alterations of the given pitch. Accidentals may be either flat (♭) or sharp (#). A *flat* sign lowers the original pitch by a semitone, or a half-step. A *sharp* raises the original pitch by a semitone, or a half-step. When looking at a piano keyboard, the black keys represent the accidentals, while the white keys represent the natural or unaltered notes in the C major scale.

Key Signature

In the above TABlature illustration, each altered note is indicated with a sharp sign immediately before the effected note. When music appears in sheet music form, the composer often does not indicate each altered note as it appears in the music. Instead, he or she uses something called a *key signature*. A key signature comprises the altered notes that occur within the song, and is located on the staff immediately following the treble clef sign. The accidentals are placed upon a line or a space. On which ever line or space the accidental is placed upon, then every occurrence of that note throughout the song is altered according to the sign. The only way that this rule can be broken is if there is a *natural sign* (♮) placed before the note within the song. The following is the key signature that is used in all Native American flute music that is written in TABlature:

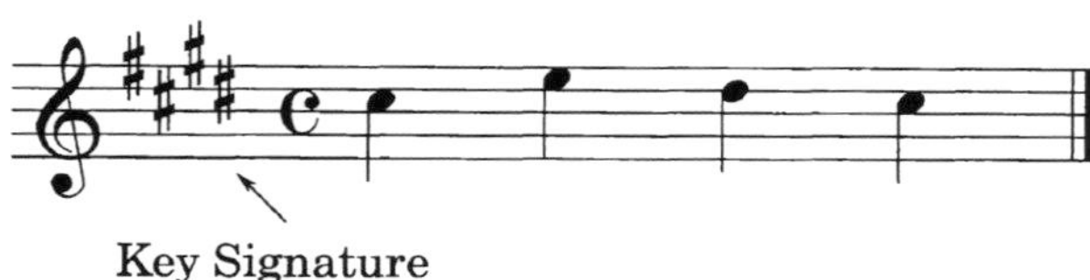

Notice that there are four sharps: on the F line, on the C line, on the G line, and on the D line. This means that these four notes will always be played with the sharp fingering for that TABlature note each time it appears in the music, unless it is preceded by a natural sign or follows an identically pitched note with a natural sign within the same measure. Please remember that once a note is preceded by a sign in a given measure it always retains that sign within the same measure, even though it appears only the first time the note is used within a measure. Musically, a treble clef with these four notes expressed as sharps is said to have a key signature of E Major.

Compare the following two examples of an eight-note range from the TABlature for the six-hole Native American flute. The first example is without a key signature and the other has the E Major key signature. The key signature makes the composer's job somewhat less stressful as he or she does not have to remember to use a sharp sign in front of the appropriate notes, since they are already indicated by the key signature. Be sure that you are comfortable with the key signature concept before going on, especially as it applies to the TABlature key of E Major.

Most reasonably well-constructed five-hole and six-hole Native American flutes should come close to performing a range of 14 notes, more or less. Do not be alarmed if yours does not, for each flute, regardless of range, has many songs to sing.

Because of the methods and materials used in the construction of the Native American flute, there is variety in the tuning of each individual instrument. In general, each Native American flute is a unique instrument, whether it be "original" or of contemporary manufacture. At times, even flutes made by the same maker and with the same fundamental key will show variations in the pitches of certain notes over the total range of the instrument.

Native American flutes are not chromatic instruments and only sometimes diatonic in the sense of true Western art music. Please note that chromatic instruments are capable of producing all 12 pitches represented by the black and white keys within a given octave of the piano, and diatonic instruments are capable of producing seven pitches within a given octave of the piano [i.e. Do-Re-Mi-Fa-Sol-La-Ti-Do].

The majority of European-originated musical instruments have structured "keying" systems based upon chromatic scales, which execute specific individual pitches in either the treble clef, bass clef, alto clef, or tenor clef, depending upon the specific range of the instrument. As Native American flutes generally lack any form of consistency as to a relationship between the pattern of holes being covered and specific musical notes, the only practical way of being able to notate music so that others might be able to read it and approximate a song is by using a TABlature system. This system specifies a notation of a certain note which corresponds to a pattern of covered and uncovered holes. Regardless of the key of your flute and if you follow the TABlature system, the song should be able to be reproduced on your flute.

Theoretically, when a professional looks at the first note of the TABlature [F# - all holes covered] he or she hears and/or visualizes the sound made by depressing the black key just after the first white F key following middle C on the piano keyboard. It is a very specific pitch. However, when you cover all holes on your Native American flute and depending upon its key, it will most likely be some pitch other than F#. Remember that the key of an instrument is its lowest fundamental note, which, in the case of the Native American flute, is the sound produced with all holes covered. Therefore, it is good to know that the TABlature pitches are really somewhat arbitrary. Feel free to forget about this technical fact, as it is of little relevance to you with regard to your learning and utilization of the TABlature system.

This TABlature system is explained in greater detail in the book written by R. Carlos Nakai and James DeMars entitled *The Art of the Native American Flute*. It is distributed by Ken Light of Amon Olorin Flutes in Montana via the following address and phone number: Ken Light, 492 Lemlama Lane, Arlee, MT 59821; Phone: 1-406-726-3353. It can also be obtained by contacting Canyon Records Productions at: 3131 West Clarendon Avenue, Phoenix, Arizona, 85017; Phone: 1-800-268-1141. In addition to a detailed explanation of the Native American flute TABlature system, the book also covers musical styles, pitch and TABlature relationships, writing and arranging in

TABlature form, a guide to understanding music notation, as well as the various musical symbols used in standard music notation and how they apply to the Native American flute.

At the end of this chapter are two identical sheets showing the TABlature fingering systems. Please remove one of the sheets and cut it into three separate parts. These references can then be placed on your music stand at the bottom of, or adjacent to, the music on which you are working. For more permanent reference you will find it highly beneficial to laminate each of the pieces. For my own personal use, I laminate the five- and six-hole TABlature fingering charts back-to-back and even have a set that I reduced on the copier, and laminated, so that it will fit within my shirt pocket.

TABlature Fingering Charts

TABlature
Four-Hole Native American Flute

By Tim R. Crawford

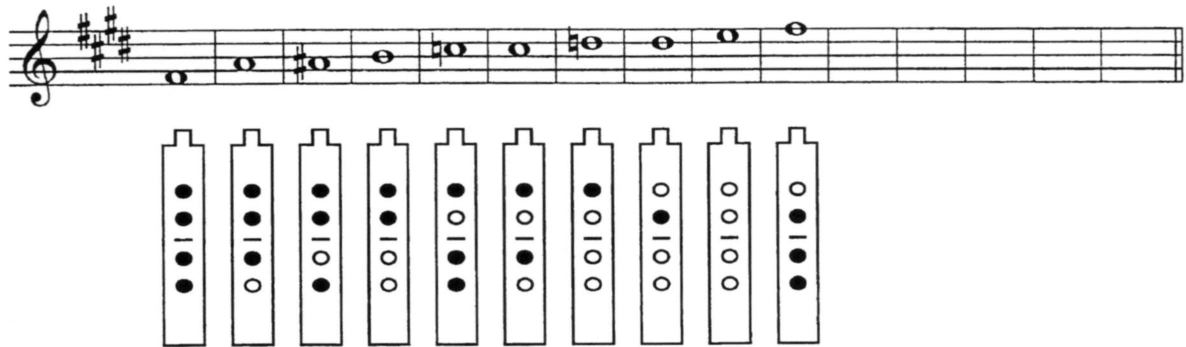

TABlature
Five-Hole Native American Flute

Originally Created By R. Carlos Nakai

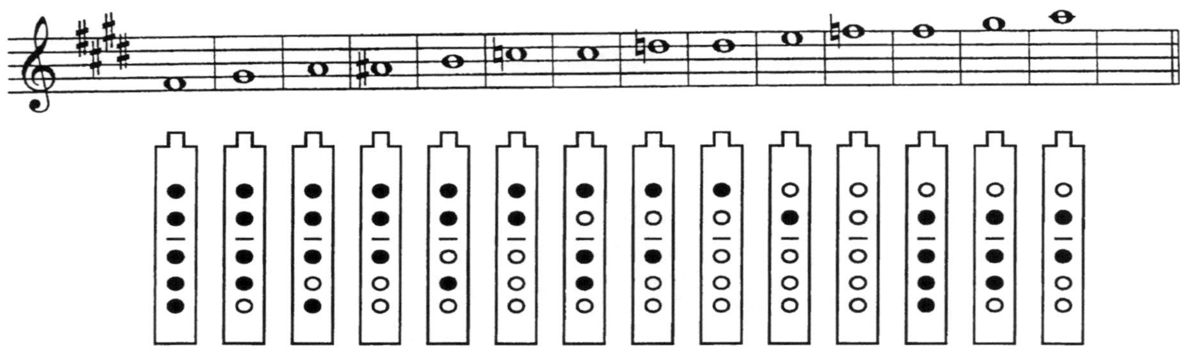

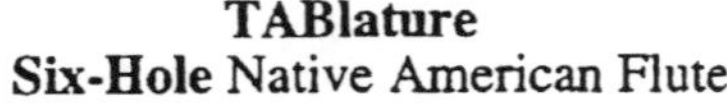

TABlature
Six-Hole Native American Flute

Originially Created By R. Carlos Nakai

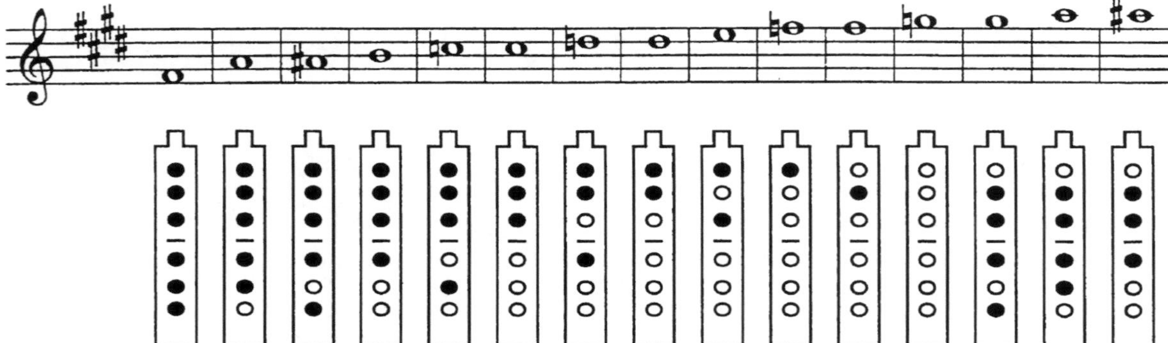

TABlature Fingering Charts

TABlature
Four-Hole Native American Flute

By Tim R. Crawford

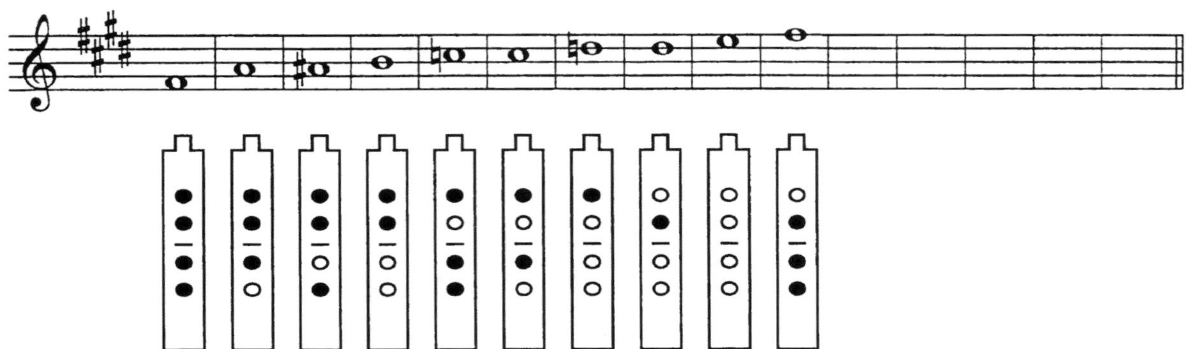

TABlature
Five-Hole Native American Flute

Originally Created By R. Carlos Nakai

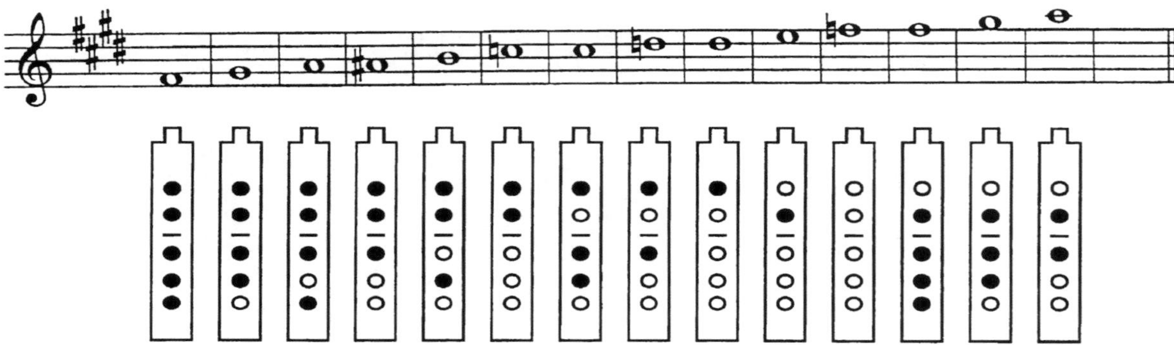

TABlature
Six-Hole Native American Flute

Originially Created By R. Carlos Nakai

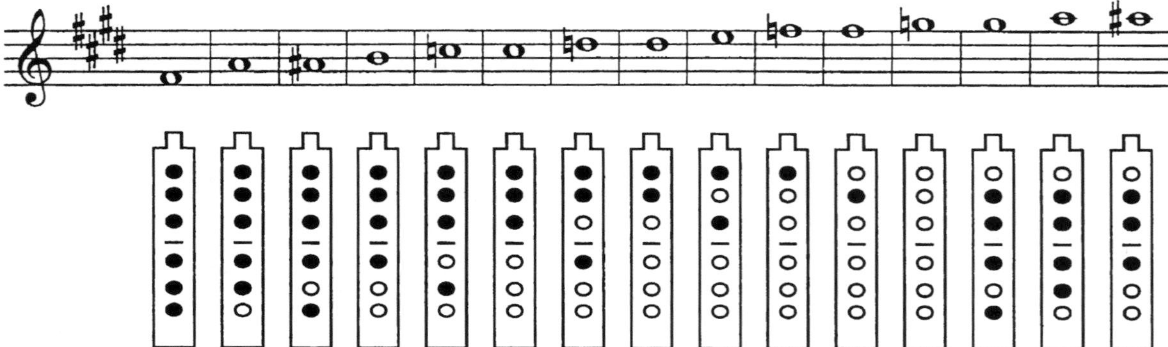

Introduction to the TABlature Exercises

Five-Hole Native American Flute

In this chapter, there are eight exercises for you to practice, followed by five traditional songs which were chosen for their familiar melodies. This was done to help you feel comfortable with reading TABlature. It is suggested and strongly advised that you play and study each individual exercise a minimum of eight times before moving on to the next exercise. In addition, I would also recommend that you only do one new exercise on any given day. It would also greatly help your learning process if, before beginning a new exercise, you return to the first exercise and repeat each previous exercise at least one time, up through the most recent exercise. Optionally, two TABlature self- scoring tests have been included for you to try when you feel comfortable with your TABlature learning progress. I suggest that you make a couple of copies of these pages in order to practice your knowledge. After completing each page, self-score to see how well you are doing.

Keep in mind that the TABlature is in the key of E Major. This means that, unless otherwise labeled, the following notes are always understood to be sharp: F, C, G, and D - note the sharp [#] symbols on the staff lines to the right of the treble clef. Furthermore, understand that each set of staff lines with a treble clef in these exercises is one measure, in the absence of any other measure-separating bars being present. As such, a note will always retain its previous "sign" until specifically changed within any given measure. As an example, on the first measure of the first exercise, please note that the C is indicated as a natural instead of being a C# as the key signature requires. But when the C appears again it shows no natural or sharp sign, therefore it will retain the natural sign given to the note earlier within the measure.

As you will most likely be anxious to play a song, go ahead and try "Michael Rowed the Boat Ashore," after completing the first four lessons. For convenience, I may only show the fingering diagram one time for identical adjacent notes, but be sure to play the note the correct number of times for the traditional music as indicated on the staff lines.

Try to learn the names of the TABlature notes, as well as the fingering. Each time a new note appears in an exercise the note's name is provided, but just the one time until exercise 8. An easy way to learn the names of the notes is to remember that the notes always adhere to the following sequence, regardless of where the first note may appear: C, D, E, F, G, A, B, C. Remember that the notes that appear between the staff lines spell the word F-A-C-E, from bottom to top.

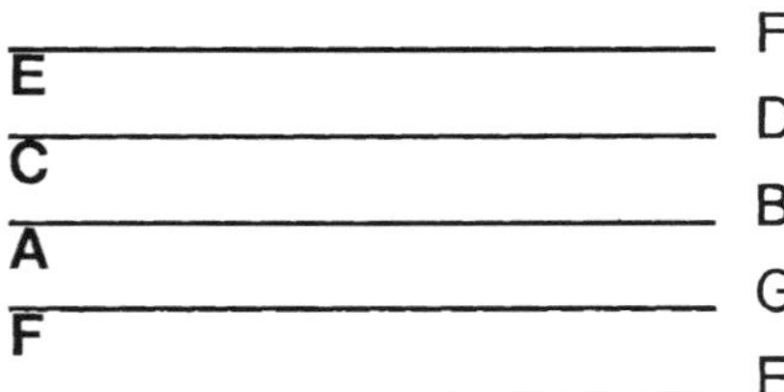

Because the Native American flute is only rarely chromatic - capable of producing all 12 pitches within an octave - it is difficult to achieve the exact pitches with all the TABlature notes shown for the traditional songs. When you feel that the pitch may not be precise, then feel free to experiment with alternative fingerings to see if you can get your flute to sound closer to the required pitch. If you do find an alternative fingering, mark the music so you will remember it for the next time you play the music. This can easily be done by using very small open and closed circles to represent the alternative fingerings done in a vertical manner, much like the TABlature fingerings. When I cannot achieve the correct pitch when playing music, I will sometimes play the note for a shorter period of time than indicated and make the next note a bit longer. Often, this helps to smooth over the pitch differences. I may also slip in some grace notes to smooth the section over.

Suggested Study Plan for the Five-Hole Flute

Day 1: Exercise 1, 8X

Day 2: Exercise 1, 1X; Exercise 2, 8X

Day 3: Exercise 1, 1X; Exercise 2, 1X; Exercise 3, 8X

Day 4: Exercises 1 through 3, 1X each; Exercise 4, 8X; "Michael Rowed the Boat"

Day 5: Exercises 1 through 4, 1X each; Exercise 5, 8X; "Michael Rowed the Boat;" "Hush Little Baby"

Day 6: Exercise 1 through 5, 1X each; Exercise 6, 8X; "Hush Little Baby;" "Red River Valley"

Day 7: Exercise 1 through 6, 1X each; Exercise 7, 8X; "Red River Valley;" "Amazing Grace"

Day 8: Exercise 1 through 7, 1X each; Exercise 8, 8X; "Amazing Grace;" "Aura Lee"

Optional: Self-Test 1 and Self-Test 2

CONGRATULATIONS!

Please Note: It is important to all students of this instrument that we share a common standard or language by which to read and write our music. The established system, as used within this book, for both the five- and six-hole Native American flute is credited to R. Carlos Nakai. Since the creation of these standard systems, there has continued to be some controversy regarding the choice of notes, or indicators, that accompany specific fingerings for the five-hole TABlature. The controversy has mostly revolved around the G# indicator for the second fingering, in as much as this particular interval, or indicated pitch change from the fundamental, does not seem to accurately reflect the overwhelming majority of contemporary five-hole Native American flutes.

In April of 2000, I wrote to Mr. Nakai indicating that the simple fix to this controversy would be to preserve his original fingerings, but substitute the notes, or indicators, for the six-hole TABlature in place of his original five-hole TABlature. This would eliminate the G# indicator.

Just prior to going to print with this edition, I learned from Mr. Nakai that he is making a change in the second finger position by substituting an A indicator in place of the original G# indicator for the five-hole TABlature. However, I have been unable to verify what effect this change may or may not have on his original fingerings and when this change will, in fact, be published. As a result, this book continues to reflect his original system. I apologize to the reader for any inconvenience that this edition may create if Mr. Nakai does alter his system, which will, in all probability, become the new standard for all of us. I will address any changes that may occur in a future printing.

Five-Hole Native American Flute TABlature: Exercise 1

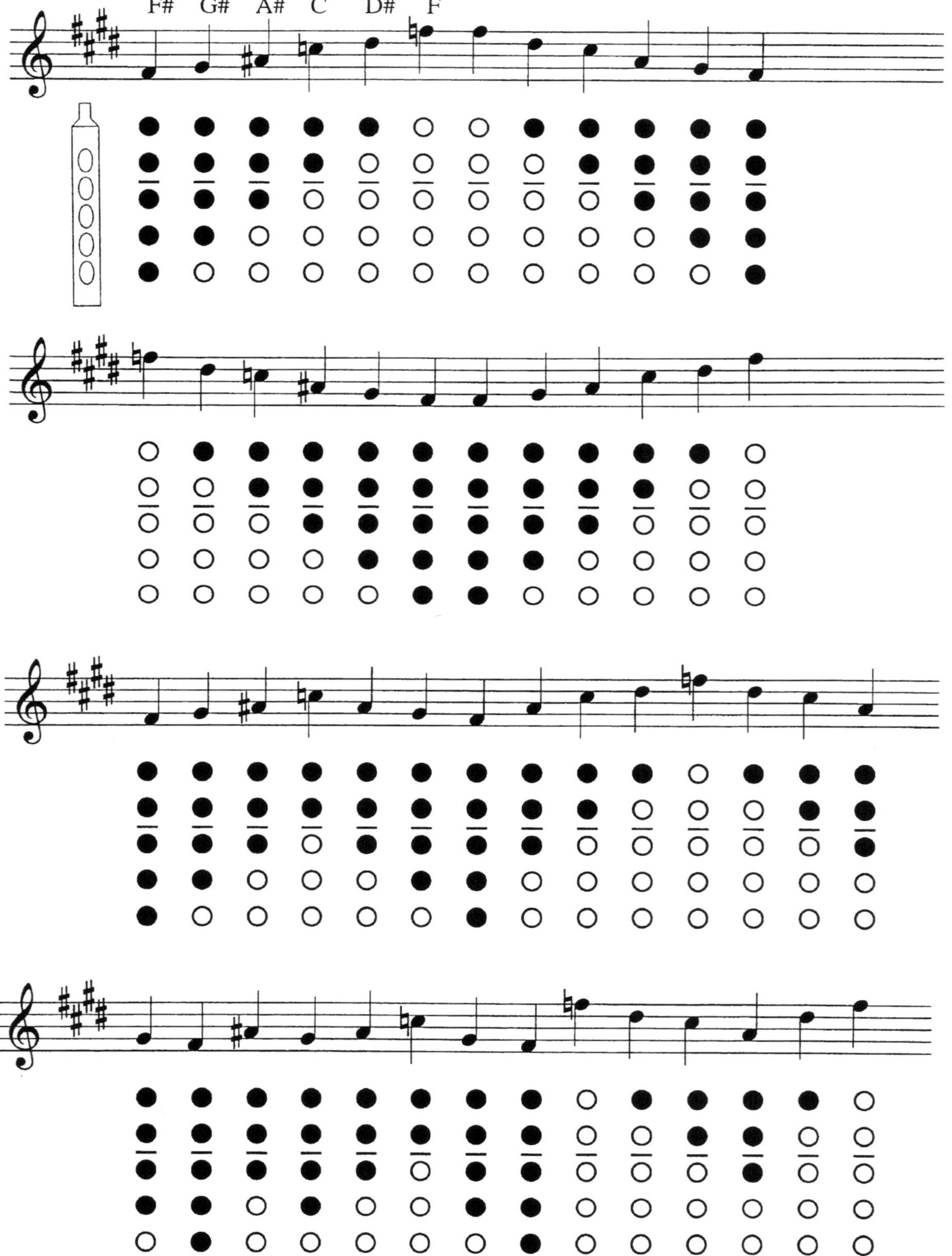

Five-Hole Native American Flute TABlature: Exercise 2

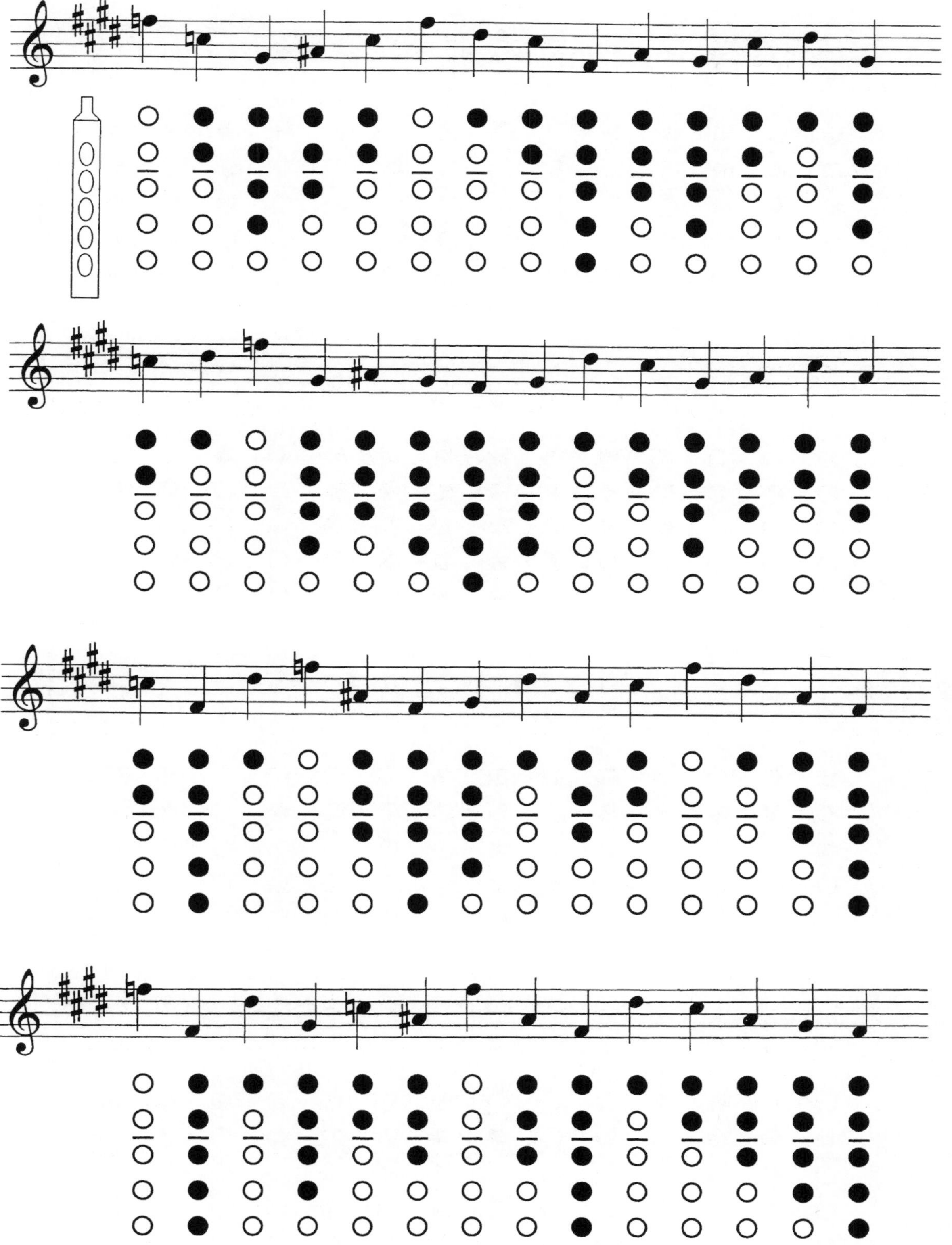

Five-Hole Native American Flute TABlature: Exercise 3

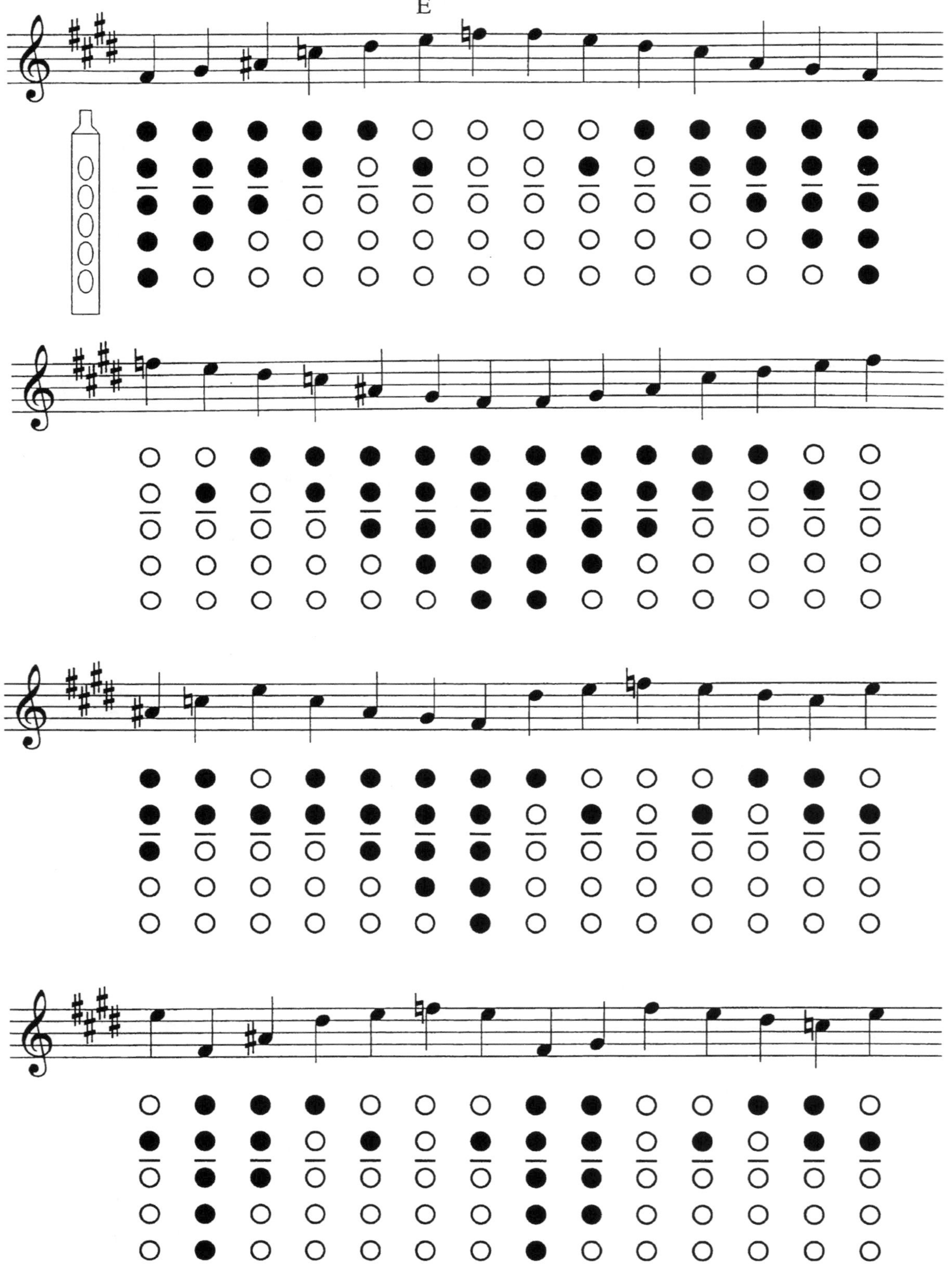

Five-Hole Native American Flute TABlature: Exercise 4

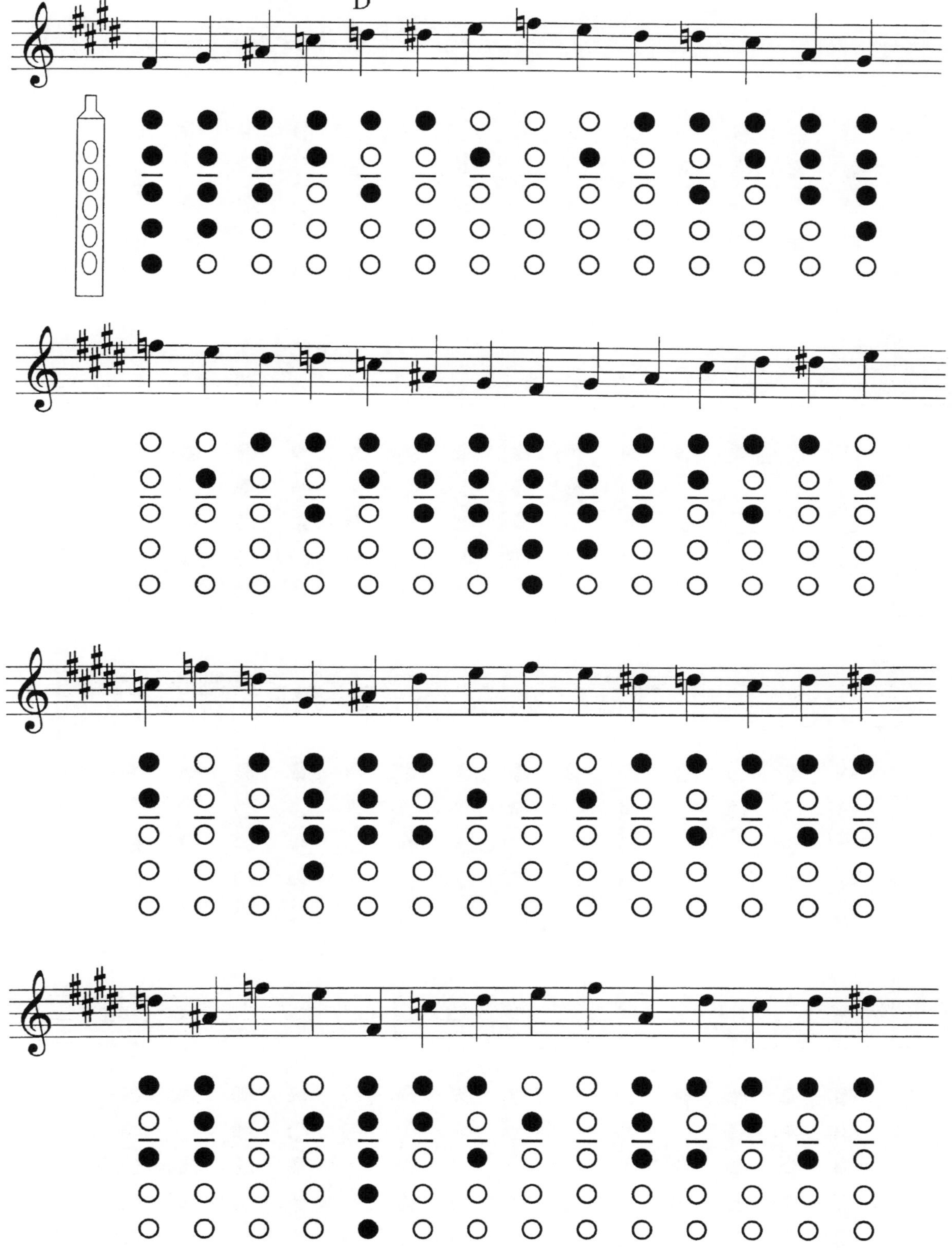

Five-Hole Native American Flute TABlature: Exercise 5

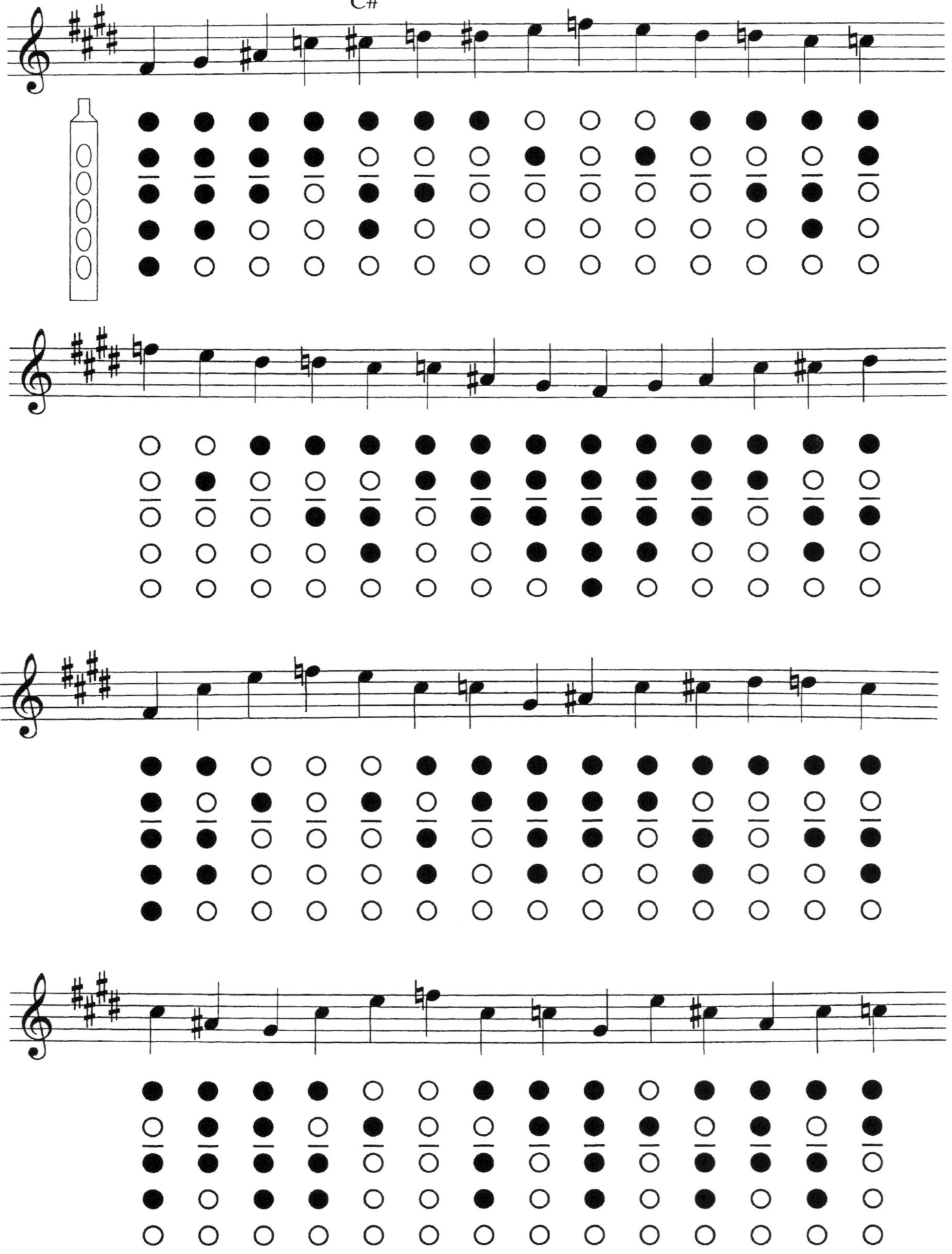

Five-Hole Native American Flute TABlature: Exercise 6

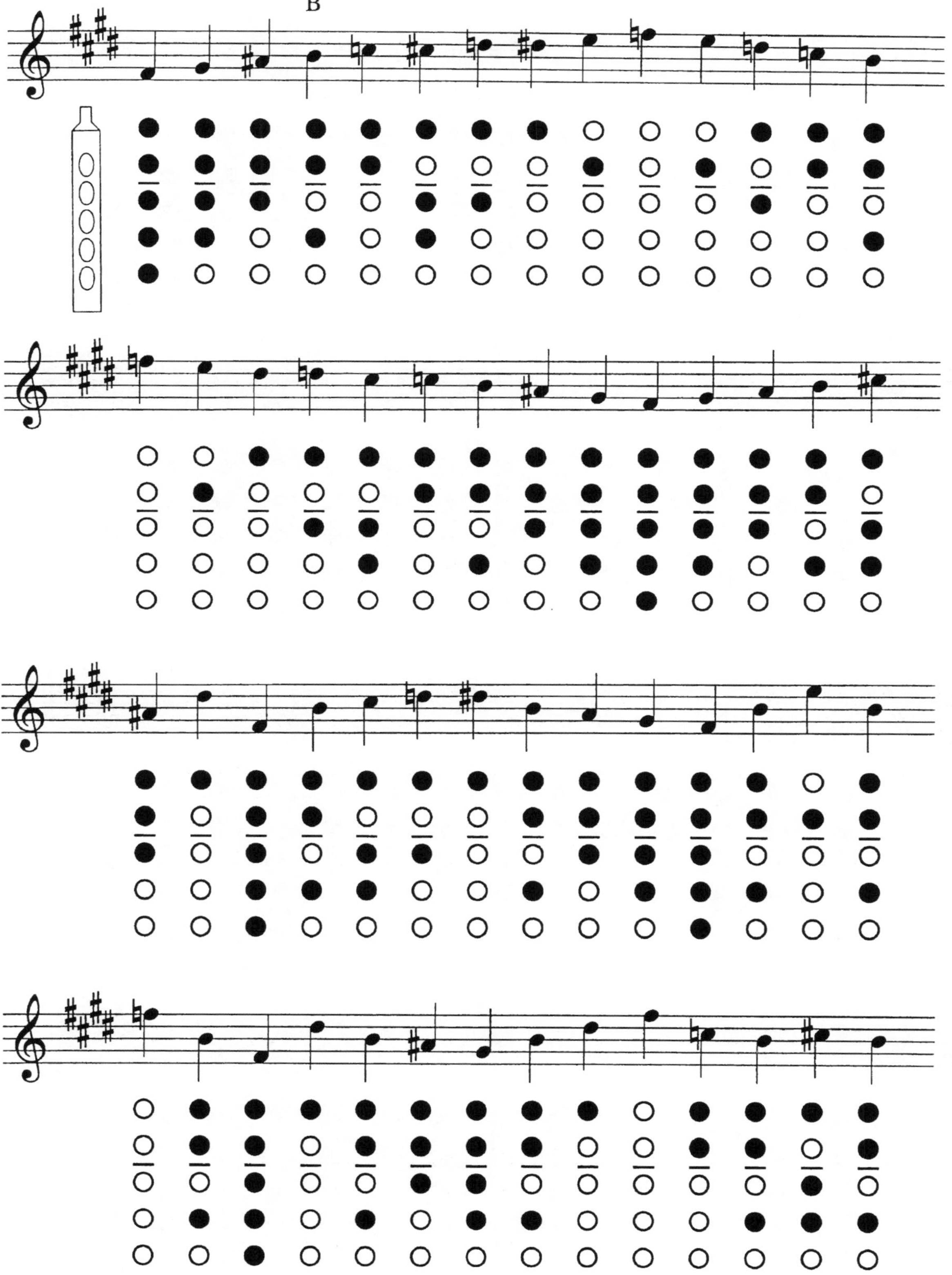

Five-Hole Native American Flute TABlature: Exercise 7

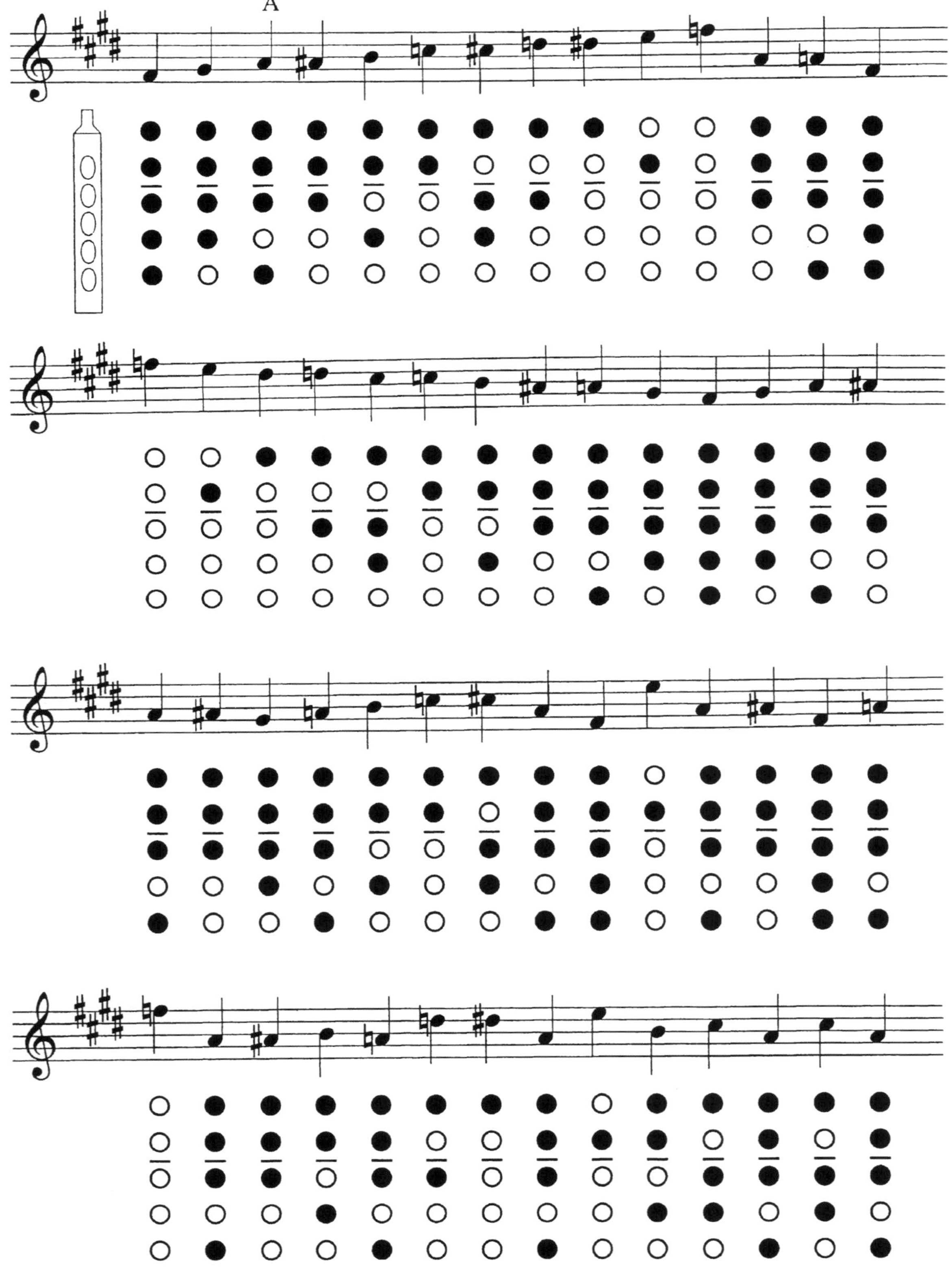

Five-Hole Native American Flute TABlature: Exercise 8

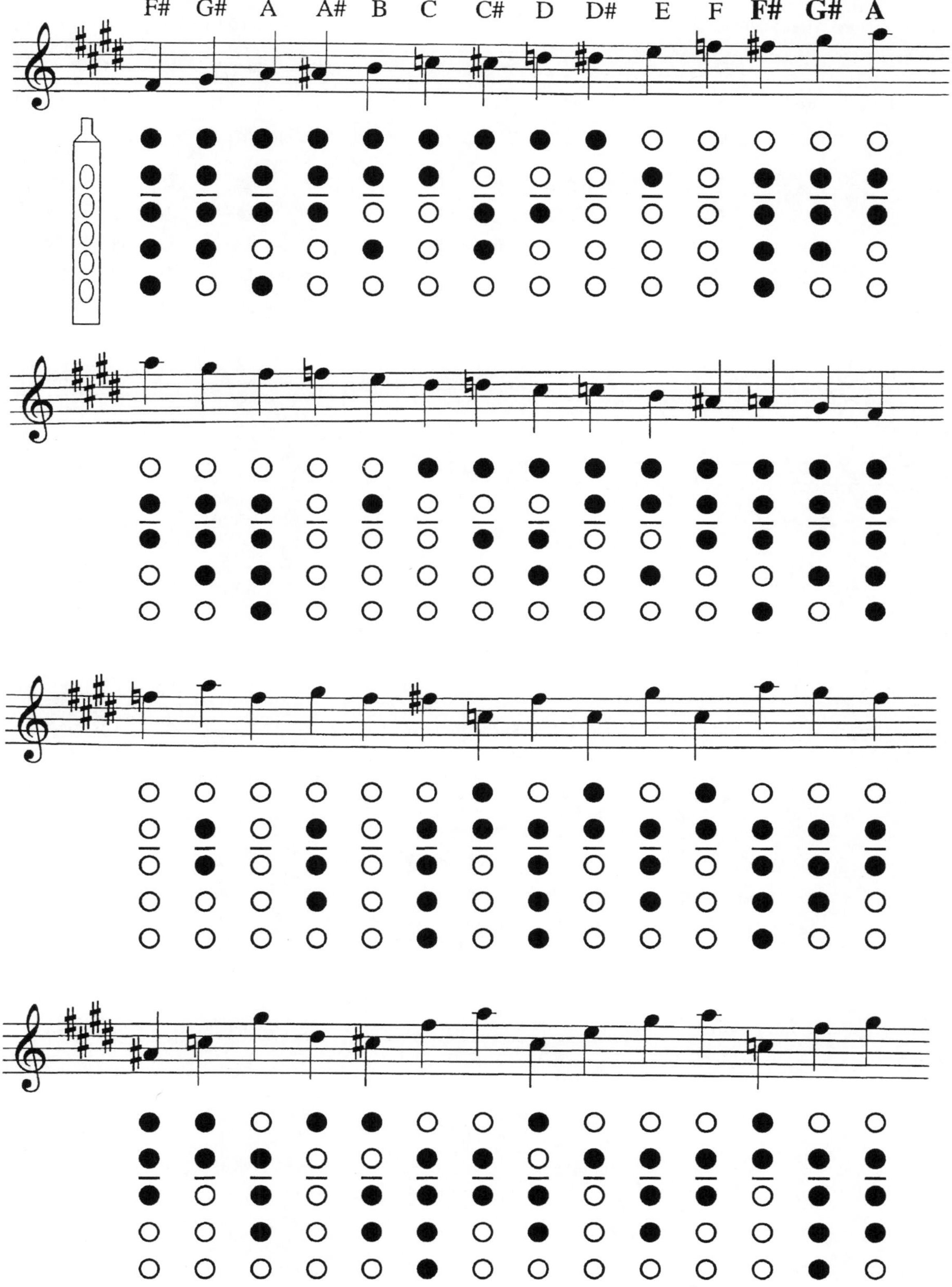

AMAZING GRACE

TABlature
Five-Hole Native American Flute

Traditional
Transposed by Tim R. Crawford

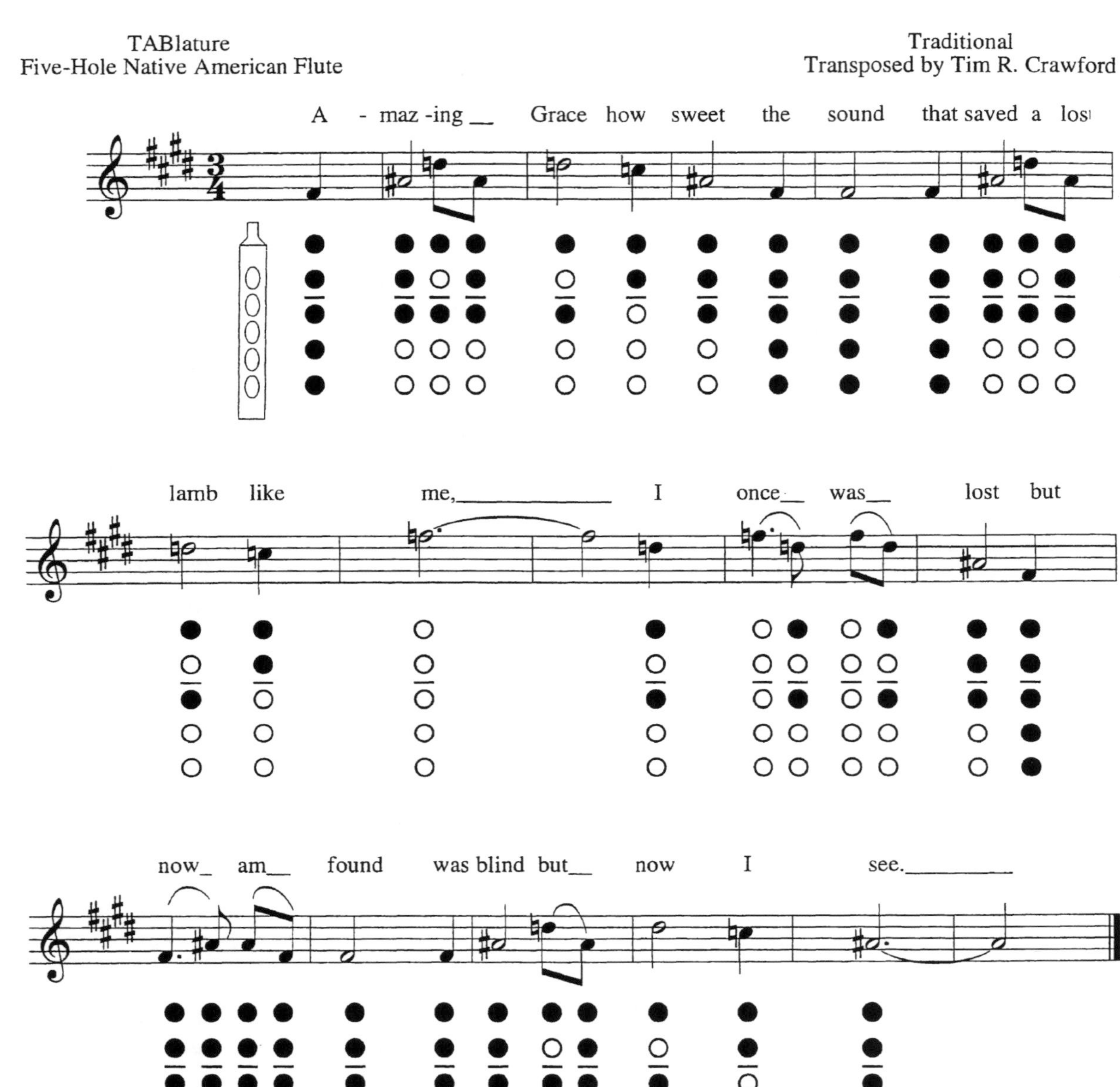

Aura Lee

TABlature
Five-Hole Native American Flute

Traditional
Transposed by Tim R. Crawford

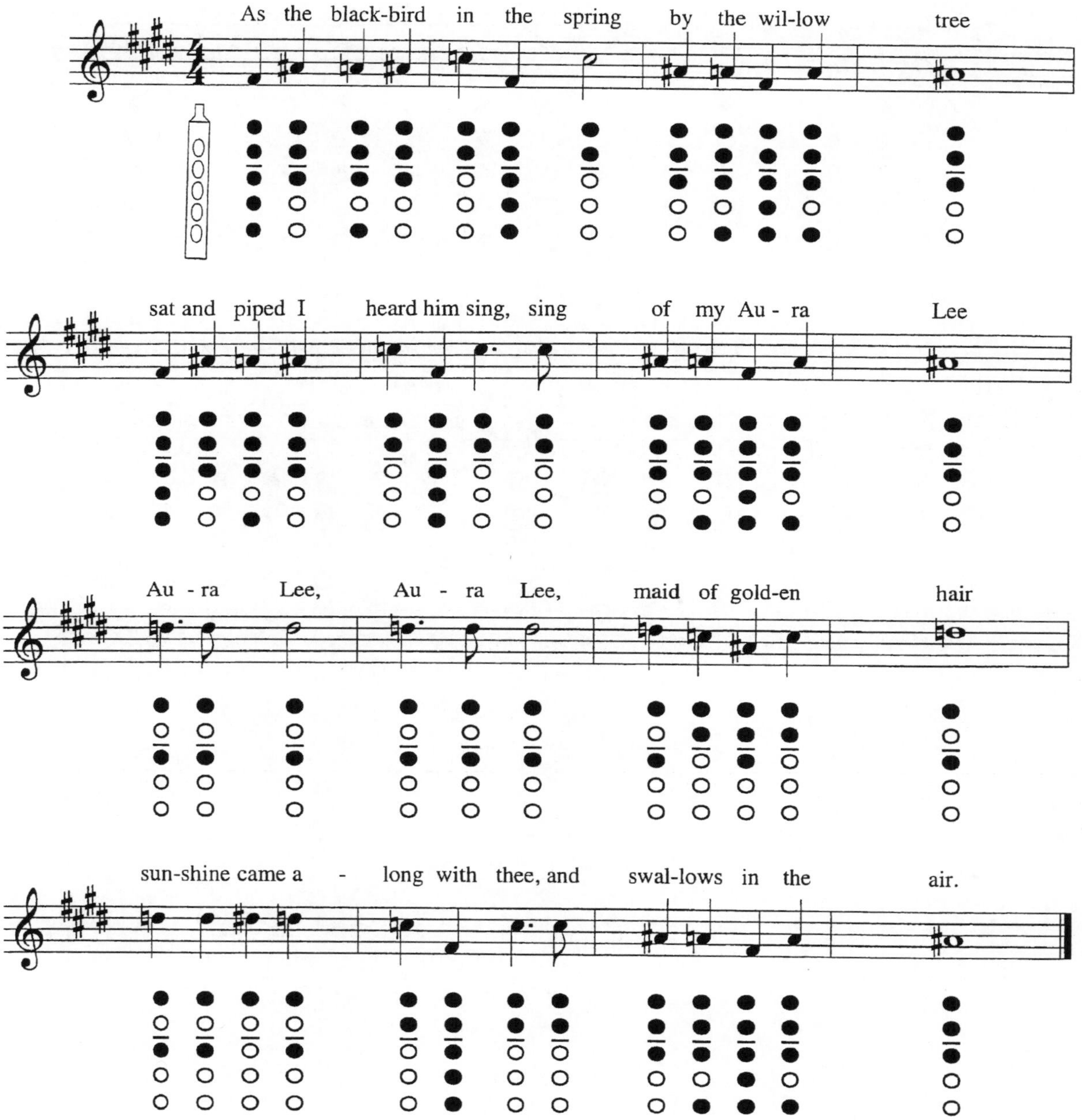

As the black-bird in the spring by the wil-low tree

sat and piped I heard him sing, sing of my Au - ra Lee

Au - ra Lee, Au - ra Lee, maid of gold-en hair

sun-shine came a - long with thee, and swal-lows in the air.

Hush Little Baby

TABlature
Five-Hole Native American Flute

Traditional
Transposed by Tim R. Crawford

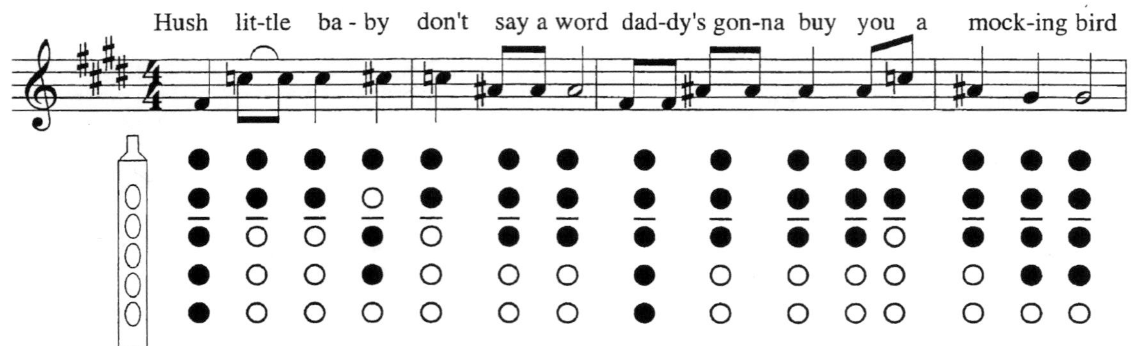

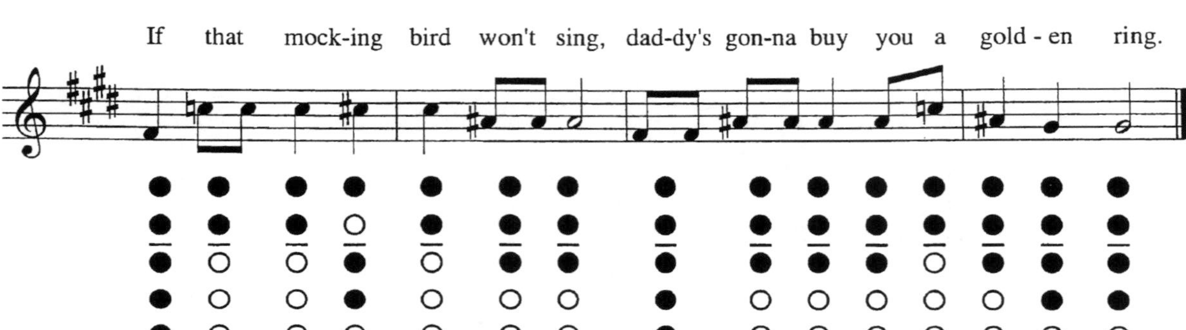

Michael, Row The Boat Ashore

TABlature
Five-Hole Native American Flute

Traditional
Transposed by Tim R. Crawford

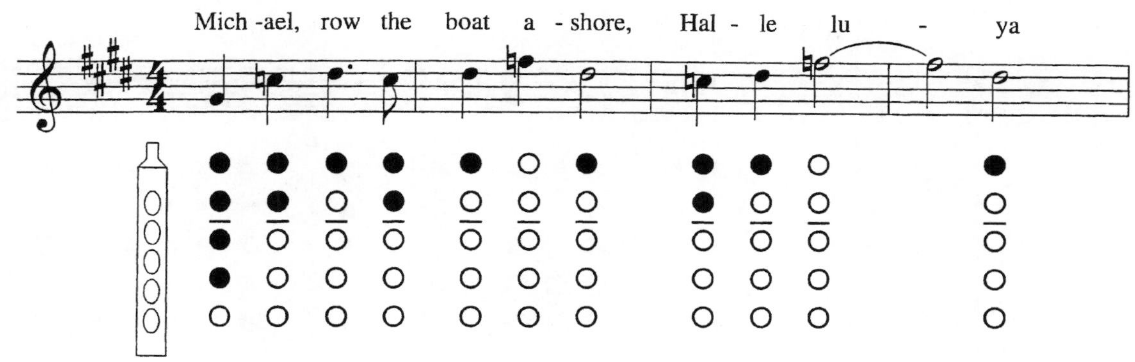

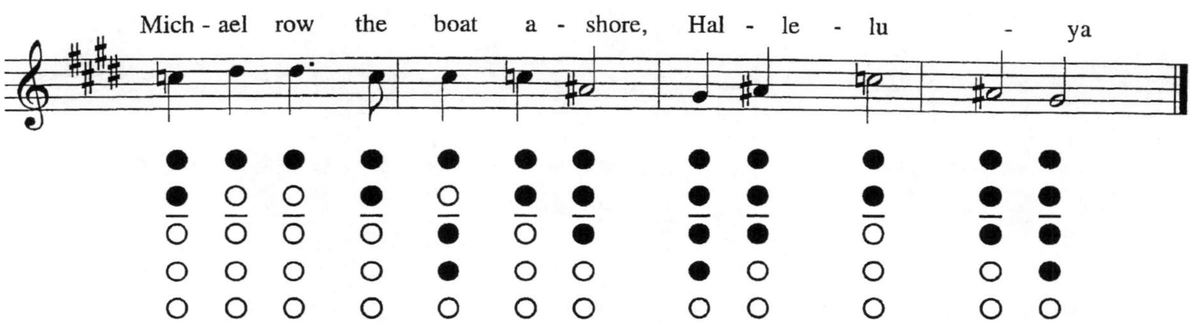

Red River Valley

TABlature
Five-Hole Native American Flute

Traditional
Transposed by Tim R. Crawford

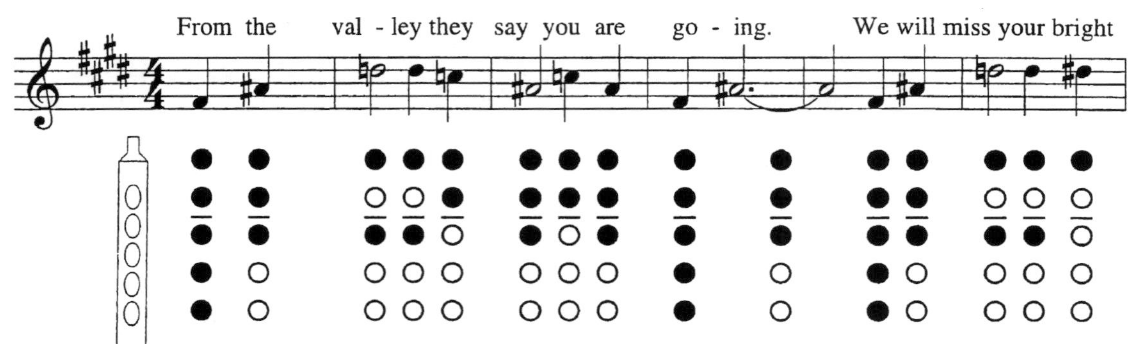

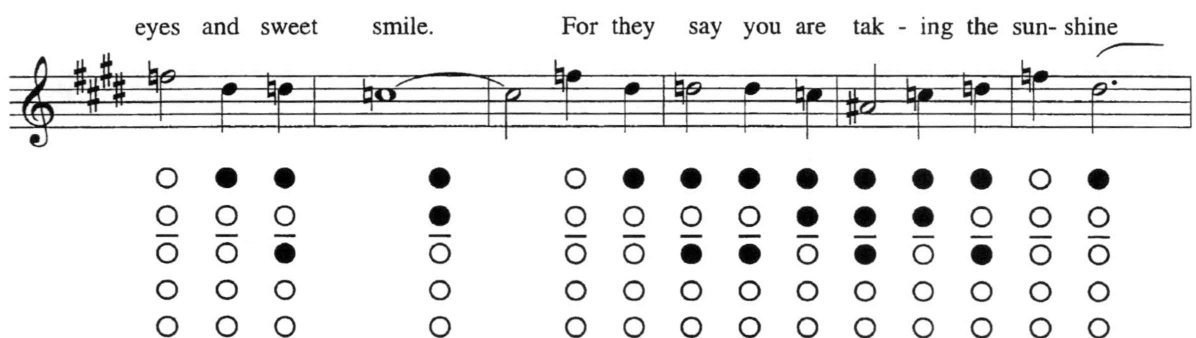

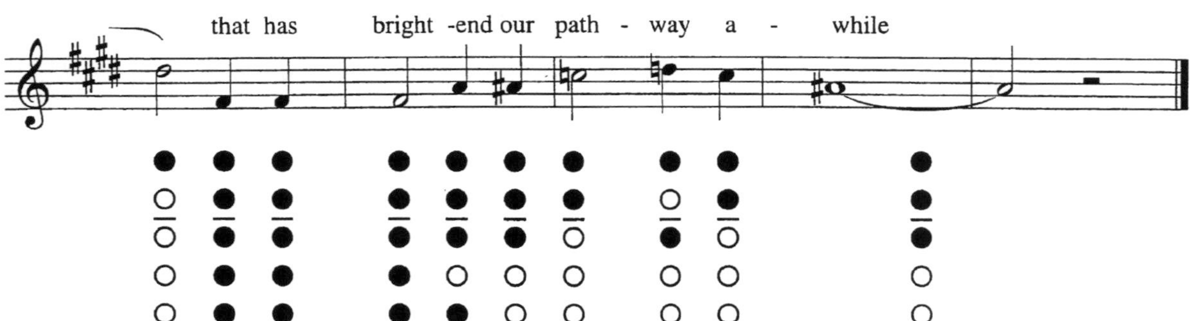

Notate your own traditional song!

Five-Hole Native American Flute TABlature: Self-Test 1

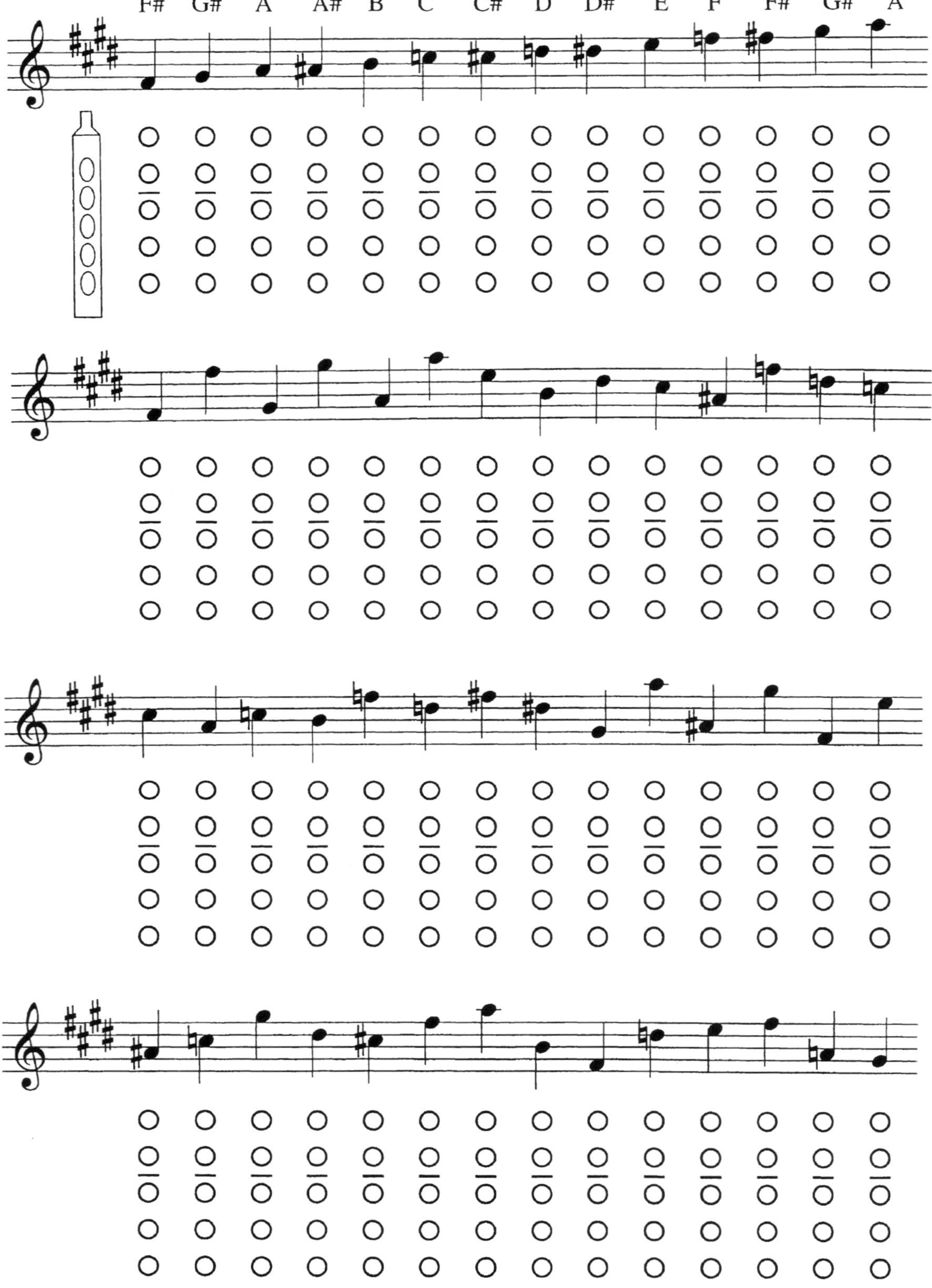

Five-Hole Native American Flute TABlature: Self-Test 2

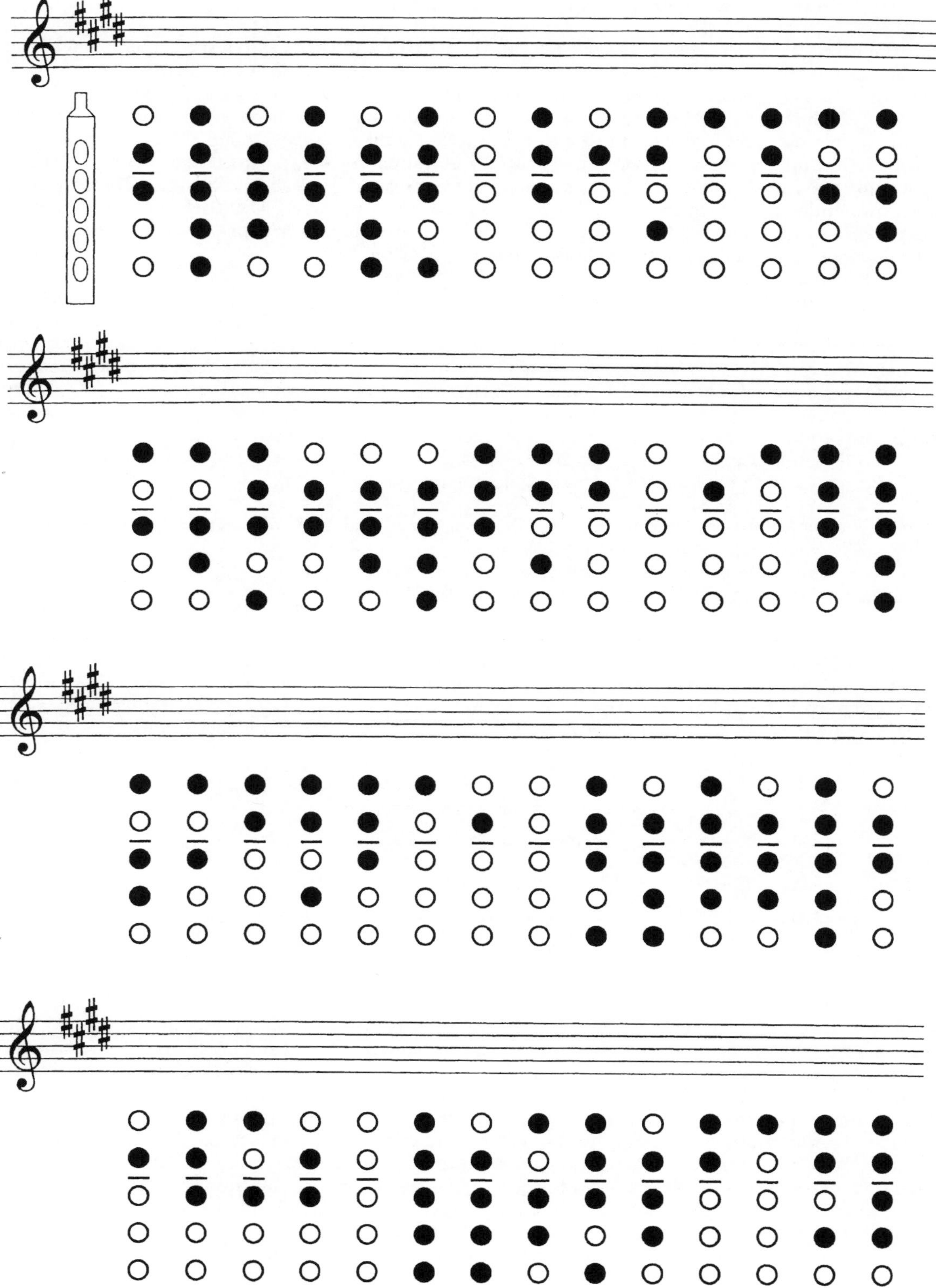

Introduction to the TABlature Exercises

Six-Hole Native American Flute

In this chapter, there are eight exercises for you to practice, followed by five traditional songs which were chosen for their familiar melodies in order to help you feel more comfortable with reading TABlature. It is suggested, and strongly advised, that you play and study each individual exercise a minimum of eight times before moving on to the next exercise. In addition, I would also recommend that you only do one new exercise on any given day. It would also greatly help the learning process if, before beginning a new exercise, you go back to the first exercise and repeat each previous exercise at least one time, up through the most recent exercise. Optionally, two TABlature self-scoring tests have been included for you to try when you feel comfortable with your TABlature learning progress. I suggest that you make a couple of copies of these pages in order to practice your knowledge. After completing each page, self-score to see how well you are doing.

Keep in mind that the TABlature is in the key of E Major. This means that, unless otherwise labeled, the following notes are always understood to be sharp: F, C, G, and D - note the sharp [#] symbols on the staff lines to the right of the treble clef. Furthermore, understand that each set of staff lines with a treble clef in these exercises is one measure, in the absence of any other measure-separating bars being present. As such, a note will always retain its previous "sign" until specifically changed within any given measure. As an example, on the first measure of the first exercise please note that the C is indicated as a natural, instead of being a C# as the key signature requires. But when the C appears again it shows no natural or sharp sign as it will retain the natural sign given to the note earlier within the measure.

As you will most likely be anxious to play a song, go ahead and try "Michael Rowed the Boat Ashore," after completing the first four lessons. For convenience, I may only show the fingering diagram one time for identical adjacent notes, but be sure to play the note the correct number of times for the "traditional" music as indicated on the staff lines.

Try to learn the names of the TABlature notes, as well as the fingering. Each time a new note appears in an exercise the note's name is provided, but just the one time until exercise 8. An easy way to learn the names of the notes is to remember that the notes always adhere to the following sequence, regardless of where the first note may appear: C, D, E, F, G, A, B, C. Remember that the notes that appear between the staff lines spell the word F-A-C-E, from bottom to top.

Because the Native American flute is only rarely chromatic - capable of producing all 12 pitches within an octave - it is difficult to achieve the exact pitches with all the TABlature notes shown for the traditional songs. When you feel that the pitch may not be precise, then feel free to experiment with alternative fingerings to see if you can get your flute to sound closer to the required pitch. If you do find an alternative fingering, mark the music so you will remember it for the next time you play the music. This can easily be done by using very small open and closed circles to represent the alternative fingerings done in a vertical manner, much like the TABlature fingerings. When I cannot achieve the correct pitch when playing music, I will sometimes play the note for a shorter period of time than indicated and make the next note a bit longer. Often, this helps to smooth over the pitch differences. I may also slip in some grace notes to smooth the section over.

Suggested Study Plan for the Six-Hole Flute

Day 1: Exercise 1, 8X

Day 2: Exercise 1, 1X; Exercise 2, 8X

Day 3: Exercise 1, 1X; Exercise 2, 1X; Exercise 3, 8X

Day 4: Exercises 1 through 3 1X each; Exercise 4, 8X; "Michael Rowed the Boat"

Day 5: Exercises 1 through 4 1X each; Exercise 5, 8X; "Michael Rowed the Boat;" "Hush Little Baby"

Day 6: Exercises 1 through 5, 1X each; Exercise 6, 8X; "Hush Little Baby;" "Amazing Grace"

Day 7: Exercises 1 through 6 1X each; Exercise 7, 8X; "Amazing Grace;" "Aura Lee"

Day 8: Exercises 1 through 7 1X, each; Exercise 8, 8X; "Aura Lee;" "Red River Valley"

Optional: Self-Test 1 and Self-Test 2

CONGRATULATIONS!

Notes:

Six-Hole Native American Flute TABlature: Exercise 1

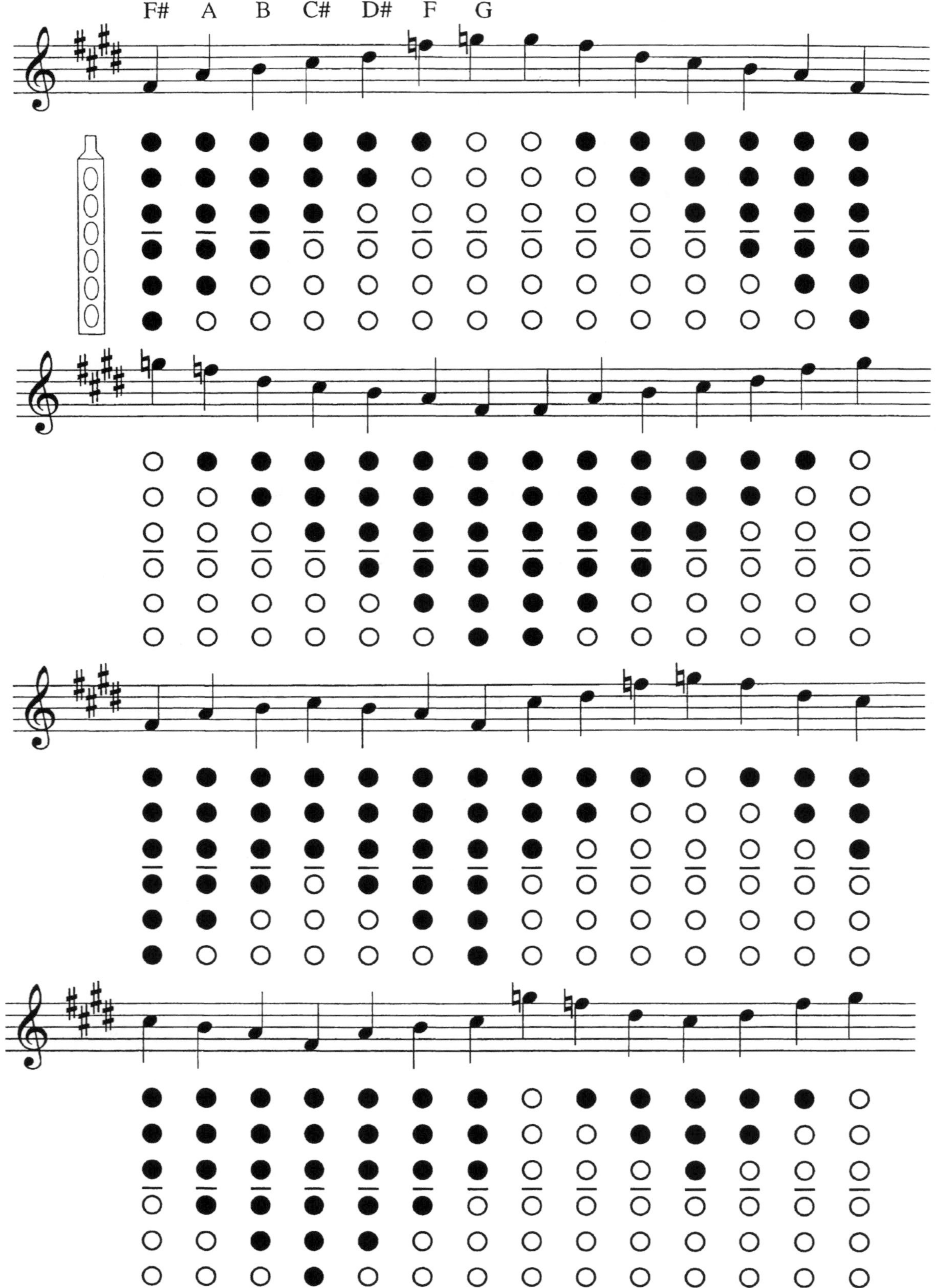

Six-Hole Native American Flute TABlature: Exercise 2

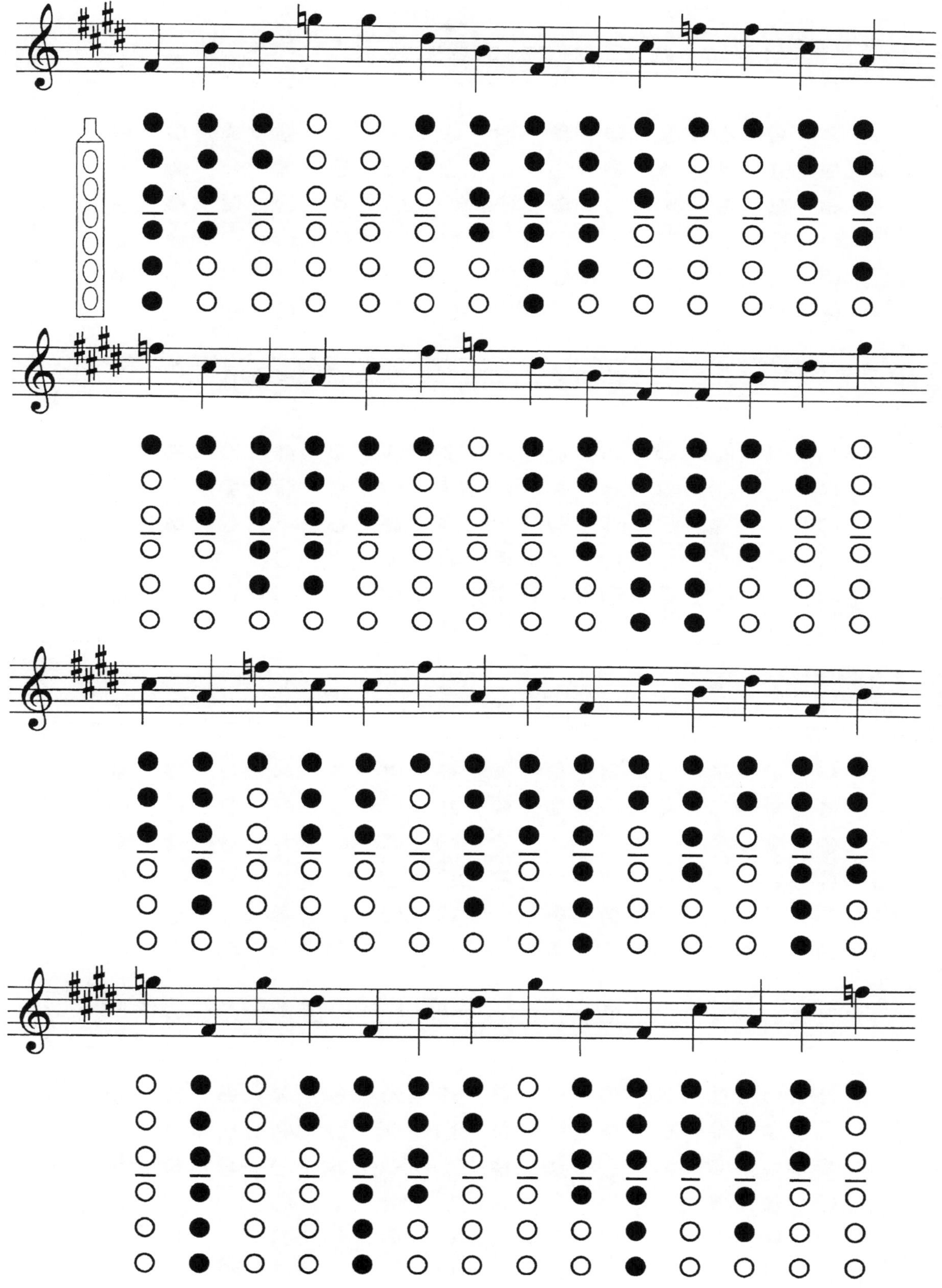

Six-Hole Native American Flute TABlature: Exercise 3

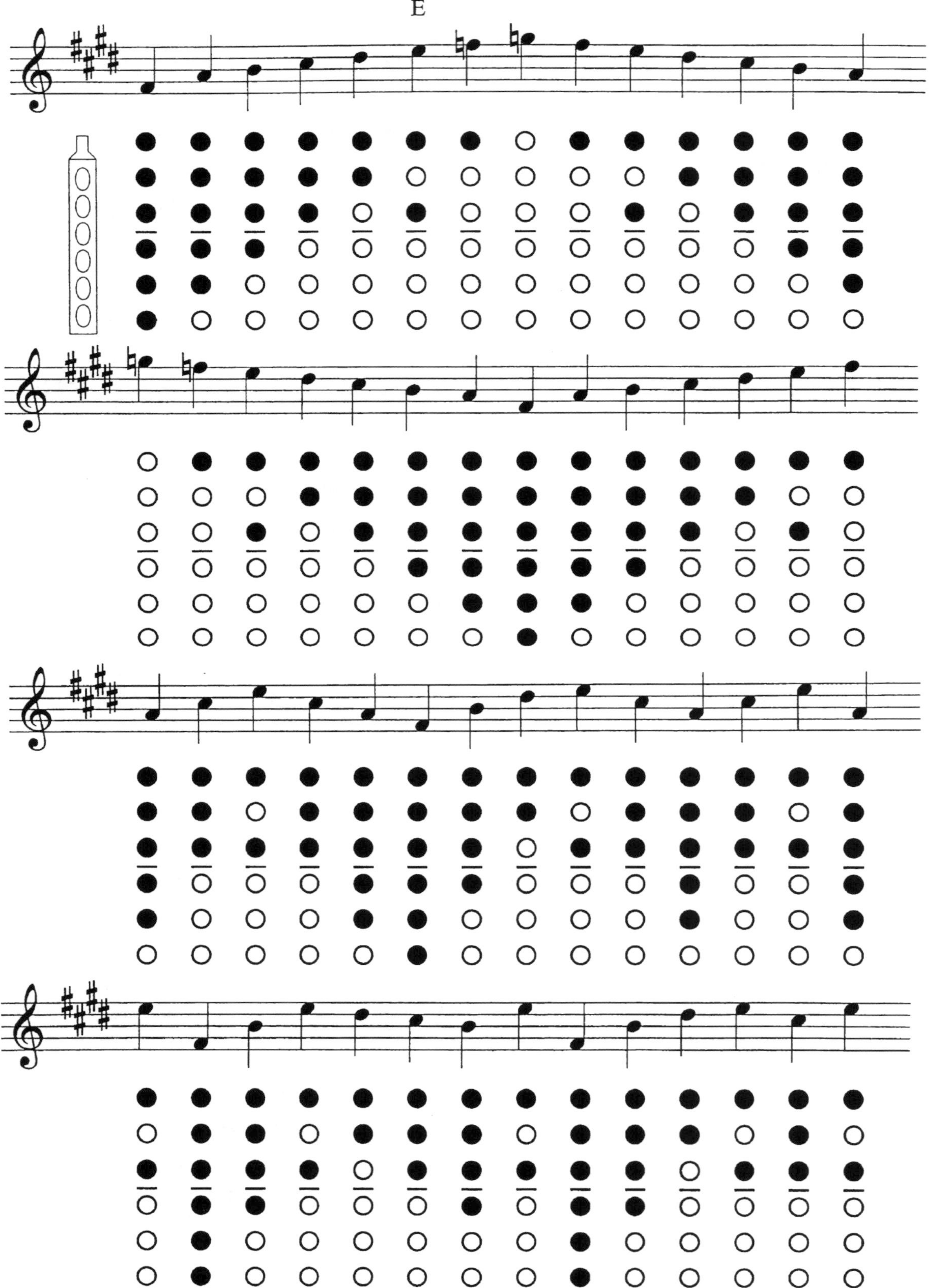

Six-Hole Native American Flute TABlature: Exercise 4

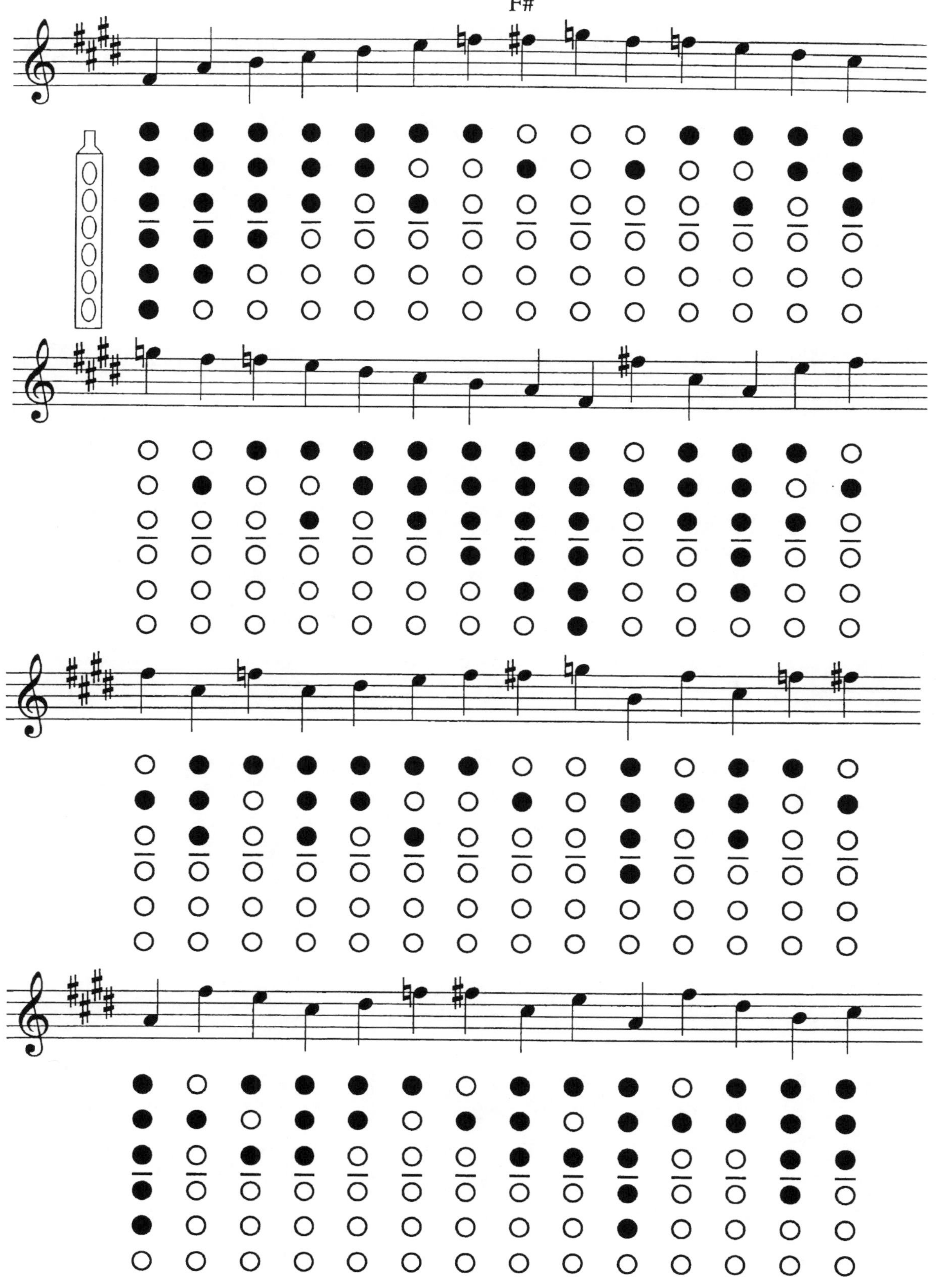

Six-Hole Native American Flute TABlature: Exercise 5

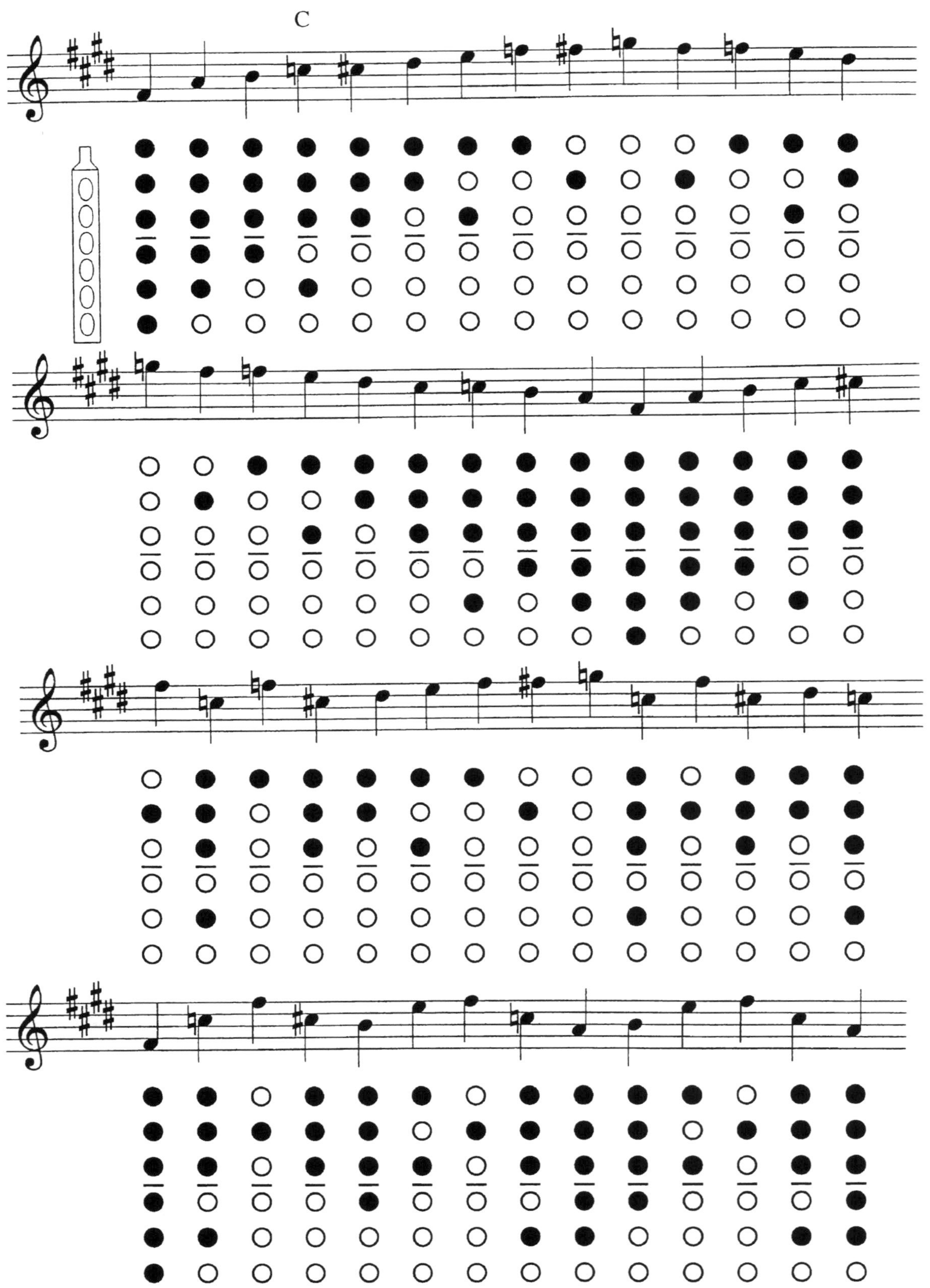

Six-Hole Native American Flute TABlature: Exercise 6

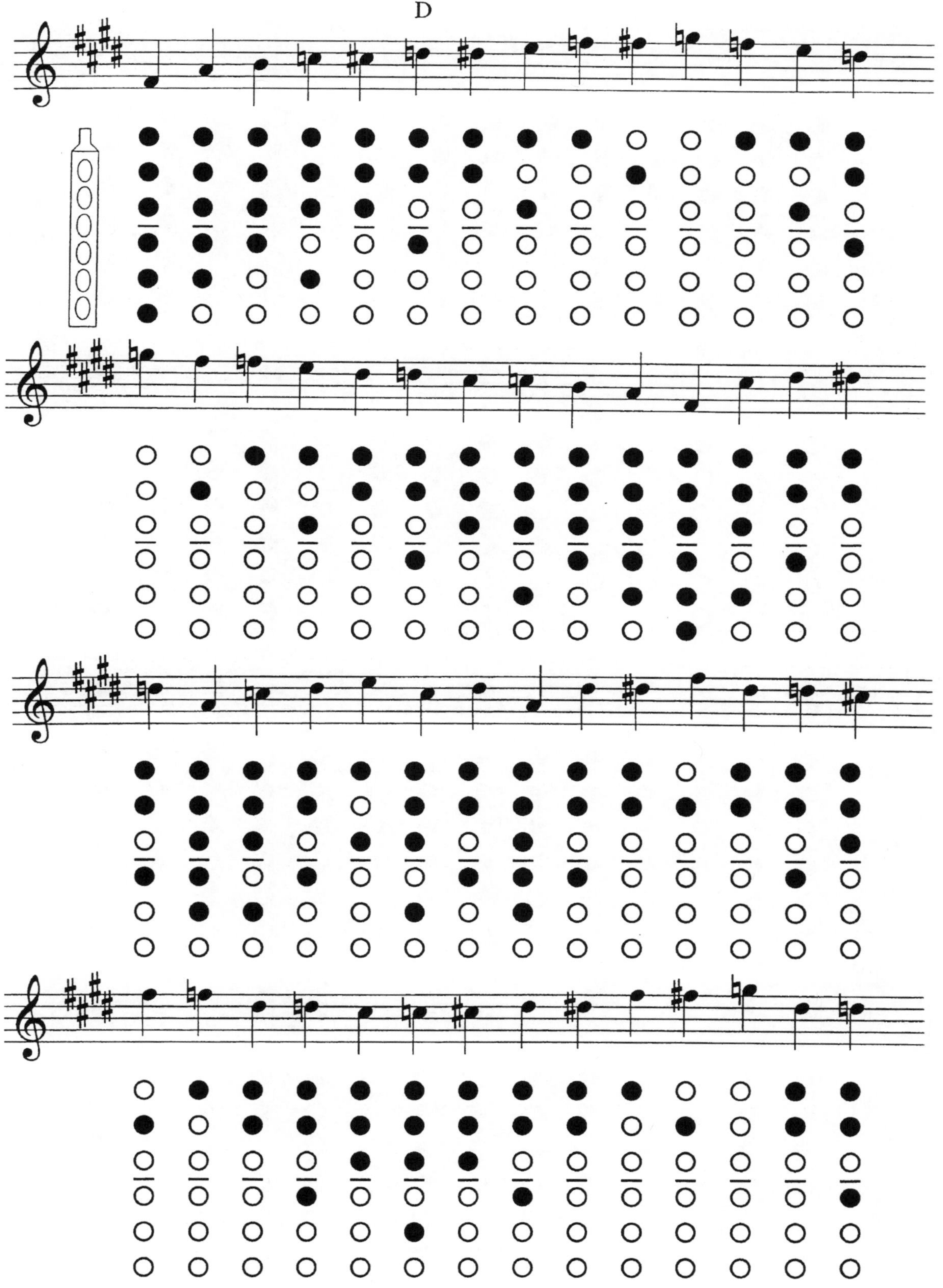

Six-Hole Native American Flute TABlature: Exercise 7

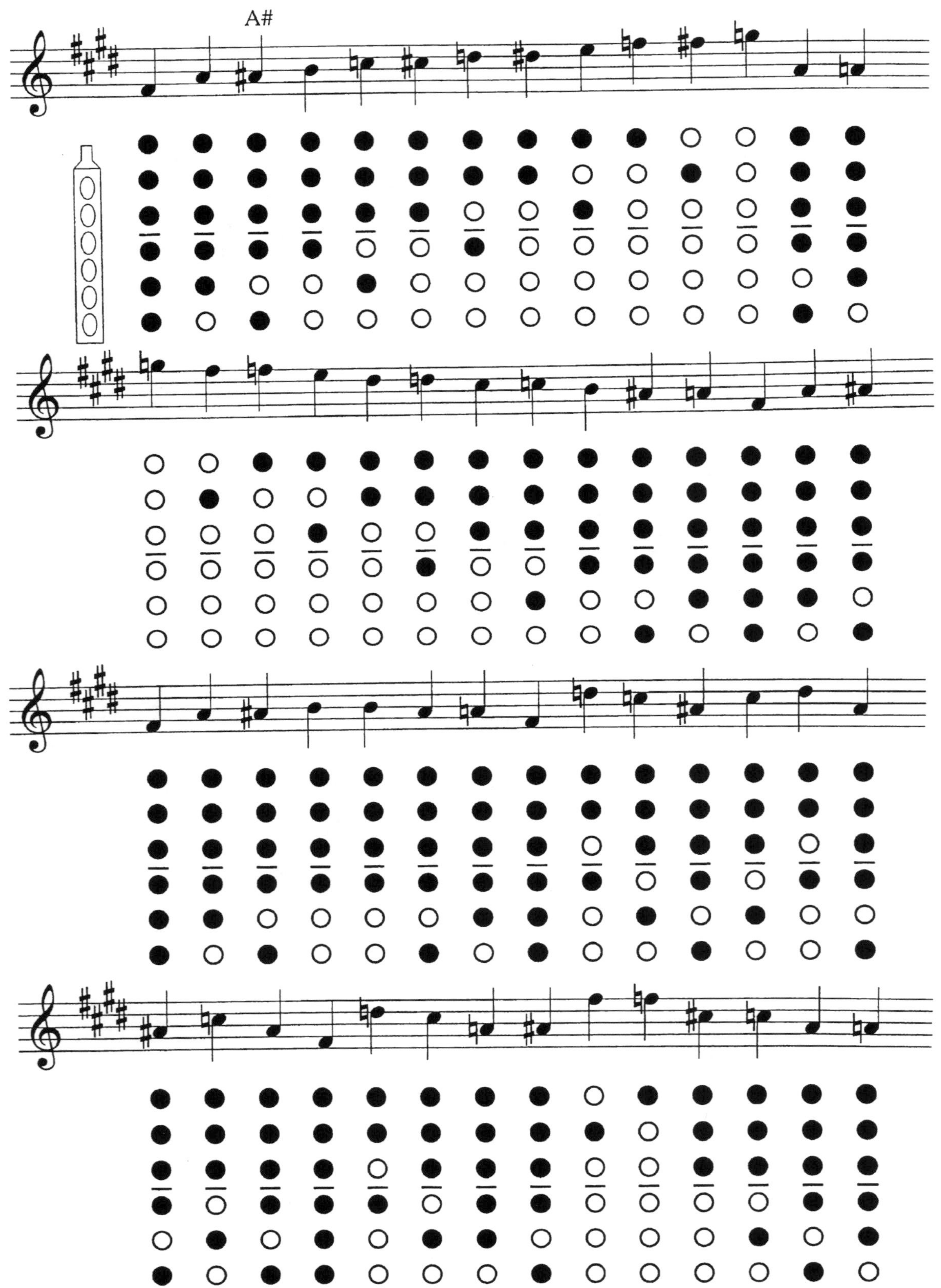

Six-Hole Native American Flute TABlature: Exercise 8

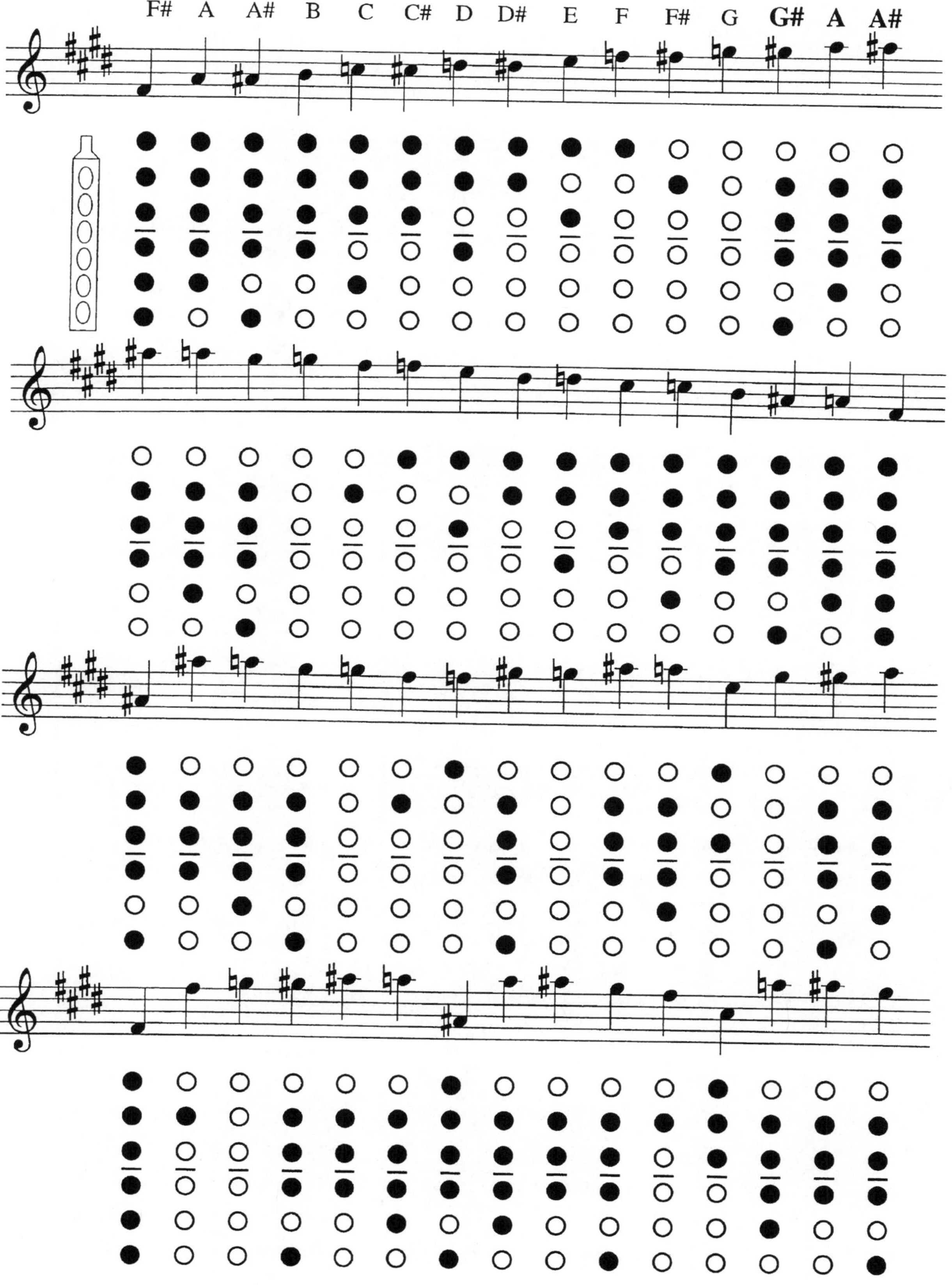

AMAZING GRACE

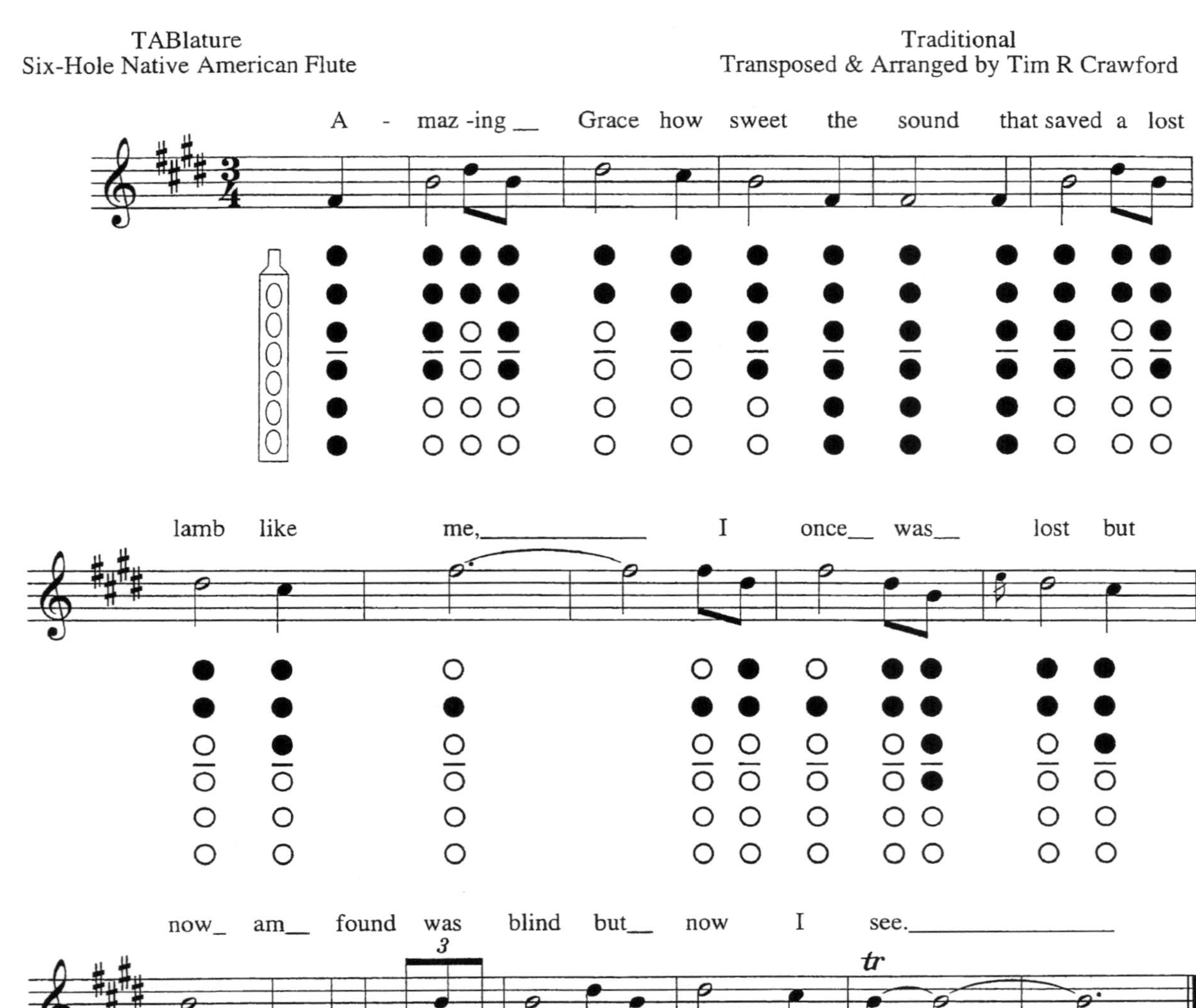

Aura Lee

TABlature
Six-Hole Native American Flute
Traditional
Transposed by John Sarantos
& Tim R. Crawford
As the black-bird in the spring by the wil-low tree
sat and piped I heard him sing, sing of my Au - ra Lee
Au - ra Lee, Au - ra Lee, maid of gold-en hair
sun-shine came a - long with thee, and swal-lows in the air.

Hush Little Baby

TABlature
Six-Hole Native American Flute

Traditional
Transposed by John Sarantos
& Tim R. Crawford

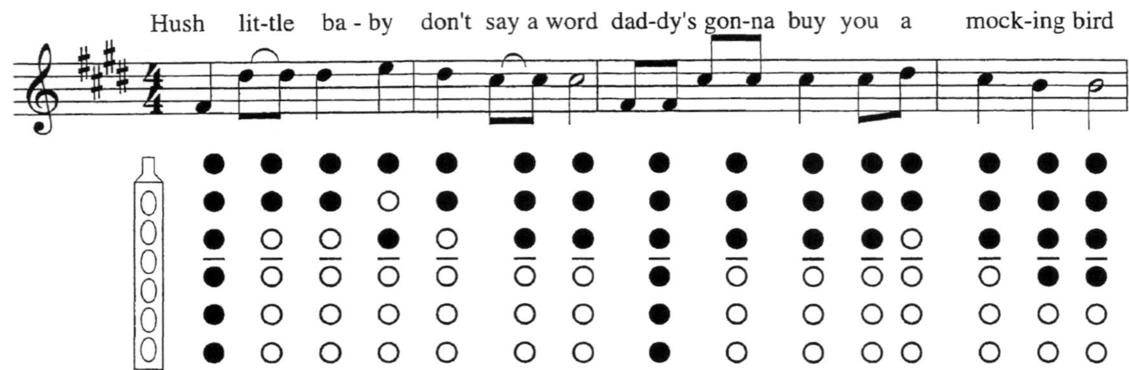

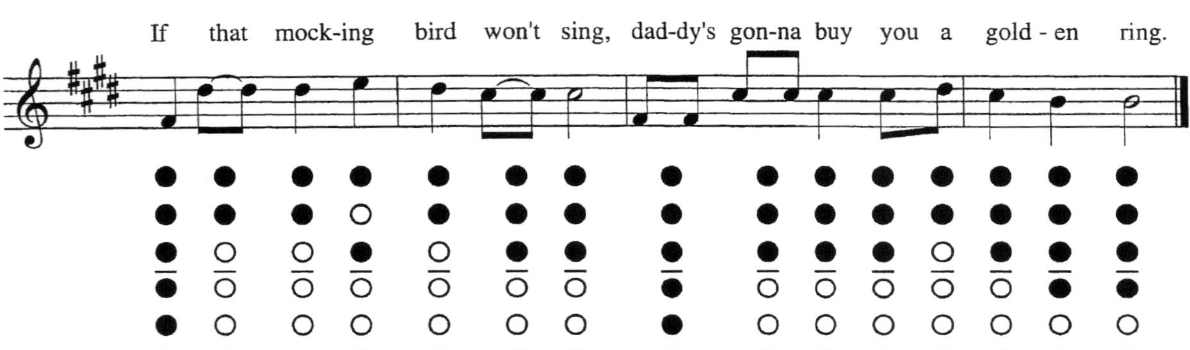

Michael, Row The Boat Ashore

TABlature
Six-Hole Native American Flute

Traditional
Transposed by John Sarantos
& Tim R. Crawford

Red River Valley

TABlature
Six-Hole Native American Flute

Traditional
Transposed by Tim R. Crawford

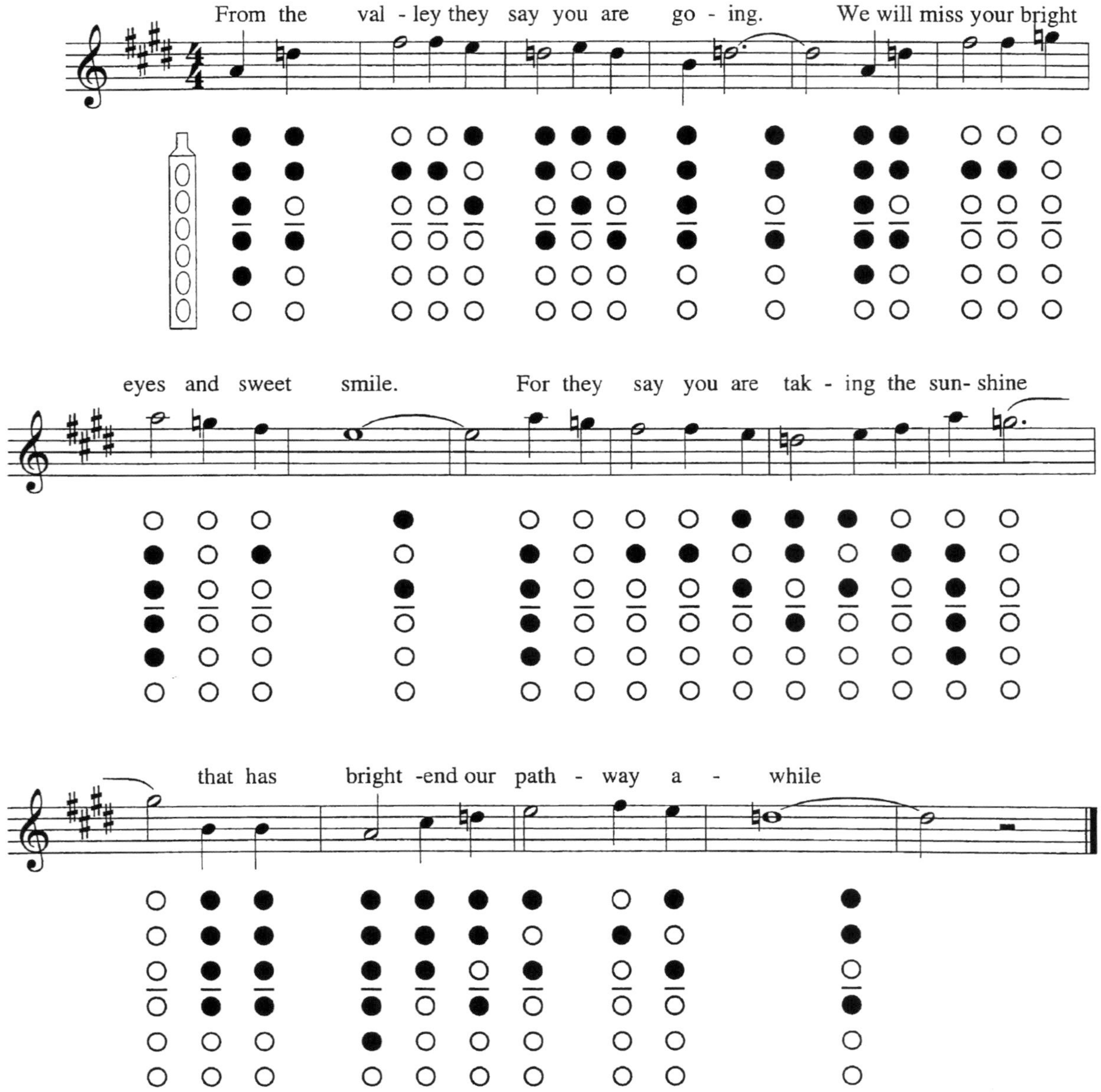

From the val - ley they say you are go - ing. We will miss your bright

eyes and sweet smile. For they say you are tak - ing the sun- shine

that has bright -end our path - way a - while

Six-Hole Native American Flute TABlature: Self-Test 1

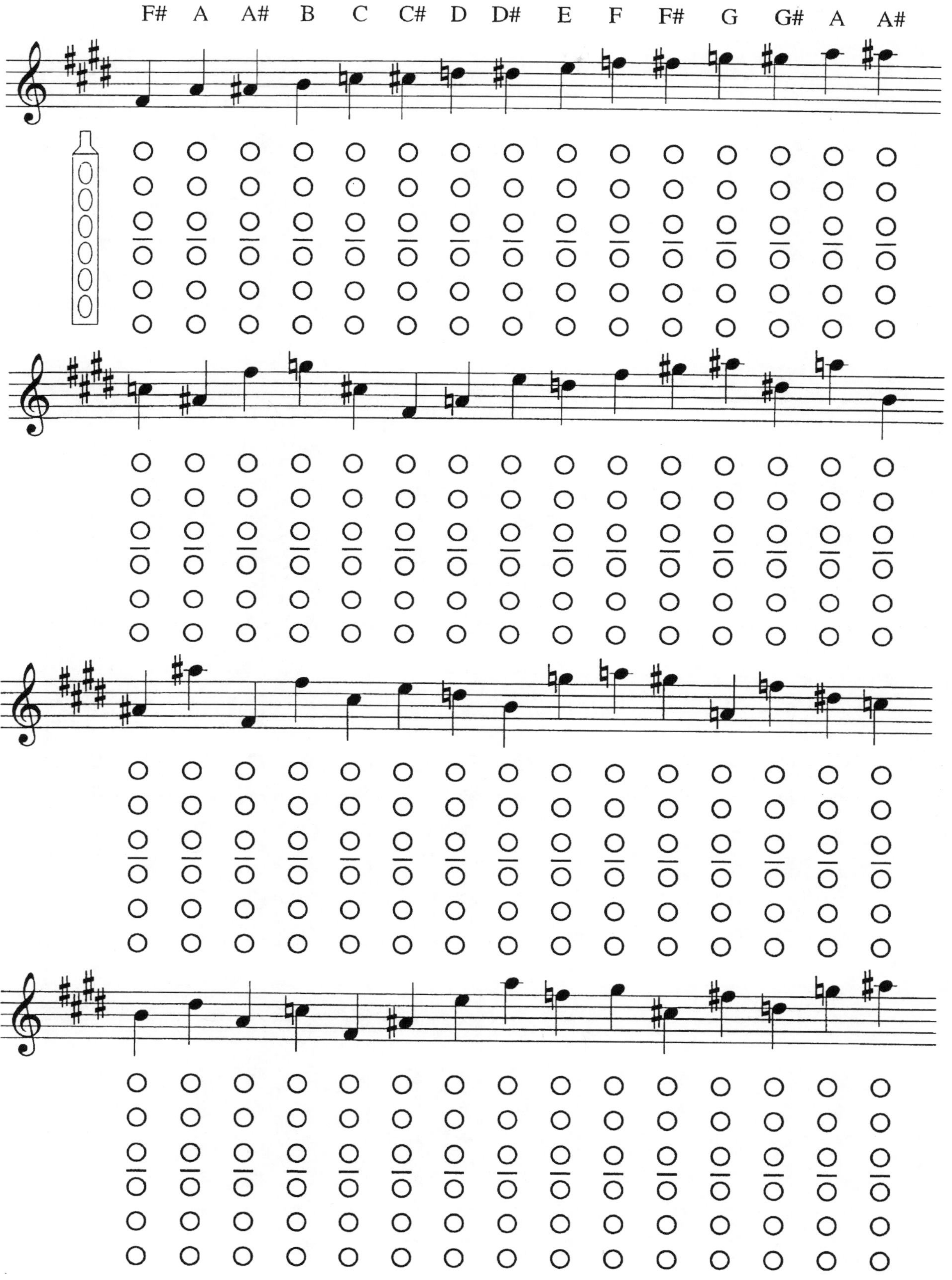

Six-Hole Native American Flute TABlature: Self-Test 2

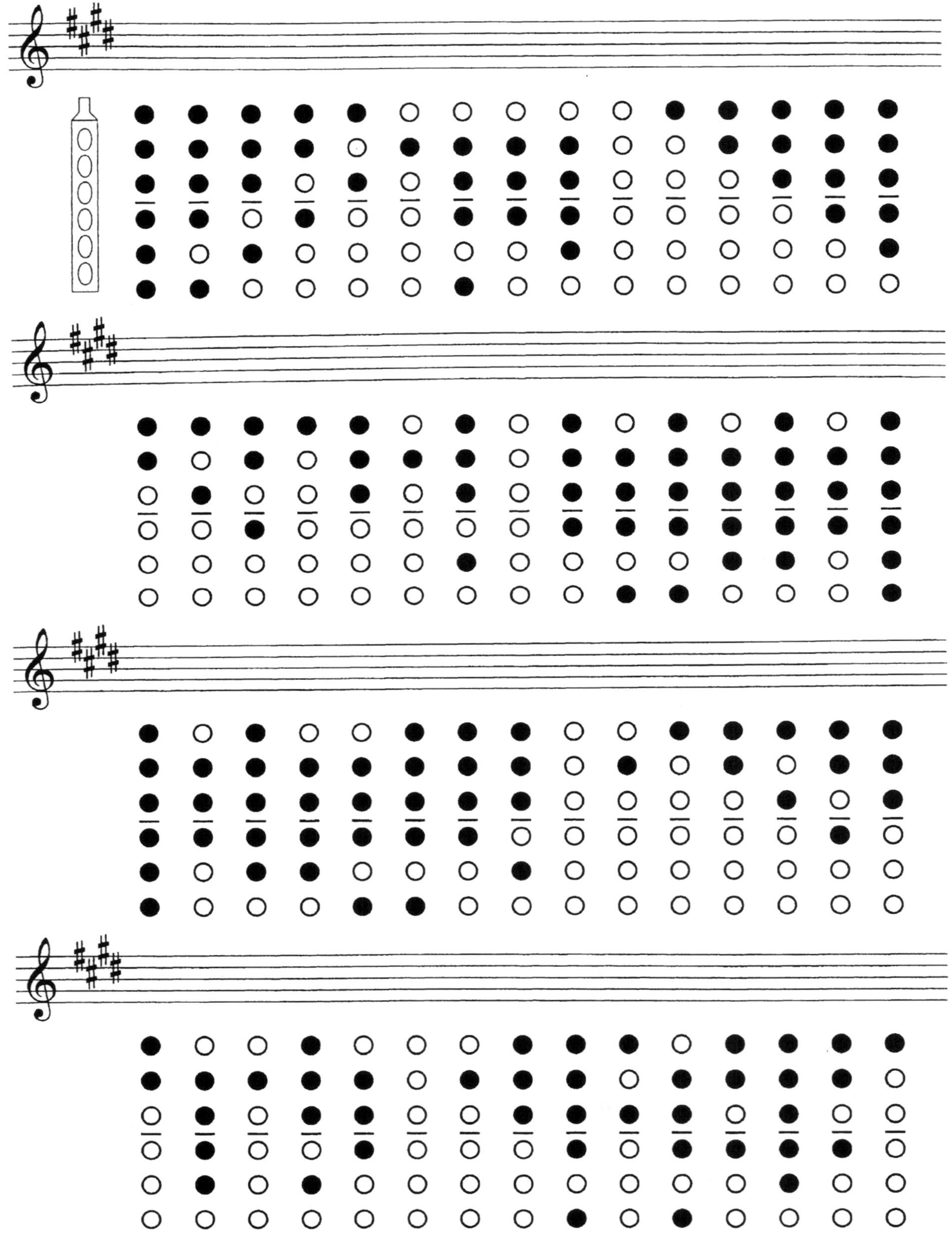

Early Flute Music of the Indigenous Peoples

Prior to the invention of the phonograph, transcriptions of the music of indigenous peoples of North America into Western music notation was accomplished in the field by a very limited number of early anthropologists/ethnomusicologists by simply listening to the music as it was either played or sung. One of the earliest of these researchers was Dr. Theodore Baker of Germany who made a number of transcriptions in 1880. His work was followed by Dr. Franz Boas in 1883-1884 who worked with a culture that was then referred to as the Central Eskimo. In addition, during 1884, Alice C. Fletcher published 10 songs from the Omaha culture of which she had made field transcriptions (Densmore, 1942). With the invention of the phonograph, researchers were able to make wax cylinder records in the field and then transcribe the music from these cylinders into Western musical notation at their convenience or later with the help of assistants.

One of the earliest documented recording series' are those that Alice C. Fletcher made among the Omaha people in Nebraska around 1890, although it is believed that the first use of the phonograph was probably by Jesse Fewkes who, in April of 1890, recorded the songs of the Passamaquoddy people in Maine (Densmore, 1942). It would appear, however, that the majority of these early and even subsequent field recordings were of vocal music. As an example, in the book *A Study Of Omaha Indian Music*, a total of 92 songs are presented that were transcribed from wax cylinder records. Of this total, only two are presented as having been transcribed from flute recordings made in the 1890s (Fletcher, 1994). I tend to believe that some of the "original" or indigenous songs published in recent years for the Native American flute originated with vocal recordings. However, as Frances Densmore stated: "In some tribes it's said that certain songs may either be sung or played on the flute, and the Menomonee said that love songs were imitations of flute melodies" (Densmore, 1942).

On the other hand, of specific interest to this topic, Densmore also wrote that she had to be very discreet about the vocal love songs as they were not "traditional" in our sense of general understanding, but rather a development brought to the indigenous peoples by the Europeans. Densmore states:

> "This is not a native custom [vocal love songs] and is usually connected with evil magic or intoxication. Love songs, in the old days, were sung to add intrigue of various sorts... A Papago said, 'If a man gets to singing love songs we send for a medicine man to make him stop.' In one tribe I was warned that if I recorded love songs, the fine old men would have nothing to do with my work." (Densmore, 1942)

Frederick R. Burton who spent time with the Ojibwa at the turn of the last century wrote that, as far as he could determine, tunes were not created for the flute as it was used in place of the lover's voice.

> "The flute, therefore, does not figure as a means to instrumental music, which was wholly unknown to the Aboriginal Indian, but as a substitute for the voice; and in the making of love songs, care is often taken that they shall be capable of reproduction on the flute." (Burton)

My limited research for transcriptions of indigenous music, specifically for the flute, included an examination of books written by four early anthropologists/ethnomusicologists: 14 books by Frances Densmore, two books by Alice C. Fletcher, one book by Frank Speck, and one book by Natalie Curtis. I was only able to identify a total of 20 songs specifically for the Native American flute, with 14 of these being transcriptions from wax cylinder records of flutes being played. The remaining six were from vocal recordings, in the apparent absence of a flute player, in order to provide the music that was believed to be for the flute. Without a doubt, there are more transcriptions in existence specifically from recordings of the flute, but nowhere near the abundance of vocal recordings. Densmore noted that during the period between 1907 and 1941 more than 2,600 records had been transcribed and transferred to various archives representing approximately 39 different cultures, the bulk of which going to the Smithsonian. She went on to say that these transcriptions did not represent all of the records that had been actually recorded (Densmore, 1942). There was, unfortunately, no indication as to how many of these transcriptions were from flute recordings as opposed to vocal recordings. As an example of the limited transcriptions of original music for the Native American flute, *Yuman and Yaqui Music* by Frances Densmore contains only two complete flute songs versus 128 vocal songs, although two other short flute melodies are given some reference.

Of the 20 transcriptions that I have been able to acquire that were specifically for the flute, I am presenting seven of them that I consider to be reasonably representative of this very limited group. Only one of the seven, "Yuchi Love Song," is presented for both the five- and six-hole Native American flute, with the rest being for the six-hole flute. "The man who gave this tune, 'Yuchi Love Song,' exclaimed something like the following when he had finished: 'Oh, if some girls were only here! When they hear that they cry and then you can hold them. It makes them feel lonesome. I wish some were here now. I feel badly myself' " (Speck, 1909). The arrangements that I have made of these transcriptions are relatively minor and represent an attempt to present the music in a manner contemporary with the original transcriptions, in a musical context that can also be easily followed by the reader.

One of the most well known perspectives on indigenous music was written by Edward Wapp, a descendent of Curtis Pequahno (Potawatomi) and Jes Wapp (Sauk/Fox), both of whom were Native American flute players.

> "Music in a culture will change as the culture changes. For the courting flute, change has occurred, both contextually and musically. It will probably never be heard again in its traditional context, nor will the many old and beautiful love songs that were once used to court young women be heard again. But, the beauty of the flute and the music that it can produce will never be lost, even though many new changes have and will yet occur." (Wapp, 1984)

Federal Cylinder Project

Due to the pioneering efforts of Thomas Edison, the wax cylinder phonograph became commercially available in 1889. These spring-wound units were comparable in size and weight to today's portable sewing machines, and they proved to be practical for ethnomusicologists to use when making field recordings. The size of these early cylinders were about the same diameter as today's small soup cans and about one and a half times as long.

During the nation's bicentennial period, renewed interest from American Indians in their own cultural heritage prompted the American Folklife Center, a division of the Library of Congress, to "inaugurate the Federal Cylinder Project, a project to organize, catalog, duplicate for preservation, and ultimately disseminate the contents of those old cylinders and thus to permit them to serve the process of cultural reflection and renewal in late twentieth-century America" (Brady, et al.). The majority of the cylinder collections in the archives of the Library of Congress consist of music and spoken word recordings that document the music and lore of Native American cultures, although the collection also consists of recordings from every continent.

Initially, the Federal Cylinder Project, with support from the Smithsonian Institution, began cataloging and duplicating all of the cylinders in their collection in 1979. One of the primary participants in this project, Erika Brady, has written a book entitled *A Spiral Way: How the Phonograph Changed Ethnography* which I highly recommend to those with an interest in the history of these early wax cylinder recordings (Brady).

According to the inventory listed in Volume 1 of the Federal Cylinder Project published in 1984, they were successfully able to catalog and duplicate 6,400 cylinders of music from 135 various Native American cultures (Brady, et al.). While some of the cylinders only contain a single recording, others have up to nine individual recordings.

After the initial cataloging and duplication of the wax cylinders, the next part of the project was to divide the cylinders up into geographic areas and then, in succeeding volumes, publish a catalog of the individual recordings on each cylinder. Volume 2 of the Federal Cylinder Project was published in 1985 and covered the northeastern and southeastern portions of the United States. The cultures included within the Northeastern Catalog are: Chippewa, Fox, Iroquois, Kickapoo, Menomonee,

Passamaquoddy, Sauk, Shawnee, and Winnebago. The cultures included within the Southeastern Catalog are: Alabama, Catawba, Cherokee, Chitimacha, Choctaw, and Seminole (Gray and Lee).

Volume 3 of the Federal Cylinder Project was published in 1988 and covered the Great Basin/Plateau and the northwest coast/arctic cultures. The cultures included in the Great Basin/Plateau Catalog are: Nez Perce, Okanagon, Thompson, Ute, and Yakima. The cultures included within the Northwest Coast/Arctic Catalog are: Carrier, Clackamas Chinook, Clayoquot, Comox, Eskimo, Halkomelem, Ingalik, Kalapuya, Kwakiutl, Makah, Nitinat, Nootka, Quileute, Shasta, Squamish, Tlingit, Tismshian, Tututni, and Umpqua (Gray, 1988).

Volume 5 of the Federal Cylinder Project was published in 1990 and covered the California and Southwestern cultures, along with the Central American and South American cultures. The cultures included in the California Catalog are: Cahuilla, Chumash, Costanoan, Diegueno, Gabrielino, Hupa, Karuk, Kitanemuk, Klamath, Konkow, Konomihu, Luiseno, Miwok, Mono, Nomlaki, Pomo, Serrano, Wailaki, Yokuts, Yuki, and Yurok. The cultures included in the Southwestern Indian Catalog are: Apache, Cocopa, Maricopa, Mohave, Papago, Pima, Quechan, and Yaqui (Gray and Schupman).

Unfortunately, no further volumes have been published. This leaves a large gap for researchers and descendants of many cultures.

In late August of 2001, I e-mailed the American Folklife Center for information on the status of the missing volumes, 4, 6, and 7. These volumes would have covered the southwestern Pueblo, Navajo, and the Plains cultures, among other cultures. I received the following reply on September 5, 2001, from Judith Gray, a reference specialist and editor of the existing volumes:

> "Those catalogs are not done and will probably never be published, except perhaps on-line, even if the manuscripts were ever completed. I am the 'last remnant' of the Federal Cylinder Project staff, but my work is now unrelated to cylinder cataloging except on very rare occasions. So, I can make no promises about any sort of time schedule. There are rough-drafts of most of the Plains cylinder collections, but there are almost none for any of the Pueblo or Navajo collections. Perhaps, if you ever have occasion to come to Washington, D.C., you can look through the content lists of various cylinder collections to see if there are any flute melodies among them."

An examination of the 1,231 pages of the existing three volumes that catalog the individual songs on each individual wax cylinder that were successfully duplicated yield a total of 34 songs that would be of interest to students of the Native American flute. As some of them are vocals in imitation of the Native American flute, and a few are duplicates, there were actually only 20 songs that were direct Native American flute recordings. I have included the catalog information and description for those 34 songs as follows:

The Federal Cylinder Project - Volume 2

Chippewa Indian Music. The Alice C. Fletcher Collection; Cylinder No. 850; AFS NO. 20,324: 13; Collector No. Fl. 198: Song 2) [Love Song, in imitation of flute performance style].

Menomonee Indian Music. The Frances Densmore Collection; Cylinder No. 3,183; AFS No. 10,687: B7-B8; BAE Cat. No. 1646; 1647: Song 1) [Flute melody (1) - - 1646] and Song 2) [Flute Melody (2) - - 1647].

Cylinder No. 3,184; AFS No. 10,687: B9-B10; BAE No. 1648; 1649: Song 1) [Flute Melody (3) - - 1648 and Song 2) [Flute Melody (4) - - 1649.

Menomonee Indian Music. The Alanson Skinner Collection; Cylinder No. 6,821; AFS No. 8905; B5: Song 1) [Flute love song].

Winnebago Indian Music. The Frances Densmore Collection; Cylinder No. 3,295; AFS NO. 10,710: A1-A2/10,711: A2-A3: Song 5) [Flute Melody (a) - - 1865, Song 6) [Fragments of flute melody], Song 7) [Repetition of 1865] and Song 8) [Flute Melody (b) - - 1866.

Cylinder No. 3,299; AFS NO. 10,710: B3; BAE CAT NO. 1862;1863: Song 3) [Love song (b) - - 1863; flute version] and Song 5) [Love song (b) - - 1863; sung version].

Winnebago Indian Music. The Alice C. Fletcher Collection; Cylinder No. 834; AFS No. 20,323: 14; Collector No. Fl. 182; Box 12, No. 2: Song 2) [Flute melody (love song)] and Song 3) [Flute melody Sac and Fox song].

Cylinder No. 853; AFS No. 20,325: 3; Collector No. Fl. 201: Song 1) [Flute melody (love song)] and Song 2) [Flute melody (love song)].

Cylinder No. 863; AFS No. 20,325: 14; Collector No. Fl. 21: Flute melody [single song]

Winnebago Indian Music. The Paul Radin Collection; Cylinder No. 1,821; AFS No. 21,358: 3: Song 1) [Flute Melody] and Song 2) [repetition]

Choctaw Indian Music. The Frances Densmore Collection; Cylinder No. 3,812; AFS No. 21,265: 14: Whistle Melody [3 cuts].

The Federal Cylinder Project - Volume 3

Flathead Indian Music. The Claude Everett Schaefer Collection; Cylinder No. 190; AFS NO. 11,024: A1-A2; Collector No. A1-A4: Song 1) [Flute melody].

The Federal Cylinder Project - Volume 5

Gabrielino Music. The Hohn Peabody Harrington Collection; Cylinder No. 1352; AFS NO. 20,346: 8; S.I. No. 00001083: Song 1) Popiim'an Pi'mokvol song; w/bone whistle].

Karuk Music. The Helen Heffron Roberts Collection; Cylinder No. 144**; AFS No. 19,874: 2; Collector No. 1A,a-1A,g: Song 2) [Flute tune sung by Phoebe - - 1a,b; taught Phoebe by an old flute player].

Cylinder No. 92; AFS No. 19,874: 4; Collector No. 3a-3g: Song 1) [War Dance Song—3a; unidentified whistle performer].

Cylinder No. 98; AFS No. 19,875: 4; Collector No. 9a-9f: Song 6) [The Song of the Eel, Flute melody - - 9f].

Cylinder No. 135; AFS No. 19,881: 2: Song 1) [Flute tune - -47a] and Song 2) [Flute tune, repetition of 47a - - 47b].

Konomihu Music. The Helen Heffron Roberts Collection; Cylinder No. 118; AFS NO. 19,878: 4; Collector No. 30a-30j: Song 2) [War Dance Song - - 30b; headman w/flute].

Northern Pomo Music. Cylinder No. 273; AFS No. 11,029: A1-A4; Collector No. 9a-9d: Song 3) [Flute tune, Pomo love song - - 9c] and Song 4) [Repetition of preceding tune - - 9d].

Cylinder No. 274; AFS No. 11,029: A5-A6; Collector No. 10a-10c: Song 2) [Jim Brown's Flute Piece - - 10b].

Huichol Music. The Carl Sofus Lumholtz Collection; AFS No. 11,017: B2; Original No. 18; AMNH CAT No. 272: Song 1) [Blowing Flute].

Papago (Tohono O'Odham) Music. The Frances Densmore Collection; Cylinder No. 2648; AFS No. 10,613: A1-A2; BAE CAT No. 967; 968: 1) [Four fires on the ground - - 967; connected with story of the origin of the flute].

Cylinder No. 2649; AFS No. 10,613: A3-A4; BAE CAT No. 969; 970: 1) [The girls are approaching -- 969; connected with story of the origin of the flute].

Cylinder No. 2649; AFS No. 10,613: A3-A4; BAE CAT No. 969; 970: 1) [The girls are approaching -- 969; connected with story of the origin of the flute].

In the early fall of 2001, I made a request to the American Folklife Center Reference Committee for an estimate to copy all of the above referenced selections from their duplicate copies. It was my thought, aside from the contributions to the "Early Flute Music of the Indigenous Peoples" chapter within this book, that it would be a worthwhile endeavor for these recordings to be issued on a CD. This would be of significant educational and musical interest. As of April 2002, I have not received a response to my inquiry.

Based upon the results of the three detailed reference volumes of the Federal Cylinder Project and my other research over a number of years, it is my estimate that there may exist up to 50 individual recordings of the Native American flute on the early wax cylinder recordings.

Note: The Library of Congress Folk Recordings, through their Archive of Folk Culture, possesses a number of recordings of American Indian music. It is available on 20 individual cassettes. The organization's Web site provides a listing by culture and song title. I was unable to determine whether or not any of those songs might possibly be a recording of the Native American flute from the descriptions provided. The Web site address is: http://lcweb.loc.gov/folklife/folkcat.html

Love Song

TABlature
Five-Hole Native American Flute

Yuchi (Speck, 1909)
Arranged by Tim R. Crawford

Love Song

TABlature
Six-Hole Native American Flute

Yuchi (Speck, 1909)
Transposed & Arranged by Tim R. Crawford

Chippewa Melody

TABlature
Six-Hole Native American Flute

Chippewa (Densmore, 1913)
Transposed & Arranged By Tim R. Crawford

Flageolet Melody

To Bring Forth Snow (from a legend)

TABlature
Six-Hole Natie American Flute

Mandan & Hidatsa (Densmore, 1923)
Transposed & Arranged By Tim R. Crawford

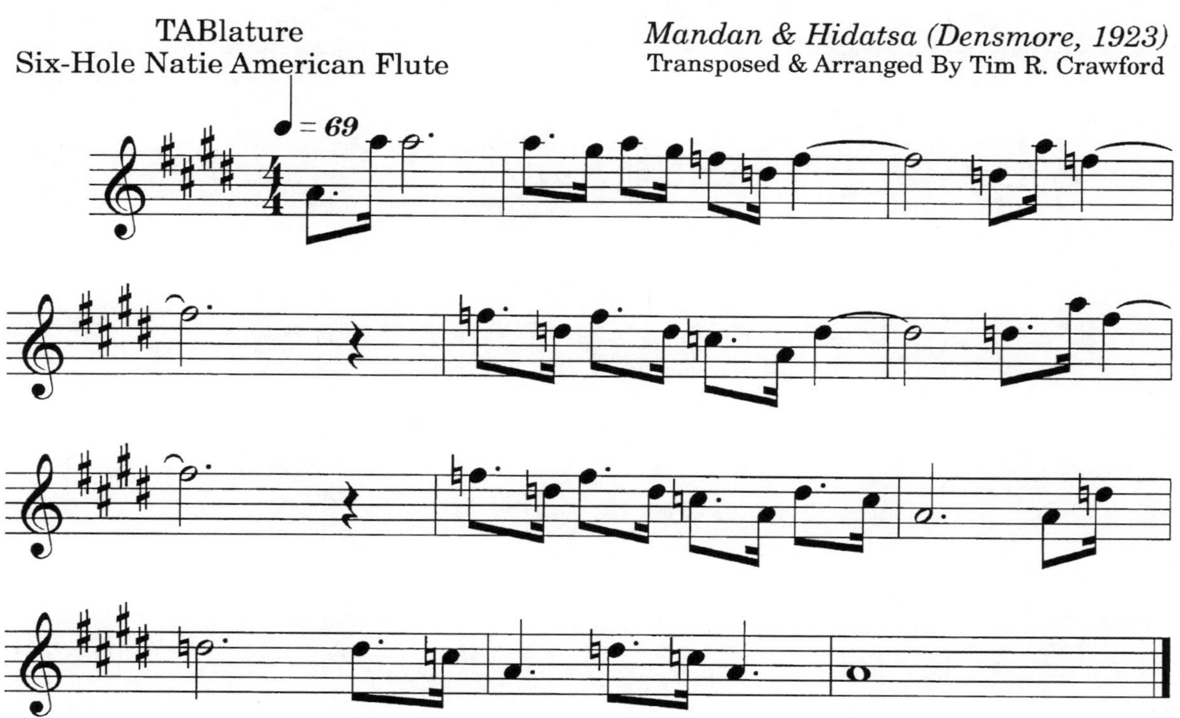

Flute Melody No. 2

Flute Melody No. 3

Love Call

TABlature
Six-Hole Native American Flute

Omaha (Fletcher, 1900)
Arranged By Tim R. Crawford

Slow to Moderate

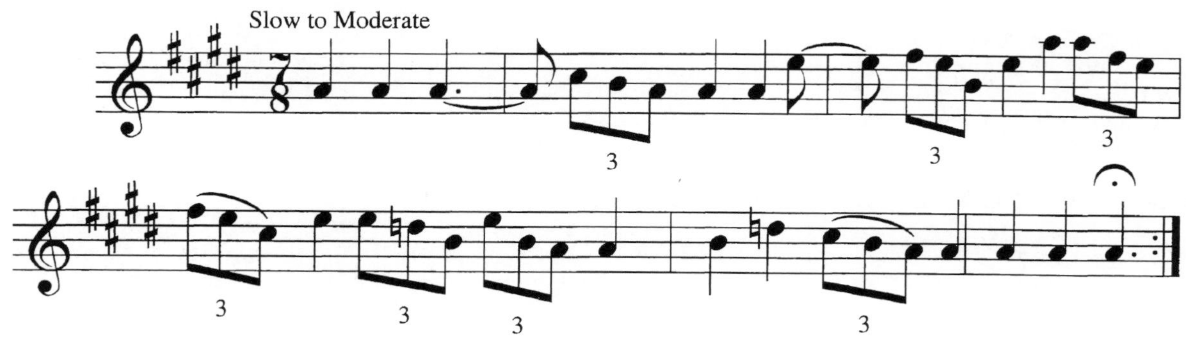

Flageolet Piece

(No. 91)

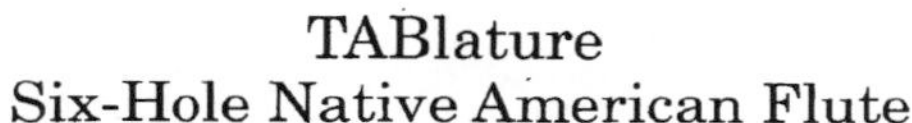

TABlature
Six-Hole Native American Flute

Omaha (Fletcher, 1893)
Arranged By Tim R. Crawford

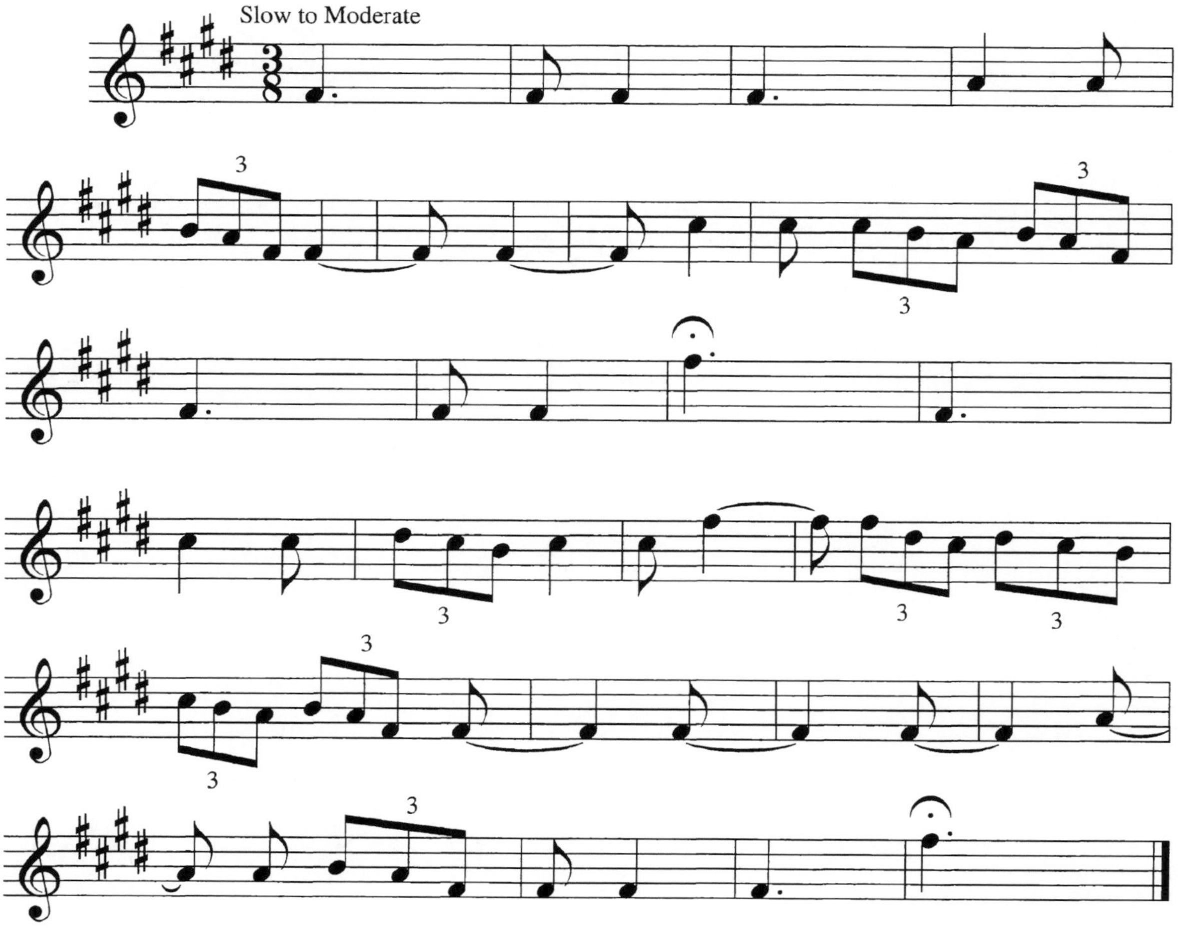
Slow to Moderate

About the Music

Each of my own songs presented here reference the key or tuning of the Native American flute that was used in the creation of that song. This reference has created some unanticipated confusion on the part of readers in previous editions who were concerned that they could not play a specific song unless they owned a flute in the key; this is simply not true. My music, for the most part, can be played on any instrument, with number of finger holes being equal. Therefore, ***please ignore the key or tuning reference*** and play the music with which ever flute you own or happen to be favoring at the moment. The intervals [steps between the notes] will basically follow most instruments, regardless of key, and the song will play just fine. However, as individual flutes have variations in their own intervals, sometimes a song may not sound "right," even if played in the referenced key; therefore, if a song does not sound quite "right" to you, try playing it on a different flute.

Above all else: **DO IT YOUR WAY! EXPERIENCE THE MAGIC!**

Please feel free to take liberty with the notes, their duration, or anything else contained within the music. I may or may not play my own music as written, depending upon the vicissitudes of my mood at that moment. In all actuality, I seldom play a song in quite the same way each time that I perform it.

Interestingly, the Native American flute may very well be the "ultimate instrument" for improvisational music, which is probably in keeping with its origins. I once listened to a professional musician explain that she had taken up playing the Native American flute because she was tired of the strict musical discipline that she was required to maintain when playing a silver concert flute. She went on to explain that she believed that it was too limiting of her desire to express herself through music. She stated that the Native American flute satisfied her need for musical self-expression. Also, a former professional musician informed me that he had given up playing the piano professionally for a variety of reasons, but so loved music that he was grateful for having discovered the flute as it allowed him to continue to enjoy music, and to enjoy it his way! Finally, a music teacher, with many years of teaching experience, confided to me that she too was grateful for the discovery of the Native American flute, as she felt that it gave to her much greater freedom to explore her own musical creativity without concern for the discipline of "classical" music.

Thus, if you are a trained musician, I would suggest that you forget about the rigid rules of meter and rhythm that you have struggled to master all of these years and let yourself go with the flow that you feel building from within yourself. You might discover a new musical dimension and freedom with this uniquely North American solo instrument.

Use my music to help stimulate your own musically creative side, for those of you who are intermediate or advanced players. If you are a new student then this music will help you to learn to play the Native American flute, as well as introduce you to various playing techniques. Then, as you continue in the development of your own confidence, you too will be stimulated to create your own music.

The original songs within this book for the Native American flute that I have composed are presented in alphabetical order and are separated into three sections: four-hole, five-hole, and six-hole.

In addition, I have two recordings that present 21 of these songs. *Voices* (1998) contains 12 songs from this book, while *In Remembrance* (2001) contains 9 songs from this book. The CDs are $15.95 each, plus $1.50 shipping and handling, postpaid by check or cash. Please send funds made payable to: WindWalker, P.O. Box 946, Cannon Beach, OR, 97110-0946. Sorry, credit cards are not accepted.

Note to Educators

With the development of the TABlature system, you now have an opportunity to present the Native American flute in a classroom setting. This third edition of *Flute Magic: An Introduction to the Native American Flute* readily offers to you a workable text and musical exercise book that will help guide students along the learning path. Special pricing is available for educational institutions and teachers. Please write directly to: WindWalker P.O. Box 946, Cannon Beach, OR, 97110-0946 for this option. **Special Note:** *Flute Magic* is available in either comb binding or perfect binding.

Flute Options

The making of wooden flutes requires considerable experience. The talent to accomplish the required hand work with the wood can be very significant. Also, there is a considerable investment of time on the part of the builder/artisan in flute making. All of these elements play a role in, as well as other business and material costs, the price that each individual flute builder must charge for his or her product.

Through the years, I have had several educators comment to me that they would like to introduce the Native American flute to their classes but were frustrated in their pursuit of relatively low-cost flutes that they judged their students could afford, especially in the lower grade levels. They have also been frustrated in locating such a source that could readily supply the low-cost flutes in quantity for classroom use.

Today, many flute builders, who have probably also heard these same comments, realize that today's buyer of inexpensive models are tomorrow's potential customer for their more expensive handcrafted models. Thus, they have endeavored to create some lower cost alternatives to help encourage this potential. Some of the builders of wooden Native American flutes who have been able to work out designs and construction techniques that enable them to offer wood models as low as, or close to, $75 each are: High Spirits Music - Arizona; Love Flutes - California; Windspirit - California; 'Chris Ti Coom' Flutes - Colorado; and Earth Rhythms - Texas. Surprisingly, Butch Hall of Native American Flutes in Texas has informed me that they are able to offer flutes in classroom quantities in the $49 price range. There are most likely other makers who offer low-cost models. Therefore, please see the list of flute builders in Appendix G, alphabetized by state, and contact them all.

Additionally, several of these builders offer excellent-value, low-cost wood kits. However, be aware of the hazards of some wood dusts and the possible need for adequate ventilation and/or respiratory protection. A significant Web site dealing with respiratory protection and wood working is: www.riparia.org/toxicwoods.htm Flute makers offering flute kits are as follows:

Stellar Musical Products - Washington
Following Generations Music - Oregon
White Deer Indian Traders - Wisconsin
Butch Hall Native American Flutes - Texas

Butch Hall offers some very attractive pricing, in quantity, of newly-designed quality flute kits which only require gluing, sanding, and a finish. They are readily available, in bulk, for classroom use. Pricing is as follows: 1-24, $25 each; 25-99, $15 each; 100+, $12.50 each. Shipping is extra.

Ken Light of Amon Olorin Flutes in Montana has introduced a PF-Series flute that is made of molded plastic and is readily available in quantity for [at the time of this writing] $59.95, plus $5 shipping and handling. You actually receive one head piece and two separate body tubes. One of the body tubes is a G minor tuning, while the other body tube is an F# minor tuning. Thus, the students will actually have two different flutes with which to learn and practice. A drawstring cloth bag is included. The PF-Series flute appears to be an excellent value, has a reasonable tone quality, and would appear to be fairly constant in timbre from flute to flute. I am very impressed with the overall appearance and functionality of these Native American-styled plastic flutes and consider these instruments to be worthy for serious classroom use.

At the time of this printing, I am aware of only two flute builders offering inexpensive flutes made of PVC: Brad Sanders of Walking Wind Flutes in Westport, Washington, and Jan Pickard of Compass Rose Events in Broomfield, Colorado. Jan's PVC flutes are built with a removable mouthpiece which she advertises as a benefit for easy disinfection. [See the "Flute Builders" appendix for further contact information for these two individuals.]

In addition, an interesting option for PVC flutes exists on flute builder Scott Loomis' Web site. Here, he has plans and instructions for making a six-hole PVC flute for $1. Scott's Web site address is as follows: www.loomisflute.com

With all of this discussion about low-cost flutes, it is important to remember that there are flute artisans whose flutes, while more costly, are very much worth every dollar paid. Many of these same flutes will be tomorrow's prized heirlooms sought after by new generations of players who have heard of these "Stradivariuses." Today, you have a wonderful opportunity to own one of these future heirlooms and to thereby expose the younger generations, which you are influencing, to the options available for their own future consideration. Give it some serious thought, as the "pool" of flute artisans is quite small and requires the support of everyone to ensure that this unique North American instrument continues to thrive.

Note: As a general caution, the reader should be aware that all or some individual woods, finishes, and PVC products can potentially have some negative health impact, depending upon manufacture and use. Flutists are encouraged to discuss their concerns with a health care provider and/or other qualified professionals.

Additional TABlature and Finger Chart Sources

***The Art of the Native American Flute* [1996]** by R. Carlos Nakai and James DeMars, with additional material by David P. McAllester and Ken Light. Available from Canyon Records Productions [1-800-268-1141].

***Feathered Pipe Memories* [2000]** by Carl Bludts, published by Rabbitdog Publishing, 1808 Lauderdale Road, Louisville, KY, 40205. A book/CD package featuring 14 original and traditional songs. While all of the songs are in TABlature, 11 of the songs are also in finger chart notation. In addition, the book contains poetry by Joan Johannes.

The Four Directions by Carl Bludts. A book/CD package featuring 20 traditional Native American songs and original compositions by Belgian flute player Carl Bludts. The songs are written in both Nakai TABlature and finger chart notation.

***Hymns for the Native American Flute, With Inspirational Quotes and Sayings* [2002]** by Gary Stokum and Dr. Kathleen Joyce-Grendahl. This book is comprised of instructions on transcribing music into the R. Carlos Nakai TABlature system, TABlature charts for the five- and six-hole Native American flute, biographies of the authors, and 64 hymns. Available from: Dr. Kathleen Joyce-Grendahl, 310 Ash Wood Drive, Suffolk, VA 23434.

***INAFA Songbook, Volume 1* [2002]** compiled by the International Native American Flute Association [INAFA]. Included are 34 songs by INAFA members, with a forward by R. Carlos Nakai. There is an introduction and a description of the musical symbols and terms used throughout the book. The songs are in the form of solos, duets, and trios. Proceeds benefit the INAFA. Available for $15, which includes shipping and handling, from: INAFA, 310 Ash Wood Drive, Suffolk, VA 23434.

***A Kokopelli Circle of Friends* [1999]** collected by Wayne McCleskey and John Sarantos. Available from Wind Warrior Publications, 4026 N.E. 55th Street, Suite D, Seattle, WA, 98105. Twenty-eight songs, in TABlature, contributed by 15 people including Robert Sweetriver Bellus, Carl Bludts, Christine Ibach, Joel Shaber, Jan Kirlew, Dr. Kathleen Joyce-Grendahl, and others.

***A Kokopelli Christmas, Songs for the Winter Season* [1998]** by Wayne McCleskey and John Sarantos. Available from Wind Warrior Publications, 4026 N.E. 55th Street, Suite D, Seattle, WA, 98105. Approximately 100 Christmas and seasonal songs from around the world transcribed by the authors into the Nakai TABlature system for the six-hole Native American flute.

A Kokopelli Songbook for the Contemporary Native American Flute, Volume I: Folk and Traditional Songs by Wayne McCleskey and John Sarantos. Available from Wind Warrior Publications, 4026 N.E. 55th Street, Suite D, Seattle, WA, 98105. Approximately 24 songs transcribed by the authors into finger chart form [not TABlature] for the six-hole Native American flute.

Oregon Flute Circle Notebook as contributed by members of the Oregon Flute Circle [OFC] and collated by Sherrie Kuhl. Contact information: OFC, Sherrie Kuhl, 26476 Powell Road, Eugene, OR, 97405. This is a very nice three-ring binder of songs in TABlature, most of which have finger diagrams. Music includes original songs, as well as other standard favorites.

***Songs of the White Buffalo Woman* [1998]** by Anne Kimble Howard. Available from Rabbitdog Publishing, 1808 Lauderdale Road, Louisville, KY, 40205. Sixty tunes from the extensive Frances Densmore collection of original Native American flute songs, as well as vocal songs, transcribed by the author into the Nakai TABlature system for the six-hole Native American flute.

***Under One Sky: 41 Traditional Native American Songs for the Contemporary Native American Flute* [six-hole version]** by John Sarantos and Wayne McCleskey. Songs are written in both the Nakai TABlature and finger chart notation.

References

Austin, Terry. "Greetings." E-mail to Tim R. Crawford. 3 April 2002.

Bennett, Roy. *Music Dictionary*. New York: University of Cambridge Press, 1995.

Boulton, Laura. *Musical Instruments of World Cultures* [Revised Edition]. New York: Intercultural Arts Press, 1975.

Bierhorst, John. *A Cry From the Earth: Music of the North American Indians*. New Mexico: Ancient City Press, 1979.

Brady, Erika, et al. *The Federal Cylinder Project, Volume 1, Introduction and Inventory*. Washington D.C.: Library of Congress, 1984.

Brady, Erika. *A Spiral Way, How the Phonograph Changed Ethnography*. Mississippi: University Press, 1999.

Brown, Harry. "Making the American Indian Flute." *Woodwind Quarterly* 7, [1994]: 32 - 49.

Burton, Frederick R. *American Primitive Music*. New York: Moffat, Yard and Company, 1909.

Bushy, Robert Garrison. "Native American Flute File." Arizona: Heard Museum Library, n.d.

Buss, Judy Epstein. "The Flute and Flute Music of the North American Indians." Thesis - University of Illinois at Urbana-Champaign, 1977. A master's degree thesis detailing song forms, melodic intervals, structures, pillar tones, cadences, etc., for both vocal and flute melodies.

Canadian Museum of Civilization Corporation, [Web site] "Musical Instruments" Web site address: http://www.civilization.ca/aborig/stones/instref/inidx.htm#bull

Catlin, George. *George Catlin and His Indian Gallery*. Smithsonian American Art Museum. New York: W.W. Norton & Company, 2002.

-----. *The North American Indians, Volume 1 and Volume 2*. New York: Dover Publications, 1973.

Conlon, Paula. "The Flute of the Canadian Amerindian." Thesis - Carleton University, 1983. Master's degree thesis with detail of approximately 100 flutes that Conlon studied in museums. Also discusses the history, development, and music of the Native American flute.

Crawford, Tim R. Personal photographs of a collection temporarily on display at the Heard Museum - Phoenix, Arizona.

Cunningham-Summerfield, Ben. "Yalulu." *News From Native California: An Inside View of the California Indian World,* Vol. 2.4 (1998): 35 - 37.

Curtis, Natalie, ed. *The Indians' Book: Songs and Legends of the American Indians*. New York: Dover Publications, Inc., 1968.

Davis, John. Personal interview. 28 March 2002.

Densmore, Frances. *The American Indians and Their Music*. New York: The Womans Press, 1936.

-----. *Chippewa Music - II*. Smithsonian Institution, Bureau of American Ethnology, Bulletin 53. Washington, D.C.: Government Printing Office, 1913.

-----. *Handbook of the Collection of Musical Instruments in the United States National Museum*. United States National Museum, Bulletin 136. Washington, D.C.: Government Printing Office, 1927.

-----. *Mandan and Hidatsa Music*. Bureau of American Ethnology, Bulletin 80. Washington, D.C.: Government Printing Office, 1923.

-----. *Papago Music*. Smithsonian Institution, Bureau of American Ethnology, Bulletin 90. Washington, D.C.: Government Printing Office, 1929.

-----. *Seminole Music*. Smithsonian Institution, Bureau of American Ethnology, Bulletin 161. Washington, D.C.: Government Printing Office, 1956.

-----. *The Study of Indian Music*. Smithsonian Institution, The Smithsonian Report for 1941. Washington, D.C.: Government Printing Office, 1942.

-----. *Yuman and Yaqui Music*. Smithsonian Institution, Bureau of American Ethnology, Bulletin 110. Washington, D.C.: Government Printing Office, 1932.

Diamond, Beverley, M. Sam Cook, and Franziska von Rosen. *Visions of Sound: Musical Instruments of First Nationals Communities in Northeastern America*. Chicago: The University of Chicago Press, 1994.

Fages, Pedro. *A Historical, Political, and Natural Description of California, Written for the Viceroy in 1775*. Translated by Herbert Ingram Priestley. Berkeley: University of California Press, 1937.

Fletcher, Alice C. *Indian Story and Song From North America* [Reprint]. Nebraska: University of Nebraska Press, 1995.

-----. *A Study of Omaha Indian Music* [Reprint]. Nebraska: University of Nebraska Press, 1994.

Gendar, Jeannine. "Buzzers, Bows and Bull Roarers." *News From Native California: An Inside View of the California Indian World*, Vol. 11, No. 4, Summer 1998: 40

Gilman, Benjamin. "Hopi Songs." *Journal of American Ethnology and Archaeology, Volume 5*. Massachusetts: The Riverside Press, 1908.

Gomez, J.P. E-mail to Tim R. Crawford. 4 March 2002.

Gray, Judith. *The Federal Cylinder Project, Volume 3, Great Basin / Plateau Indian Catalog, Northwest Coast / Arctic Indian Catalog*. Washington, D.C.: Library of Congress, 1988.

Gray, Judith, and Dorothy Sara Lee. *The Federal Cylinder Project, Volume 2, Northeastern Indian Catalog, Southeastern Indian Catalog*. Washington, D.C.: Library of Congress, 1985.

Gray, Judith, and Edwin Schupman, Jr. *The Federal Cylinder Project, Volume 5, California Indian Catalog, Middle and South American Indian Catalog, Southwestern Indian Catalog-I*. Washington, D.C.: Library of Congress, 1990.

Hackett, Tom. "Bullroarers." *Bulletin of Primitive Technology*, Volume 2, No. 4, 1992: 70.

Hamilton, Anna Heuerman. "The Music of the North American Indians." *The Etude Magazine*, July 1945: 376.

Hammond, George and Agapito Rey. *Narratives of the Coronado Expedition 1540-1542*. Coronado Historical Series, Vol. 2. New Mexico: The University of New Mexico Press, 1940.

Hensley, Betty Austin. *Thurlow Lieurance Indian Flutes*. Kansas: n.p., 1990.

Herndon, Marcia. *Native American Music* [Norwood Editions]. California: University of California - Berkeley, 1982.

Jeancon, Jean Allard and Frederic H. Douglas. *Indian Musical and Noise-Making Instruments* [Leaflet No. 29, 1931]. N.p.: Denver Art Museum, Department of Indian Art, 1957.

Jones, Dr. Oliver W. Telephone interview. 7 February 2002.

-----. Personal photograph collection, taken at the Smithsonian Institute, circa 1980.

Joyce, Dr. Kathleen. *The Native American Flute in the Southwestern United States: Past and Present*. Virginia: RainDance Publications, 1996.

Lieurance, Thurlow. *Songs of the North American Indian.* Philadelphia: Theodore Presser Co., 1920.

LittleJohn, Hawk. Personal e-mail to Tim Crawford. 21 October 1998.

-----. Personal e-mail to Tim Crawford. 17 November 1998.

Loomis, Scott. E-mail to Tim R. Crawford. 12 March 2002.

Mason, Bernard. *How to Make Drums, Tomtoms and Rattles*. New York: Dover Publications, Inc., 1974.

Mazie, David M. "Music's Surprising Power to Heal." *Reader's Digest World*. August 1992.

Morris, Elizabeth Ann. "Basketmaker Flutes From the Prayer Rock District, Arizona." Society for American Archaeology. *American Antiquity Journal* 24.4, 1959.

-----. *Basketmaker Caves in the Prayer Rock District, Northeastern Arizona*. Anthropological Papers of the University of Arizona 35. Arizona: The University of Arizona Press, 1980.

Nakai, R. Carlos. E-mail to Tim Crawford. 2 April 2002.

Payne, Richard W. *The Hopi Flute Ceremony*. Oklahoma: Toubat Trails Publishing Company, 1993.

-----. *The Native American Plains Flute*. Oklahoma: Toubat Trails Publishing Company, 1999.

-----. "The Plains Flute." *The Flutist Quarterly*, Volume 13, No. 4, 1988: 11-13.

-----. Telephone interview. 12 April 2001.

Price, Lew Paxton. *Creating and Using Grandfather's Flute*. California: n.p., 1995.

-----. *Creating and Using the Native American Love Flute*. California: n.p., 1994.

-----. Letter to Tim R. Crawford. 26 October 1999 and 6 May 2001.

-----. *Native North American Flutes*. California: n.p., 1990.

Randel, Don Michael, ed. *The New Harvard Dictionary of Music* [8th edition]. Massachusetts: The Belknap Press of Harvard University Press, 1996.

Riemer, Mary F. "Instrumental and Vocal Love Songs of the North American Indians." Thesis - Wesleyan University, 1978. A master's degree thesis that details the distribution of the Native American flute throughout North America, emphasizing both vocal and instrumental love songs.

Seder, Theodore A. *Old World Overtones in the New World*. University Museum Bulletin, Volume 16, No. 4. Philadelphia: University of Pennsylvania, 1952.

Slifer, Dennis, and James Duffield. *Kokopelli: Flute Player Images in Rock Art*. New Mexico: Ancient City Press, 1994. A very comprehensive and informative guide.

Smallridge, Michael. E-mail to Tim Crawford. 3 April 2002.

Speck, Frank G. *Ethnology of the Yuchi Indians* [Reprint]. New Jersey: The Humanities Press, 1976.

Stroud, Ward. *How to Play Your Native American Style Flute* [pamphlet]. Sisters, Oregon: n.p., n.d.

Sturtevant, William C. [Editor] *Handbook of the North American Indians, Volume 6, Subarctic.* Washington, D.C.: The Smithsonian, 1981.

-----. *Handbook of North American Indians, Volume 8, California.* Washington, D.C.: The Smithsonian, 1978.

-----. *Handbook of the North American Indians, Volume 9, Southwest.* Washington, D.C.: The Smithsonian, 1979.

-----. *Handbook of the North American Indians, Volume 10, Southwest.* Washington, D.C.: The Smithsonian, 1983.

-----. *Handbook of the North American Indians, Volume 11, Great Basin.* Washington, D.C.: The Smithsonian, 1986.

-----. *Handbook of the North American Indians, Volume 13, Plains.* Washington, D.C.: The Smithsonian, 2001.

-----. *Handbook of the North American Indians, Volume 15, Northeast.* Washington, D.C.: The Smithsonian, 1978.

Tomak, Curtis H. *Eastern States Archeological Federation Journal, Volume 22.* Gary L. Fogelman, comp. - *Indian Artifact Magazine* February 1995.

Tschopik, Harry Jr. Introduction. *Music of the American Indians, Southwest.* Ethnic Folkways Library No. FE-4420, 1951. Eight-page accompaniment to the 33 RPM record. Tschopik, at the time, was an Assistant Curator of Ethnology at the American Museum of Natural History.

Voegelin, Erminie W. "Shawnee Musical Instruments." *American Anthropologist, Volume 44.* Wisconsin: American Anthropological Association, 1942

Waldman, Carl. *Atlas of the North American Indian.* New York: Facts On File, 1985.

Wapp, Edward R. *The American Indian Courting Flute: Revitalization and Change.* Sharing a Heritage: American Indian Arts. Contemporary American Indian Issues Series No. 5, Los Angeles: UCLA, 1984. UCLA Publications Services Department.

-----. Letter to author. 1 July 2001.

-----. "The Sioux Courting Flute: Its Tradition, Construction, and Music." Thesis - University of Washington, 1984. A master's degree thesis that is an excellent reference on the origin and designs of the Native American flute within the Sioux culture. Also, it contains a comprehensive list of other references.

Wead, Charles Kasson. *Contributions to the History of Musical Scales.* Smithsonian Institution Annual Report, 1900. Washington, D.C.: Government Printing Office, 1902.

Westley, Marian. "Music Is Good Medicine." *Newsweek.* 21 September 1998.

Winchell, Newton Horace. "Aborigines of Minnesota." Minnesota Historical Society. Minnesota: The Pioneer Company, 1911.

Wolf, Russell. *Native Flutes: Over 250 Photos of Authentic 19th Century Native American Flutes* [CD-ROM Documentary]. Texas: n.p., 2002.

Additional Resources

Ball, Jeffrey K. and Bruce A. Whitten. *Trailhead of the American Indian Courting Flute*. Maryland: n.p., 1994.

Crowl, Christine. *The Hunter and the Woodpecker*. South Dakota: Tipi Press, 1990.

Deloria, Ella C. and Jay Brandon, trans. "The Origin of the Courting Flute." *Museum News* 22.6 [1961]. South Dakota: W.H. Over Museum - State University of South Dakota.

Densmore, Frances. *Choctaw Music*. Smithsonian Institution, Bureau of American Ethnology, Bulletin 136. Washington, D.C.: Government Printing Office, 1943.

-----. *Northern Ute Music*. Smithsonian Institution, Bureau of American Ethnology, Bulletin 76. Washington, D.C.: Government Printing Office, 1922.

-----. *Menomonee Music*. Smithsonian Institution, Bureau of American Ethnology, Bulletin 102. Washington, D.C.: Government Printing Office, 1932.

-----. *Music of the Acoma, Isleta, Cochiti, and Zuni Pueblos*. Smithsonian Institution, Bureau of American Ethnology, Bulletin 165. Washington, D.C.: Government Printing Office, 1957.

-----. *Southwest Museum Papers* No. 10. California: Southwest Museum, 1936.

-----. *Teton Sioux Music and Culture*. Nebraska: University of Nebraska, 1992.

Dunham, Mike. "Cultural Resurgence." *Anchorage Daily News* 16 August 1996.

Edgar, Robert S. *The Native American Flute Book* [3rd edition]. California: Rabbits' Run Press, 1996.

Elchstaedt, Peter. "Ed Wapp Leads Flute Resurgence." *Art Spirit,* Vol. 1 Spring, 1995. New Mexico: Institute of American Indian Arts.

Erdoes, Richard, ed. *The Sound of Flutes and Other Indian Legends: As Told by Lame Deer, Jenny Leading Cloud, Leonard Crow Dog, and Others*. New York: Pantheon Books, 1976.

Goble, Paul. *Love Flute*. New York: Bradbury Press, 1992.

Hacker, Paul. *Winds of the Past - Guide to Playing the Native American Flute*. Oklahoma: n.p., 1995.

Hofsinde, Robert ["Gray Wolf"]. *Indian Music Makers*. New York: William Morrow and Company, 1967.

Hopkin, Bart. *Air Columns and Toneholes: Principles for Wind Instrument Design*. Nicasio, California: Experimental Musical Instruments, 1999.

Lacapa, Michael, ed. *The Flute Player: An Apache Folktale*. Arizona: Northland Publishing, 1990.

Light, Ken. "The Renaissance of the Native American Flute." *Woodwind Quarterly* 2 (1993): 54 - 66.

Lohmann, Charles J. "Sharing the Music." *Native Peoples Magazine* Spring, 1995: 44 - 50.

Nakai, R. Carlos and James DeMars. *The Art of the Native American Flute*. Arizona: Canyon Records Productions, 1996.

Nettl, Bruno. *Music in Primitive Culture*. Massachusetts: Harvard University Press, 1956.

Pareles, Jon. "American Indian Music Helps a Culture." *New York Times* 4 December 1990.

Powell, E. D. *The Indian Love Flute, Vols. 1 and 2*. Arizona: n.p., 1986.

Roberts, Rick. *Gift to the People: The Native American Flute*. Massachusetts: n.p., 1995.

Shearer, Tony. *The Praying Flute*. California: Naturegraph Publishers, Inc., 1987.

Simonelli, Richard. "A Conversation With Native Flutist R. Carlos Nakai." *Winds of Change* Autumn, 1992.

Slack, Claudia. "Kokopeli." *Artists of the Sun* 20 August 1981. Official Indian Market Publication.

Spotted Eagle, Douglas. *Voices of Native America*. Utah: Eagle's View Publishing, 1997.

Steward, Julian H. *Myths of the Ownes Valley Paiute*. California: University of California Press, 1936.

Varble, Bill. "Dreaming a Life." *Mail Tribune* 25 March 1994.

Walker, Dave. *Cuckoo for Kokopelli*. Arizona: Northland Publishing Company, 1998.

Videos

Crafting Your Own Native American Flute with Lee Lacroix.
Video includes a full-scale dimensional drawing to aid in flute construction.
Contact: Lee Lacroix at 1-800-339-3902; www.echoespast.com/index.html

First Breath
A private flute lesson with Douglas Spotted Eagle.
Contact: Oregon Flute Store at 1-888-88-FLUTE; www.oregonflutestore.com

Songkeepers: A Saga of Five Native Americans Told Through the Sound of the Flute
A documentary of the Native American flute's history and evolution.
Contact: INAFA at 1-757-923-1978; www.inafa.org

Toubat: A Journey of the Native American Flute
Narrated by Tom Bee, this video centers around flute historian Dr. Richard Payne
Contact: Oregon Flute Store at 1-888-88-FLUTE; www.oregonflutestore.com

Working With the Heart in the Wood
A two-part flute making video by Raymond RedFeather of Heartwood Flutes
Contact: Raymond RedFeather at 1-719-742-5781; www.heartwoodflutes.com

TABlature Music

Four-Hole Native American Flute

HOPE

TABlature
Four-Hole Native American Flute
"D" Tuning

by Tim R. Crawford

SPRING

TABlature
Four-Hole Native American Flute
"D" Tuning

by Tim R. Crawford

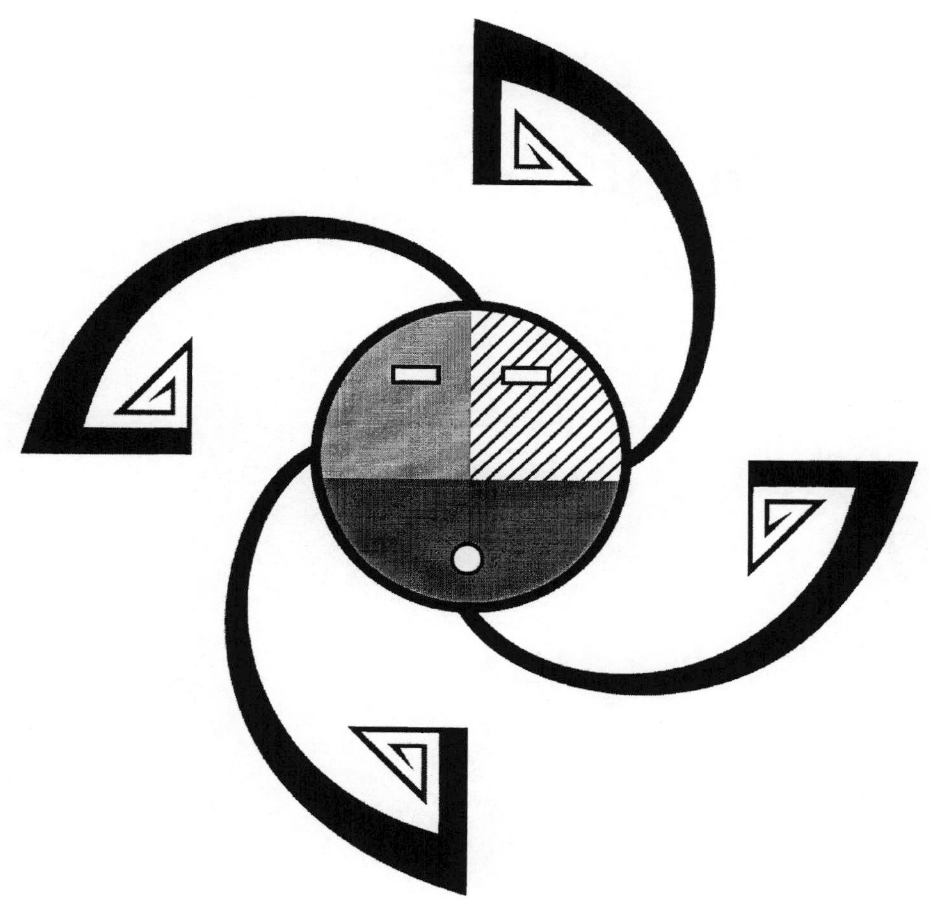

TABlature Music

Five-Hole Native American Flute

ANCIENT WOOD

BROKEN HEART

TABlature
Five-Hole Native American Flute
"G" Tuning

by Tim R. Crawford

tr

DESTINY

TABlature
Five-Hole Native American Flute
"G" Tuning

by Tim R. Crawford

FRIENDS

TABlature
Five-Hole Native American Flute
"G" Tuning

by Tim R. Crawford

HORIZONS

TABlature
Five-Hole Native American Flute
"D#" Tuning

by Tim R. Crawford

p
p
p
♩ = 60

MEDICINE WIND

TABlature
Five-Hole Native American Flute
"G" Tuning

by Tim R. Crawford

PASSAGES

TABlature
Five-Hole Native American Flute
"G" Tuning

by Tim R. Crawford

Note: At the caesuras, insert voices - a capella.

REFLECTIONS

TABlature
Five-Hole Native American Flute
"G" Tuning

by Tim R. Crawford

WATCHING YOU

TABlature
Five-Hole Native American Flute
"E" Tuning

by Tim R. Crawford

pp
pp
p
pp
p

TABlature Music

Six-Hole Native American Flute

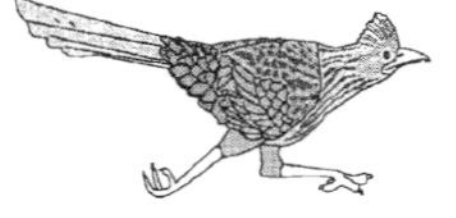

ALONE

TABlature
Six-Hole Native American Flute
"F#" Tuning

by Tim R. Crawford

p
pp

BEGINNINGS

TABlature
Six-Hole Native American Flute
"E" Tuning

by Tim R. Crawford

D.S. al Coda
tr
pp
p
ppp

CLOUD WATCHER

TABlature
Six-Hole Native American Flute
"G" Tuning

by Tim R. Crawford

pp
tr
tr
tr
pp

1
2
tr

COALS

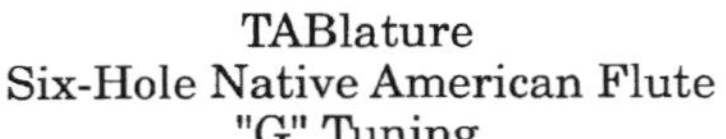

by Tim R. Crawford

Slowly

COME TO ME

TABlature
Six-Hole Native American Flute
"G" Tuning

by Tim R. Crawford

EAGLE FLIGHT

TABlature
Six-Hole Native American Flute
"A" Tuning

by Tim R. Crawford

tr
tr
tr
p
p

***Note: In measures three and six, it is okay to skip these measures. To play what is indicated, use an all-open fingering, raise two octaves, and improvise.**

EARTH SPEAKS

TABlature
Six-Hole Native American Flute
"G" Tuning

By Tim R. Crawford

p
p
p

EMBERS

TABlature
Six-Hole Native American Flute
"D" Tuning

by Tim R. Crawford

tr

tr

HAPPY SONG

TABlature
Six-Hole Native American Flute
"A" Tuning

by Tim R. Crawford

HEAR MY HEART

TABlature
Six-Hole Native American Flute
"D" Tuning

by Tim R. Crawford

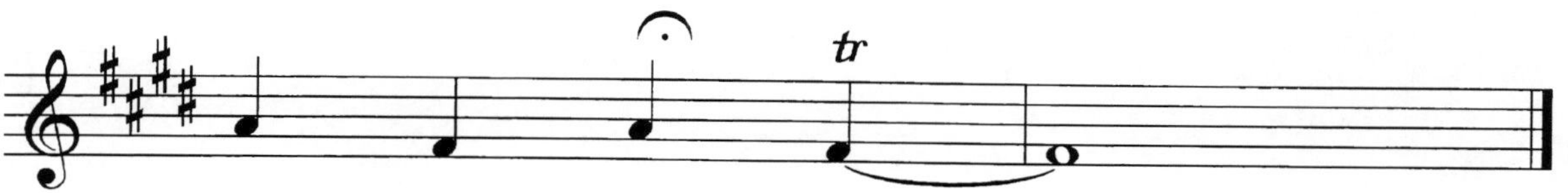
tr

LEAVES

TABlature
Six-Hole Native American Flute
"F#" Tuning

by Tim R. Crawford

p
tr
tr
p
pp

LISTEN

TABlature
Six-Hole Native American Flute
"C4" Tuning

by Tim R. Crawford

The Earth Has Music For Those Who Listen.

~ William Shakespeare ~

LONGING

TABlature
Six-Hole Native American Note
"F#" Tuning

By Tim R. Crawford

Slowly With Great Feeling

tr
p
p
tr
tr
p
tr
p
p
p
p
pp

MOON'S LIGHT

TABlature
Six-Hole Native American Flute
"F#" Tuning

By Tim R. Crawford

Note: At the caesura points, insert vocables.

MOUNTAIN SUNRISE

TABlature
Six-Hole Native American Flute
"G" Tuning

by Tim R. Crawford

OLD WAYS

TABlature
Six-Hole Native American Flute
"A" Tuning

by Tim R. Crawford

tr
D.C. al Coda

REACHING OUT

STORY CIRCLE

TABlature
Six-Hole Native American Flute
"G" Tuning

by Tim R. Crawford

tr

Taste the Wind

TABlature
Six-Hole Native American Flute
"A# " or " F#" Tuning

By Tim R Crawford

Create your own song!

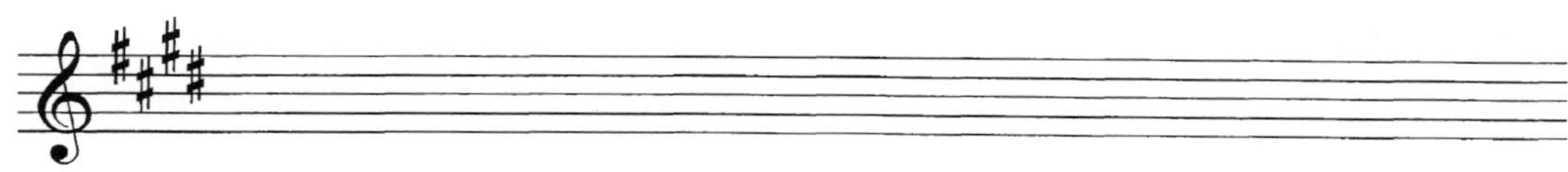

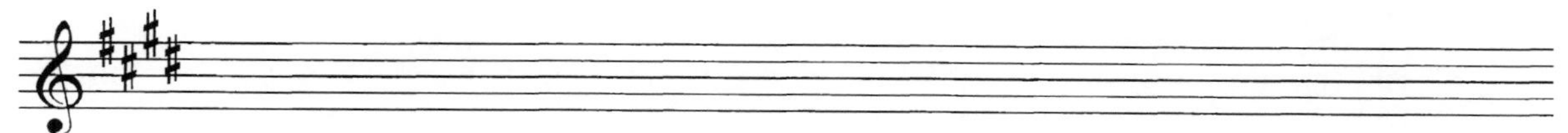

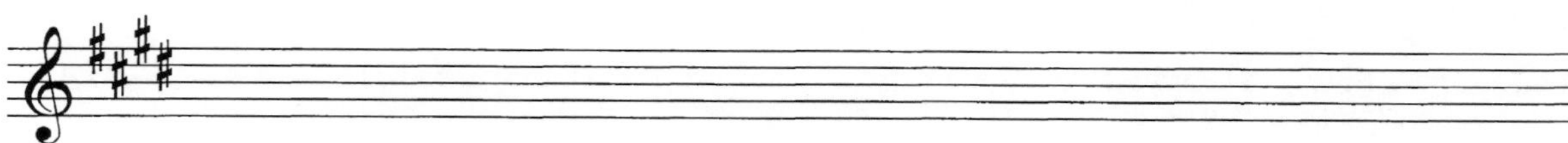

Song Writing

Getting Started

Native American flute builder and recording artist Ward Stroud has an inspirational experience that he likes to relate when it comes to writing songs:

> "At a ceremony years ago, a very interesting man wandered up to where I sat on the side of a mountain playing my flute. After listening to me for a while, he got up to leave. I stopped playing my flute and asked him who he was and from where comes. He told me that he was a Tibetan monk and had been wondering from country to country and had spent most of his life learning of the spiritual ceremonies of different peoples. We had a good talk about our different experiences and, after saying our goodbyes, we parted company. As he was walking away, he stopped and turned to me and gave me one of the most significant gifts that I have ever been given. He said to me, 'Son, if you ever need inspiration for a song just look around you. Our Earth Mother will supply you with all the music you need. Do you see the trees in the distance? Notice the tree line against the horizon? Play the tree tops like a musical score, the taller the trees the higher your notes. The lower the tree, the lower the note. Start here [he motioned to the far left] and play the tree line as if it were sheet music. There are songs everywhere you look, in the clouds, a flock of birds, or the shoreline in the bend of a creek.' What a beautiful gift were his words to me." (Stroud)

The Native American flute journey that we are sharing has no requirements and makes no demands upon any of us. Fulfillment is readily attainable for each of us by simply playing the instrument, regardless of our individual skill level, for our own personal satisfaction and enjoyment.

It is certainly not necessary, therefore, for anyone to write out his or her music or create a song in notated form. However, this separate experience can also be, in and of itself, fulfilling and self-rewarding for those who have an interest. I frequently receive correspondence from folks who express a desire to write out a song in TABlature but who feel frustrated at beginning the process. It is for those "frustrated" people that I am offering the following suggestions and comments.

Most folks who have not actually written a song tend to be under the assumption that song writers sit down and write a song out from start to finish; of course, it just does not happen quite this way. Songs, like written paragraphs, are built one note [word] at a time, as they are developed. This development phase is very rarely ever a single-setting accomplishment. Songs, like novels, are built from bits and pieces of concepts and ideas gathered together from several sessions and organized over time. There is a fairly easy technique, however, that can allow an individual to take that first big step in the TABlature journey. It requires minimal discipline, but some discipline, nevertheless.

You will need several tools to help you along the song writing path. Local music stores sell staff paper upon which you can enter notes and musical phrases. Or, you can simply draw the five lines of the music staff upon a piece of paper. Notating with a pencil is best, so that one can readily erase and alter musical efforts.

When you are playing your Native American flute and you create a phrase or a few "strings" of notes that sound good to your ear, stop and pick up a pencil and write the notes out on a fresh sheet of music paper. I would strongly urge you to simply write down the notes and phrases without any concern as to the song's time signature. In addition, do not be overly concerned about the note durations at this point, nor fitting notes within a specific measure, as you will find that as the process develops you will be altering the durations anyway. Much of the time, I use notation sheets that do not have any barlines on them; I simply write out the notes in a parlando style. Do this process every time you discover that appealing musical phrase or turn of notes. This is the discipline part. As you create them, save these "concept sheets" in a file folder. Perhaps the folder can be labeled "works in progress."

In addition, I highly recommend that you copy and cut out the TABlature charts into a small size so that you can lay them by your music to aid in writing down the notes. I laminate the five-hole and six-hole TABlature charts back-to-back. This provides me with a stiff card, approximately 3 inches by 7 inches, that I always keep handy for reference purposes.

Every now and then, place one of your concept sheets in front of you and see if you can add more notes and/or lengthen the phrasing. Do not expect to finish writing out the song when you start this process; simply have a goal of trying to build on to what you have previously started. Sometimes you will find that your "creative juices" are really flowing, while other times they will be stagnant. Be patient and do not expect a finished song to suddenly appear. If you are not getting anywhere, then put that sheet back into the folder and try one of your other concept sheets and see what happens. Usually you will find at least one of the songs that you can expand. Sometimes you will find that separate concept sheets can be combined to create longer ideas, as well. Not very long ago I was working with two different concept sheets that I had been intermittently working with for several months. I discovered that the two sheets shared many similarities, a relationship I had previously failed to recognize. I decided to weave them together, and now I have an almost-finished song.

Over time, you will find yourself gradually filling up many of those concept sheets, with some of them giving birth to a finished song. When you feel that a song is finished, and if a time signature is going to be used, then bar lines can be added and note durations inserted to conform to the desired time signature. None of that is necessary, however. You may opt to leave it in a free form, simply marking phrases with breath marks. With my own finished music, I prefer to use the bar lines; it is simply a personal choice.

In addition, I would not be overly concerned about your song's structure. Structure revolves around recurring musical ideas blended with contrasting ideas in a specific format, such as "aaba" or "aba" or "abaca." Having some structure does provide a logical flow to the music. This allows both the player and the listener musical reference points, thereby allowing for aural organization. While in the world of music there are some acknowledged standards of structure, structure can be whatever the author of the music wishes it to be. If it feels "right" and comfortable, then your melodic phrasings has an acceptable structure.

Keep in mind that some of your concept sheets may never grow beyond those first few notes; it is no big deal in the scheme of things. The important thing is to simply have some minimal discipline to stop and write out those good phrases when they occur and keep adding them to your folder, because some of these efforts will eventually give birth to a finished song and that is self-rewarding fulfillment. I usually have up to a dozen or so different pages of music going at the same time, with anywhere from eight or nine notes on each page. I have one unfinished song I started in 1994 that I work with from time to time. Perhaps some day I will finish it, or not.

As you advance along your song writing path, you might want to purchase a music notation program for your computer that will allow you to print out your finished works in a professional-looking format. While there are a number of options you might wish to pursue, Coda Music Technology offers programs for both the Mac and the PC, as well as for several different skill levels.

Having said all of the above concerning song writing, I should acknowledge that I also have a few "special" flutes with which I simply prefer to improvise upon, and I purposely avoid writing out any music to be used with these instruments. Improvisation is but another one of the very fulfilling rewards that this shared journey offers to each of us; so, if you remain frustrated with your TABlature writing efforts, forget about the TABlature and be comforted with playing the Native American flute and letting it take you on its own journey, wherever it may lead. If you feel like you require further inspiration, play the trees!

Appendix A

Bull Roarers

A bull roarer is simply a relatively thin piece of flat wood attached to a string and twirled in a circular manner above the head. The sound has been described as a "deep, visceral pitch" (Gendar); a "loud humming or roaring sound… Symbolizing the thunder" (Mason); "the furious yelping of enraged curs" (Hackett); "the rumble of distant thunder" (Payne, 1993); and "sounds in the clouds" (Densmore, 1929). Many other authors simply refer to the sound as wind-like. Many early cultures, not necessarily North American, believed that the bull roarer "is understood as being the voice of a spirit or a divinity" (Seder). I own several of these instruments and have recorded them as background on several of my albums. I have also used them, with assistance, in performance. [See closing note.] To me, bull roarers sound like the wind, and I use them in that context.

While the bull roarer tends to be associated with the Aborigines of Australia in much of the "popular" literature, the fact is that it was very much a ubiquitous instrument throughout most of the world, with a few exceptions such as Finland, northeast portions of Asia, and the eastern part of North America, excluding the Mattaponi (Seder).

Cultures in North America known to have used this instrument include the Achomawi, Apache, Arapaho, Athapaskans, Cahuilla, Cahto, Chumash, Cocopa, Cupeno, Diegueno, Eskimos, Gabrielino, Haida, Hopi, Juaneno, Kitanemuk, Kittitas, Kumeyaay, Luiseno, Mattaponi, Mono, Mojave, Nambe Pueblo, Naskapi Pueblo, Navaho, Nisenan, Maidu, Miwok, Nomlaki, Nootka, Ojibwa, Panamint, Papago, Pomo, Salinan, Serrano, Shawnee, Shoshone, Sinkyone, Southern Paiute, Tassinjorormiut [Caribou Inuit], Tolowa, Tubatulabal, Twea, Ute, Umatilla, Wintu, Yavapai, Yokuts, and Yuki.

Bull roarers were used for a variety of purposes, including as a toy, as signaling devices to warn away and to summon to a ceremony, in dance ceremonies, to influence weather, and for curative properties by shamans.

While wood was a common material used for bull roarers, other materials utilized include hide strips, deer ribs, horn, cactus, bones, baleen, and ivory. The length of the bull roarer varied from between 6 inches and 3 feet, while widths tended to vary from 1 inch to 3 inches. Generally being thin, the thickness varied from 3/16 of an inch to a 1/2-inch. Realize that there is no such thing as a "standardized" bull roarer; they were constructed in a variety of sizes, shapes, and materials. Contemporary bull roarers appear to be between 9 and 14 inches in length. Materials for the string included sinew and plant fibers, although contemporary makers sometimes use artificial sinew.

The bull roarer's edges were not always smooth, as they were often "toothed" and sometimes simply scalloped. Occasionally, bull roarers were made with a handle at the end of the string. Some of these handles were even longer than the bull roarers themselves.

Interestingly, in several cultures including the Tewa, Pomo, and Wimonuntci Ute, women and/or children were not allowed to see the instrument. One culture had a taboo against their children hearing the sound: "The Mountain Cahuilla of California locked their children in a room with their sacred bundle if they should happen to hear the sounds of the bull-roarer" (Seder). Yet, within the Shawnee culture, two types of bull roarers were "used by boys, especially as toys" (Voegelin).

The Hope Flute Ceremony by Dr. Richard W. Payne has an extensive description of a ceremony whose central events occur over a 9-day period. This event is hosted by one of the Hopi Flute Societies in late August of odd-numbered years. In addition to the flute, the bull roarer also plays a role in these ceremonies (Payne, 1993).

> "The business of the Flute Societies is vigorous supplication for essential rain. Prayers are offered to ensure fertility of man and beast. Relief from diseases related to lightning and weapons are also included in their prayer agenda… There was vital need for the powerful Flute Societies to draw rain clouds and lightning closely in to give life to the

> parched fields. The villagers eagerly anticipated the soft sounds of the flutes as they began practicing their new songs and played the old familiar ones in the upper stories of the houses of the flute priests."
>
> "C took the two standards with the red horse hair from the ridge under his left arm, an eagle feather, and a bull roarer in his left hand and bull roarer in his right hand and took a position north of the altar. He then waved the two standards over the altar several times, dipped the point of the bull roarer into the medicine bowls and twirled it - producing the sound of thunder. This he did six times, but always changing the bull roarers... Lomahungwa dipped his face into the spring four times, as the flutes played, took out the small cylinder, which he had previously deposited, and handed it to the small boy who then followed the two bull roarers around the spring four times, whereupon these and all but four players left and trotted away to the Flute Spring." (Payne, 1993)

The above quotes are only two instances in Payne's book in which the bull roarer is used in this ceremony. There are several more references in the book.

While it is not known if they were used together, the Yavapai culture of the Southwest used both the bull roarer and the flute when calling for rain (Sturtevant, 1983).

Currently, I am aware of only two sources for bull roarers:

Kitty Lancaster - Alaska Territorial Outpost, P.O. Box 80140, Fairbanks, AK, 99708.

Lark in the Morning, P.O. Box 799, Fort Bragg, CA, 95437; www.larkinam.com

Note: A word of caution regarding the use of this instrument. Be certain that it is securely fastened at both ends *before each use*. This spinning disk can cause property damage and personal injury to someone should it come loose while in use. Be aware of this potential danger and use it only if and when you have adequate clearance and can safely do so. Treat it with respect and be very careful about where and how it is used. It is better to be safe than sorry.

Appendix B

Eagle Bone Whistle TABlature and Information

TABlature
Eagle Bone Whistle

Suggested by R. Carlos Nakai

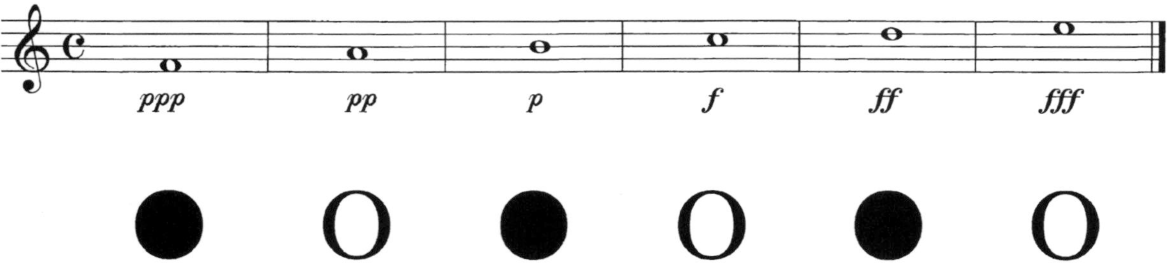

Since this is TABlature, the reader is reminded that these notes are not the actual pitches. Eagle bone whistles, as well as other similar sized whistles, produce sounds at relatively high frequencies. This TABlature is only for an eagle bone whistle open at both ends, without any finger holes. The end of the barrel is held in the crook of the index finger, so that the thumb can open and close the end portion of the barrel. Meanwhile, the index finger holding the whistle presses against the lips for leverage as the thumb opens and closes.

I have included dynamic markings to aid in finding the correct pitch. These dynamic markings are more relative than actual. The higher the actual pitch the greater the volume of air required, while the lower the actual pitch the lesser the volume of air required. This is what I am trying to illustrate with the use of the dynamic markings.

My own simulated eagle bone whistle will only manage the fundamental (F in the TABlature) with my thumb partially off the end hole. Additionally, I can manage an even higher pitched seventh note with a major effort of over blowing.

Today, most performers use a simulated eagle bone whistle made of resin; other options are turkey bone, chicken bone, or even small pieces of cane. It should be noted that federal laws prohibit the use and possession of any parts of migratory birds by non-Native Americans.

At the time of publication, eagle bone whistle blanks, and possibly even completed units, are available from the following:

Crazy Crow Trading Post, P.O. Box 847, Pottsboro, TX, 75076; Phone: 903-786-2287

Absaroka, P.O. Box 777, Dubois, WY, 82513; Phone: 307-455-2440

Oregon Flute Store, 90944 Leashore Drive, Vida, OR 97488; Phone: 1-888-88-FLUTE

If the aforementioned contacts do not work out, then try contacting other catalog dealers who handle Native American craft supplies.

The resin blanks that are currently available, which simulate one of the eagle's bones, are approximately 8 inches in length and have an inside bore diameter of approximately 1/4 of an inch. They are not too difficult to make. The somewhat flattened end is the end of the barrel where the thumb closes over the bore. The narrower end is the mouth end.

Somewhere between 2-1/2 inches and 2-1/4 inches from the mouth end make a mark on top of the blank; come back towards the mouth end approximately 1/2-inch from the first mark. With a coping saw or something similar [a knife will also work on the resin blank] from the top of the whistle at the second mark [closest mark to the mouth end], make a cut straight down about 3/32 of an inch [between 1/16 and 1/8 of an inch]. With the coping saw, now make a diagonal cut from the other mark to the depth of the first cut. This will remove a small piece from the top of the flute and expose the open bore. You will then need to form a small plug that will extend back from the first cut towards the mouth end; this does not need to be very long (1/8-inch or so). Be sure to leave a small air channel at the top for the air to pass through towards the splitting edge that was created when you made the second cut. You can use modeling clay, wax, silicone, or something similar to form this small plug. The difficult part is working it into such a small space, as it will require a thin tool with which to work. Crochet hooks will work, as well as small pieces of wire [such as 12 gauge]. You will also have to experiment with the plug placement by placing it and then blowing on the whistle to see what sounds you are able to produce. If the sound is not satisfactory, then move around and/or change the size of the air hole at the top of the plug. [See the diagram below.]

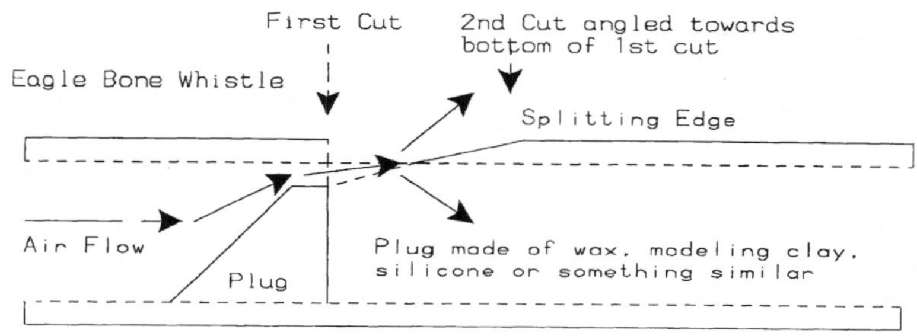

After you are finished, take a short piece of narrow leather for a neck strap and lay it on the bottom of the barrel, just in front of the cut portion of the whistle. Then, make a number of wraps with simulated sinew to hold the neck strap on to the barrel. You are finished.

Appendix C

Music, Healing, Wellness and the Native American Flute

We all know that music can soothe and comfort us, as well as provide an outlet for powerful emotions. Many of us recognize, and use to our great advantage, music as an aid for meditative and contemplative pursuits; however, less well known is that music can also be a great aid in the healing process, whether physical or mental.

It has been written that music may lower the heart rate, blood pressure, decrease anxiety and depression, and relieve pain. In at least two studies it was shown that patients who were able to listen to music before and during surgery had lower levels of stress hormones in their blood than those who were not exposed to music. In addition, one study done at California State University - Fresno demonstrated that music was the most effective supplemental [in addition to medications] therapy treatment for migraine-headache sufferers.

Clinical researchers at the University of California - Los Angeles [UCLA] School of Nursing, together with the Georgia Baptist Medical Center in Atlanta, Georgia, were able to demonstrate that prematurely born babies were more efficient users of oxygen and gained weight faster when they were exposed to soothing music. Those babies exposed to music only 90 minutes a day averaged stays of only 11 days in the Newborn Intensive Care Unit, as opposed to an average of 16 days for the control group. In addition, soothing music has been documented as relieving pain and anxiety for a variety of patients, from birthing mothers to cancer patients.

At Colorado State University's Center for Biomedical Research in Music, it was shown that stroke victims appeared to recover and/or improve their stride symmetry much faster when exposed to rhythmic dance music than those who were not exposed to the same music. A number of studies have shown that patients suffering from neurological disorders are often able to respond to music where otherwise no responses are elicited. One therapist explained how one stroke victim who was unable to speak at all gradually regained the power of speech only after starting to hum to a song that the therapist played regularly for him on her accordion. Furthermore, a Scottish study showed that daily doses of Mozart and Mendelssohn significantly improved the moods of institutionalized stroke victims, as they were less depressed and anxious than other patients within the same facility.

My first real awareness of the power of Native American flute music to potentially influence the healing of others came from a flute dealer in Michigan who, in 1992, told me a story related to my first album of Native American flute music. He said that he had sold a tape of the album to a customer who some time later returned and relayed that he had a son who had been very seriously injured in an automobile accident and was unconscious for some period of time with multiple fractures. As he had himself felt so soothed by the music, he took a cassette player to his son's hospital room to specifically play my album. He stated that even his son's doctors expressed some surprise at the physical reactions of their unconscious patient when the music was being played. The doctor apparently noted a reduction in blood pressure, as well as a reduction in the heart rate. Later, as his son was recovering and well on his way to being healed, the father simply wanted to come by and see the dealer to thank him for having sold him the tape, and with a request that the dealer also relay his appreciation to the artist for having created the album. The father felt very strongly that the music played a significant role in the physical recovery of his son from the many injures he had suffered as a result of an automobile accident.

About a year later, a mother who had tragically lost a son in a motorcycle accident thanked me for having created an album of Native American flute music that she felt helped enable her to heal some of the many emotional scars that she had acquired as a result. She explained to me that the only way she could deal with the overwhelming stress created by her loss was to sit in a darkened room, on the floor, listening to the music of the Native American flute. She further told me that she is not sure how she could have ever coped without the music.

I have had two different women tell me how, in slightly differing manners, Native American flute music appeared to be the only aid that soothed and relaxed their Vietnam war era husbands who still suffered from bouts of post traumatic stress syndrome as a result of their war-time experiences. They were very grateful to me for having created the albums, as the music of the Native American flute had really helped their relationships.

I have in my file a letter of appreciation from a massage therapist who wanted to let me know about the healing response that she had directly observed my music eliciting. She wrote that she was very much aware of how certain music "can and does initiate and enhance the healing process, but it still never ceases to amaze me." She told of a lady who was apparently tense and stressed during a massage therapy session, but as it continued on she commented on how the beauty of the music was evoking some memories of a deceased husband and brother. As the therapist then wrote: "I felt the definite release of tension and at least some of her burden."

Physiologically, it is still a mystery as to how music can accomplish the apparent benefits that it does; however, some neuroscientists believe it is quite possible that music can aid in the building and strengthening of the connections between the nerve cells within the cerebral cortex. Interestingly, in the fall of 1998, I received a correspondence from a "student" of the Native American flute who reported that he had memory and other cognitive dysfunctions as a result of a head injury incurred from an auto accident. He now feels and believes that his playing of the Native American flute created new pathways within his brain that now enable him to accomplish cognitive tasks that were otherwise previously inaccessible to him.

In February 2000, a new member of the Montana-based Internet flute circle shared the following story with the group regarding the Native American flute and his own healing experience:

> "Almost seven years ago, I was hit by a car and both of my legs were crushed. I was in the hospital for six months. I couldn't read, meditate, or do much else for a long time, due to the huge amounts of morphine I was given. The only thing I could do was to play my flute for a few minutes at a time. For another three months after I left the hospital, the doctors kept waiting to see if any new bone would be laid down in my right leg. They told me that if there was no growth by the ninth month that they would have to do a series of five surgeries to graft bone from my pelvis to my leg. At month nine there was still no new bone. We decided to go one more month. I figured that I still couldn't visualize, mediate, or what have you but that I could take this flute that was about the same size and shape of the shin bone I needed to grow and put all my breath and intention into that. For most of the tenth month I played my two flutes almost all day long. I was living alone by then in a small wheel chair accessible apartment. At month ten, I went back in for a new x-ray and there was new bone! There wasn't much, but it was enough to remove the prospect of surgery."

From my own personal experiences, as well as from much reading, there is no doubt in my mind regarding the ability of certain kinds of music to be significantly beneficial as a supplemental tool in the healing process, whether mental or physical, as well as helping us with the maintenance of our daily "wellness."

For further information on this subject, please contact the American Music Therapy Association [AMTA], an organization that offers a number of publications, as well as answers to frequently asked questions about medical therapy, how to locate a music therapist, job opportunities in music therapy, etc. AMTA can be reached at either 301-589-3300, or at their Web site - http://www.namt.com, or write to them at 8455 Colesville Road, Suite 1000, Silver Spring, MD, 20910.

Appendix D

Using the Native American Flute to Imitate a Loon's Call

During the summer of 1998, while walking along the road early one evening near the recreational cabin we own, I just happened to look out at the lake as an eagle was flying above the shoreline. As I watched the eagle approach my position and then pass, a loon wailed several times. Oh, life is good!

Sometimes at night, especially in late summer, I can hear the loons wail and answer one another from nearby lakes. Pacific loons are noted for contacting one another over long distances, and at night the sound seems to carry farther.

On two separate occasions, while playing at lake side, I felt that the loons responded to and answered my flute. On another occasion, when I was seated on a stool by the lake playing a variety of songs on several different flutes, I observed a family of loons swimming down the lake. They stopped about 25 yards away from me. My loon audience stayed in place until I finished playing. Although they made no sounds, it was obvious that they were an attentive audience.

The Loon Legend **[as told by Joe Higgs, Jr.]**

I awoke one morning to the call of an elk. The sun rained drops of light to the forest floor. I imagined the elk was singing of a glorious and wonderful morning. This was his way of giving thanks. I grabbed my flute and headed out to the lake, just as it was greeting the morning sun. I sat facing east and, first giving thanks to the Creator, gave the day a gift of song. Like the elk, I was happy. Three loons greeted me and we conversed through song.

They asked me, "Do you know from where came the voice of the flute?" I told them that I did not know. The loons began their story. Long ago their ancestors were once members of the Anishenabeg people. One of their ancestors, a little girl named Tiobi, a chief's daughter, was an important friend to the loon. Tiobi loved the loons and would greet them everyday at the lake. She had a great respect for them and the loons respected her. Tiobi convinced her people not to hunt the loon; they were a sacred bird. She said the loons cry because they are lost and the Anishenabeg people should help them.

Tiobi woke one morning and paddled her canoe out to the center of the lake. She reached toward a lost loon in the water and said, "Don't worry my friend. I will help you find your way." But the canoe tipped over and Tiobi fell in and drowned. Tiobi's father was very sad. The next morning a loon cried out from the lake, but the chief did not hear. The loon called to the elk and said, "My friend could you please sing your morning song?" The elk sang gloriously and the chief awoke to the song. He ran down to the lake where the elk had been singing, but he found no elk. Instead, the chief saw a loon looking up at him. "I see white spots on your back and believe these are tears," said the chief. "Have you lost your way my friend?" Suddenly, the chief thought he knew the loon and felt as if he were in the presence of his daughter. He cried, "My daughter, it's you!" He felt very happy, but he also felt sad. The chief could not understand what she was saying.

So, the chief ran into the woods and called out to the Great Spirit. "Great Spirit, help me understand what my daughter, the loon, is saying. How can I talk to her so she can understand me?" Lighting flashed and hit a tree where a woodpecker had been working, and a branch fell. The chief picked it up and saw that it had holes in it, as well as holes at both ends. He blew in one side of the stick and it made a beautiful sound, just like the loon.

The chief quickly ran back to where the loon was and blew into the stick. Through song he said, "Daughter, this is a gift from the Great Spirit. It is called a flute and I will sing to you like the elk, and you will hear my heart and I will hear yours. You have lost your way and so too have all the Anishenabeg that have died by drowning. You have become the tribe of the loons and cry because you are sad. We do not hear your cry; your tears have been marked upon your back as a reminder. I will sing a song of prayer for you with the mighty and powerful gift from the Great Spirit, and you will find your way to the council table and sit among our people who will be there waiting for you."

The chief played joyously and the loons disappeared. Every year the loon reappeared and the chief knew these loons where tragedies of the people who live among the lakes.

As identified by William Barklow in the liner notes of his recording entitled *Voices of the Loons*, Loons have four different calls - hoot, tremolo, wail, and yodel, as well as several combinations of these basic four calls. The wail, the longest of the calls, is one of the most popular and distinctive calls of the loon. It can be simulated with either a six-hole G flute [my preference] or a six-hole A flute. [This particular loon imitation does not seem to lend itself very well to the popular F# flute.] It is also quite possible that there are other six-hole flutes on which the wail will work.

The wail call has been broken down into, and is characterized by, three classifications: type one, type two, or a type three (Barklow). Type one wails simply have a long fundamental note which has a small harmonic rise in the middle, but without a step change in pitch. The type two call, which the G and A flutes lend themselves well to, has a relatively short fundamental at the start then slurs up several steps for a long wail and then slurs back down for another relatively short fundamental. This is also the loon wail that is most frequently heard on the lakes in south-central Alaska.

To simulate the type one call, cover the fourth and fifth holes of the G flute while sounding the fundamental. Then, overblow the note to achieve the harmonic for the long middle portion of the wail, followed by a relaxation back down to the fundamental. It is important to realize that this wail simulation is one long slur and not separate notes. An alternative finger combination for the A flute, shown in the diagram below, is effected by covering the third and fourth holes. This produces a slightly greater range between the two pitches of the wail.

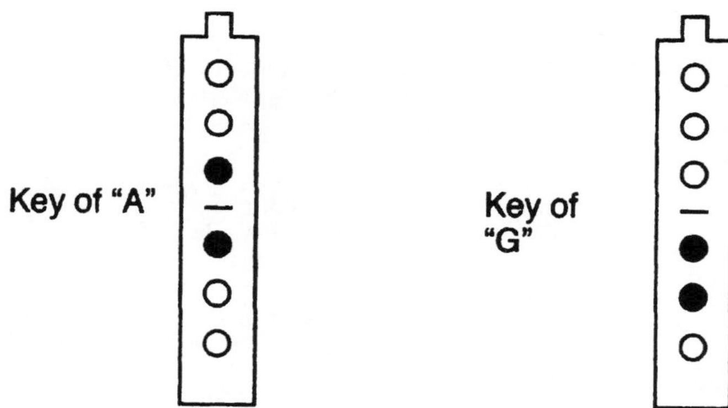

If you would like to know more about loons, or would like to purchase a recording of loons, contact the North American Loon Fund, P.O. Box 68, Mt. Pleasant, MI, 48804.

The owls are silent and the air is still,
The eagles have soared beyond the hill.

While the moon is high and shinning bright,
It appears to me that all wildlife has taken flight
As I walk across the top of the frozen snow
To check the thermometer at 26 below.

For the warmth of the sun to touch my skin
And the wail of the loons to but hear again.

Then comfort appears in the vibration of sound
As my flute lifts my soul to a much higher ground.
I am at peace as my heart I have found
From the inner warmth of this haunting sound.

~ Tim "WindWalker" Crawford ~

Appendix E

Organizations for the Native American Flute

For everyone who is interested in the Native American flute, there is an organization which is dedicated to this instrument. It is called the **International Native American Flute Association (INAFA)**. Membership is presently $20 per year and includes four issues of the organization's official publication entitled ***Voice of the Wind***, as well as a membership card and four 10 percent discount coupons honored by various flute-related retailers and flute makers. The publication includes interviews, CD reviews, book reviews, articles of varying topics concerning the Native American flute, listing of workshops, advertisements, etc. For further information, or to join this Native American flute family, please call or write to:

Dr. Kathleen Joyce-Grendahl, Executive Director
International Native American Flute Association
310 Ash Wood Drive
Suffolk, VA 23434

Phone: 757-923-1978
E-mail: INAFA@AOL.COM
http://www.inafa.org

Within the International Native American Flute Association are numerous flute circles in which members of INAFA gather locally to share their flute music and journeys. The following is a list of such organizations:

Alabama:

North Alabama Flute Circle
Contact Person: Charlie Allen
418 River Bend Drive
Huntsville, AL 35824
Phone: 256-489-1090
E-mail: clasaved1@AOL.COM
Representative to INAFA: Charlie Allen

Alaska:

Alaska Flute Circle
Contact Persons: Joan and George McCament
7666 Griffith Street
Anchorage, AK 99507
Phone: 907-346-1892
E-mail: conifer@customcpu.com
Representative to INAFA: George McCament

Arizona:

Arizona Flute Circle
Contact Person: Audrey Burk
15805 East Chicory Drive
Fountain Hills, AZ 85268
Phone: 480-816-0353
E-mail: apburk@juno.com
Representative to INAFA: Audrey Burk

Sonoran Spirits Flute Society
Contact Person: Lorrie Sarafin
730 East McKellips Road, #C327
Tempe, AZ 85281
Phone/Fax: 480-946-2036
E-mail: info@sonoranspirits.org
http://www.sonoranspirits.org
Representative to INAFA: Lorrie Sarafin

Tucson-Area Flute Association
Contact Person: RuthiE Neilan
P.O. Box 68104
Tucson, AZ 85737
Phone: 520-544-8997
E-mail: RNeilan@bigfoot.com
Representative to INAFA: RuthiE Neilan

California:

Northern California Flute Circle
Contact Person: Robert Sweetriver Bellus
P.O. Box 1010
Calistoga, CA 94515
Phone: 707-942-0101
E-mail: ncfc@naflute.com
http://www.naflute.com
Representative to INAFA: Robert Sweetriver Bellus

Southern California Flute Circle
Contact Person: Guillermo Martinez
28691 Modjeska Canyon Road
Modjeska, CA 92626
Phone: 714-649-3244
E-mail: Quetflutes@earthlink.net
Representative to INAFA: Guillermo Martinez

Sequoia Flute Circle of Central California
Contact Person: Larry Callan
1128 North Noyes Court
Visalia, CA 93291
Phone: 559-636-0723
E-mail: larryc@cos.edu
Representative to INAFA: Larry Callan

Colorado:

Pikes Peak Flute Circle
Contact Person: Clarence Sproul
810 Big Valley Drive
Colorado Springs, CO 80919
Phone: 719-591-2922
E-mail: CSproulcd@email.msn.com
Representative to INAFA: Clarence Sproul

Connecticut:

Connecticut Native American Flute Circle
Contact Person: Malcolm Shute
43 Westland Avenue
West Hartford, CT 06107
Phone: 860-561-3140
E-mail: macshute2@AOL.COM
Representative to INAFA: Malcolm Shute

Florida:

Florida Flute Circle
Contact Person: Dock Green
4850 Knights Loop
Plant City, FL 33565
Phone: 813-754-8990
E-mail: slvhawk@AOL.COM
Representative to INAFA: Nancy Abosaid

Emerald Coast Flute Circle
Contact Person: Jim Conley
500 Gulf Shore Drive, #422
Destin, FL 32541
Phone: 850-654-5650
E-mail: jim-n-e@cox.net
Representative to INAFA: Jim Conley

Indian River Flute Circle
Contact Person: Mike Knight
6695 Cairo Road
Port St. John, FL 32927
Phone: 321-639-3561
E-mail: mjknight@cfl.rr.com
http://groups.yahoo.com/group/flutecircle/
Representative to INAFA: Mike Knight

Central Florida Flute Circle
Contact Person: Dock Green
4850 Knights Loop
Plant City, FL 33565
Phone: 813-754-8990
E-mail: slvhawk@AOL.COM
Representative to INAFA: Dock Green

Georgia:

Georgia Flute Circle
Contact Person: Cecelia Turbyville
3050 Margaret Mitchell Drive, #5
Atlanta, GA 30327
Phone: 404-352-5340
E-mail: cecelia@mindspring.com
Representative to INAFA: Cecelia Turbyville

Nacoochee Heartwind Flute Circle
Contact Person: Dana Ross
1435 Boggs Road, #403
Duluth, GA 30096
Phone: 678-380-8502
E-mail: oskanankubi@earthlink.net
Representative to INAFA: Dana Ross

Idaho:

Idaho Flute Circle
Contact Person: Joel Shaber
1006 Ironside Drive
Boise, ID 83706
Phone: 208-344-7514
E-mail: jlshaber@AOL.COM
Representative to INAFA: Joel Shaber

Illinois:

Central Illinois Native American Flute Circle
Contact Person: Terry Travis
3321 Blueberry Lane
Springfield, IL 62707-8253
Phone: 217-546-0029
E-mail: ttravis@springnet1.com
Representative to INAFA: Terry Travis

Chicago Native Flutes Circle
Contact Person: Diane Willis
2226 Wilmette Avenue
Wilmette, IL 60091
Phone: 847-251-7270
E-mail: DocFlute@gerf.org
Representative to INAFA: Diane Willis

Indiana:

Indiana Flute Circle
Contact Person: Gary Cope
2742 South Manker Street
Indianapolis, IN 46203
Phone: 317-780-9048
E-mail: gwcope@earthlink.net
http://www.indianaflutecircle.com
Representative to INAFA: Gary Cope

Iowa:

Spirithawk Flute Circle of Iowa
Contact Person: David Gudith
P.O. Box 124
Sigourney, IA 52591
Phone: 641-622-3485
Representative to INAFA: David Gudith

Kansas:

Kansas City-Area Flute Circle
Contact Person: Jim Curley
11200 Johnson Drive
Shawnee, KS 66203
Phone: 913-962-9711
E-mail: JCurley171@AOL.COM
http://www.mountainmusicshoppe.com
Representative to INAFA: Jim Curley

Kentucky:
Circle of Friends Flute Circle
Contact Person: Kimble Howard
1808 Lauderdale Road
Louisville, KY 40205
Phone: 502-459-4892
E-mail: Kimble@earthlink.net
Representative to INAFA: Kimble Howard

Louisiana:
Native American Flute Circle of Louisiana
Contact Person: Stephen Twohawks Reed
13251 North Ridge Avenue
Walker, LA 70785
E-mail: twohawks@eatel.net
Representative to INAFA: Stephen Twohawks Reed

Maine:
Maine Flute Circle
Contact Person: Laura Lee Perkins
P.O. Box 37
Searsport, ME 04974-0037
Phone/Fax: 207-548-6751
E-mail: whiteowlflutes@prexar.com
Representative to INAFA: Laura Lee Perkins

Maryland:
Maryland Flute Circle
Contact Person: Robert Willasch
P.O. Box 4251
Timonium, MD 21094-4251
Phone: 410-252-0368
E-mail: BobF64@AOL.COM
http://users.erols.com/brddwolf/mdflutecircle.html
Representative to INAFA: Robert Willasch

Potomac Flute Circle
Contact Person: Dr. Ron Warren
13916 Overton Lane
Silver Spring, MD 20904
Phone: 301-879-2773
E-mail: RWMuz@AOL.COM
Representative to INAFA: Dr. Ron Warren

Massachusetts:
Woodlands Flute Circle
Contact Person: Geoffrey Evans [Running Bear]
86 Boon Road
Stow, MA 01775
Phone: 978-567-8822
E-mail: northbear@attbi.com
Representative to INAFA: Geoffrey Evans

Michigan:
Chippewa Valley Flute Circle
Contact: John Sarantos
1416 Haley Street
Midland, MI 48640
E-mail: jsarantos@earthlink.net
Representative to INAFA: John Sarantos

Minnesota:
Ten Thousand Lakes Flute Circle
Contact Person: Bobb Fantauzzo
5501 Harriet Avenue South
Minneapolis, MN 55419
Phone: 612-823-5443
E-mail: bobbfan@excite.com
Representative to INAFA: Bobb Fantauzzo

Missouri:
St. Louis Flute Circle
Contact Person: Mark Holland
P.O. Box 19735
St. Louis, MO 63144
E-mail: achild@cedarnsagemusic.com
http://www.cedarnsagemusic.com
Representative to INAFA: Mark Holland

New Jersey:
Turtle Island Flute Circle
Contact Person: Jan Kirlew
P.O. Box 72
Lebanon, NJ 08833
E-mail: jkirlew@att.net
Representative to INAFA: Jan Kirlew

New Mexico:
Southwest New Mexico Flute Circle
Contact Person: Michael Kunz
P.O. Box 657
Silver City, NM 88062
Phone: 505-534-8536
Representative to INAFA: Michael Kunz

New York:
Unawat Island Flute Circle
Contact Person: Eric P. Marczak
422 Beebe Road
Delanson, NY 12053
Phone: 518-872-9324
E-mail: epm03@hotmail.com
http://www.geocities.com/whistleworld
Representative to INAFA: Eric P. Marczak

Spirit of the Wind Flute Circle
Contact Person: Dr. L.J. Baylis
P.O. Box 575
Findley Lake, NY 14736
Phone: 716-769-7759
E-mail: tatetopa@AOL.COM
Representative to INAFA: Dr. L.J. Baylis

North Carolina:
Carolinas Flute Circle
Contact Person: George Weir
4227 Country Lane
Charlotte, NC 28270
Phone: 704-708-4211
E-mail: gweir@carolina.rr.com
Representative to INAFA: Sharon Sigmon

Uwharrie Native American Flute Circle
Contact Person: Kathi Lukens
3444 Hillsdale Court
Asheboro, NC 27205
Phone: 336-625-2190
E-mail: kathi_lukens@vfc.com
http://facstaff.gborocollege.edu/llambert/flutes
Representative to INAFA: Kathi Lukens

Ohio:

Southwest Ohio Flute Circle
Contact Person: Franchot Ballinger
Phone: 513-871-0783
Representative to INAFA: Franchot Ballinger

Northeast Ohio Flute Circle
Contact Person: Carla Holtz
8598 Whippoorwill Road
Ravenna, OH 44266-8507
Phone: 330-654-3762
E-mail: whiprwll@neosplice.com
Representative to INAFA: Carla Holtz

Oklahoma:

Oklahoma Native American Flute Society
Contact Person: Paula Conlon
500 West Boyd, Room 138
Norman, OK 73019
Phone: 405-325-1431
E-mail: pconlon@ou.edu
http://www.paulaconlon.com
Representative to INAFA: Paula Conlon

Oregon:

Oregon Flute Circle
Contact Person: Sherrie Kuhl
26746 Powell Road
Eugene, OR 97405
Phone: 541-344-7917
E-mail: gskuhl@televar.com
Representative to INAFA: Sherrie Kuhl

Cascadia Flute Circle
Contact Person: Ellen Saunders
P.O. Box 5035
Manning, OR 97125
Phone: 503-324-9320
E-mail: Aldriga@AOL.COM
Representative to INAFA: Ellen Saunders

Pennsylvania:

Flute Circle of Southwestern Pennsylvania
Contact Person: Raymond Barley
341-TE Oakville Drive
Pittsburgh, PA 15204-4326
Phone: 412-922-8931
E-mail: MusicBar-WO2C@att.net
Representative to INAFA: Raymond Barley

Dreamcatcher Flute Circle
Contact Person: Scott Edwards
3452 Pennell Road
Aston, PA 19014
Phone: 610-497-9453
E-mail: scott@warriormagician.com
http://www.warriormagician.com/dreamcatcher
Representative to INAFA: Scott Edwards

Rhode Island:

Rhode Island Flute Circle
Contact Person: George Penedo
72 Hawthorne Avenue
Cranston, RI 02910
Phone: 401-941-0718
E-mail: georgepen@AOL.COM
Representative to INAFA: Steve Bliven

Texas:

Heart of the Cedar Flute Circle
Contact Person: Debbie Garner
1605 Monterrey Drive
Garland, TX 75042
Phone: 972-276-6960
E-mail: debbie.garner@verizon.net
Representative to INAFA: Debbie Garner

Heart of Texas Native American Flute Circle
Contact Person: Clark Musgrove
202 Elm Forest Loop
Cedar Creek, TX 78612
Phone: 512-303-1698
E-mail: cmusgrov@ipsofacto.com
Representative to INAFA: Clark Musgrove

Armadillo Flute Society
Contact Person: Bill Tucker
701 Elm Street
Dallas, TX 75228
Phone: 214-860-2360
E-mail: btucker@dcccd.edu
Representative to INAFA: Bill Tucker

Utah:

EarthSong Native American Flute Circle
Contact Person: Wm. Scott Francis
518 East 4500 South #A
Salt Lake City, UT 84117
Phone: 801-277-8312
E-mail: scottfrancis@earthlink.net
Representative to INAFA: Wm. Scott Francis

Washington:

Washington Flute Circle
Contact Person: James Marshall
321 Farallone Avenue
Fircrest, WA 98466
Phone: 253-460-2716
E-mail: lowellirish@yahoo.com
http://www.zadjik.com/nafc/index.html
Representative to INAFA: Wayne McCleskey

Wisconsin:

Central Wisconsin Flute Circle
Contact Person: Tom Gustin
500 Sherman Avenue
Stevens Point, WI 54481
Phone: 715-343-0665
E-mail: trmegustin@charter.net
Representative to INAFA: Tom Gustin

Clear Water Flute Circle
Contact Person: Jane Wolf
126 South Barstow
Eau Claire, WI 54701
Phone: 715-832-3055
Representative to INAFA: Judy Willink

Madison Four Lakes Flute Circle
Contact Person: Elliot Napp
1240 Drake Street, #2
Madison, WI 53715
Phone: 608-251-6974
E-mail: enapp@meriter.com

International:

Dutch/Belgium Native American Flute Circle
Contact Person: Hans van Gurp
Koepeldwarsstraat 6
4611 JV Bergen op Zoom
The Netherlands
E-mail: Gurpie@hotmail.com

Andean Native American Flute Circle
Contact Person: Kike Pinto
Taki Andean Music Museum
Hatunrumiyoq 487-5
Cusco, Peru
E-mail: killincho@yahoo.com

Appendix F

Building Your Own Native American Flute

For many people, the option of flute building is born of necessity; for others, it is simply to satisfy some curiosity. For craft persons, flute building is simply an extension of already-acquired skills. For many other individuals, creating a flute is a natural path of satisfaction to play an instrument created by one's own hand. For those who are compelled to build their own flute, a flute kit is a practical beginning point in the process, unless you are an experienced wood worker.

Important: Before beginning any building project, you need to be informed of the hazards of wood dusts and adequate ventilation and/or respiratory protection. The dust of many woods can be toxic; therefore, please protect your health by undertaking research in order to be informed about wood. One of the Web sites that provides valuable information on this subject is as follows: www.riparia.org/toxic woods.htm

Books and Videos

The "Creating Series" by Lew Paxton Price. Highly detailed booklets available from the author at: Lew Paxton Price, P.O. Box 88, Garden Valley, CA, 95633; Phone: 530-333-9470. The available books are as follows: *Creating and Using Grandfathers Flute*, *Creating and Using the Native American Concert Flute*, *Creating and Using the Native American Love Flute*, *Creating and Using Older Native American Flutes*, *Creating and Using Smaller Native American Flutes*, *Creating and Using the Largest Native American Flutes*, and *Creating and Using Very Small Native American Flutes*.

Crafting the Native American Love Flute by Jim Adams. This is an e-Book available through the Proud Tradition Art Works Web site. Detailed instructions with numerous pictures and illustrations are within this source. Web site: www.cedarsongflutes.com

Fluteshop: A Guide to Crafting the Native American Style Flute by Russell A. Wolf. This title is available from the author at: Russell Wolf, 1945 Helen Lane, Lewisville, TX 75067 Phone: 972-221-5879; E-mail: wolf@airmail.net

The Complete How-To Book of Indiancraft by W. Ben Hunt. This book is published by the Macmillan Publishing Company. Published in 1933, this is the oldest published "contemporary" design guide.

Voices of Native America, Instruments and Music by Douglas Spotted Eagle. This is available through Eagle's View Publishing Company, 6756 North Fork Road, Liberty, UT 84310.

Crafting Your Own Native American Flute with Lee Lacroix. Video includes a full-scale drawing. Contact: Lee Lacroix at 1-800-339-3902; www.echoespast.com/index.html

Heartwood Flutes Presents Working With the Heart in the Wood. This is a two-part flute building instructional video by Raymond RedFeather: 1-719-742-5781; www.heartwoodflutes.com

Kits Sources

Following Generations Music, P.O. Box 787, Sisters, OR, 97759; Phone: 503-789-2831; www.stroudflutes.com

Butch Hall Flutes, P.O. Box 333, Weatherford, TX, 76086; Phone: 817-596-8155; www.butchhallflutes.com

Stellar Musical Products, E-2030 Phillips Lake Loop, Shelton, WA, 98584; Phone: 1-888-427-8850; www.stellarflutes.com

White Deer Indian Traders, Wisconsin; Phone: 715-344-9217; E-mail: cjgduke@coredcs.com

Appendix G

Flute Builders

I believe that the following list of Native American flute builders for both Canada and the United States is reasonably current at the time it was compiled in advance for this third edition. The list represents all of the builders, known to me, who sell directly to individual flute buyers. A few flute builders have chosen not to respond to our inquiries and a few others have specifically requested that they not be listed. Omissions are accidental and not in any way intentional. This listing, due to limited available space, does not include the many retail stores that carry many of these builders' products, as well as the inventory of others who may not sell directly to individual purchasers.

The number of individual flute makers considerably exceeds our limited collection of flutes, thus **the presence of these builders should not necessarily be construed to be an endorsement by either the author, the editor, or the publisher**. This listing is strictly offered as a courtesy to all known flute builders and as an aid to those seeking a flute. For the flute buyer, the best choice is to be able to play the flute before purchasing. In the absence of that option, the next best route is to try and do business with a builder who will allow you to return the flute if you are not satisfied with the scale and tone quality. [See the flute hygiene discussion in the "Flute Care" chapter.]

Like almost any other consumer product, you will find a wide range of pricing. Sometimes the reasons appear to be obvious and sometimes they do not. There are many variables that influence the price of a flute, such as: wood cost, as many of the woods used can be rather exotic; whether the flute is made from one or two pieces of wood; the degree to which power equipment is used in place of hand tools; the total amount of labor invested; shop costs; advertising costs; and many other expenses that you might not think of like the gas for the car to drive to purchase raw materials and attend "trade" shows, lodging costs while traveling to shows, cost of maintaining Web sites, and the cost of telephones and FAX machines.

Building a Native American flute is a skilled task and each builder should be respected for his or her commitment to market the products of their own labor. I suspect that, more often than not, the whole effort for many builders is simply a labor of love and that they must maintain a "day" job in order to support both their families and their flute building commitment.

Having said that, I have personal experience from my own travels and the purchases of friends that there are some builders in existence whose products might better serve as wall hangers rather than a musical instrument. Hopefully, the market place will weed this small minority out of business or force them to correct their poor practices. It is difficult to anticipate this problem, but you can protect yourself by requesting up front and in writing a guarantee from the builder for any mail order purchases. Insist that you be allowed to return the flute if you are not satisfied for a full refund, minus shipping and handling.

I am often asked what is the best flute for a person to purchase. Amateur astronomers have a short answer for similar questions in their field that is also applicable for a Native American flute purchase. The best telescope is the one that gets used! This is also true for flutes. If it sounds "right" and warm when you blow through the pointy end, then it will most likely be the flute that you use the most. Studying the chapter dealing with instrument key prior to a purchase will be helpful, as well.

One last caution: If someone tells you to avoid the flutes of a certain builder or a specific model of a builder, be sure and ask at least two others for their opinion before firming up a judgment. As the saying goes - "beauty is in the eye of the beholder." This is true for not only the appearance of the instrument but for the quality of the sound that it produces. Personally, I have never met a flute that I did not like, including a few wall hangers, provided that they make a reasonable sound. I have several six-hole flutes that are effectively really only three hole flutes, yet I find that each of them still has many songs to sing.

Alabama

James R. Gilliland
P.O. Box 200
Madison, AL 35758
Phone: 256-971-1518
jgflutes@yahoo.com

Dan White
Whitepath Flutes
296 Country Road, #510
Selma, AL 36701
Phone: 334-875-1983
www.whitepathflutes.tripod.com

Arkansas

Rick Heller
Beech Creek Studio
HC 33 Box 57
Pettigrew, AR 72752
Phone: 1-888-561-5585
www.rickhellerflutes.com

Nev Autrey
Wholesole Dealer Inquiries
Route #1, Box 198A
Ash Flat, AR 72513
poorfolk@centuryinter.net

Paul Pitt
Coyote Clay Flutes
P.O. Box, 1253 Harding University
Searcy, AR 72149
Phone: 501-268-1178
www.geocities.com/coyoteclay

Arizona

Alex Maldonado
5536 East San Angelo
Gladalupe, AZ 85283
Phone: 480-839-3028
maldonadoart@AOL.COM

Terry Pendergrass
932 East 6th Place
Mesa, AZ 85203
Phone: 602-610-2617

E.D. Powell
1429 West Morrow Drive
Phoenix, AZ 85027
Phone: 602-869-0355
www.cache.net/flute/

Leland Wach
Trader Lee Flutes
11001 East Grove Street
Apache Junction, AZ 85208
Phone: 602-984-5820
traderlee@gtcinternet.com

Lee LaCroix
Echoes Past
P.O. Box 1656
Oracle, AZ 85623
Phone: 1-800-339-3902
www.echoespast.com

J.P. Gomez
Heartsong Flutes
P.O. Box 2653
Sedona, AZ 86339
Phone: 928-300-4815
www.heartsongflutes.com

Odell Borg
High Spirits Music
P.O. Box 522
Patagonia, AZ 85624
Phone: 1-800-394-1523
www.highspirits.com

Michael Gulino
Moonlight Creek Flutes
11002 East Beck Lane
Scottsdale, AZ 85259
Phone: 480-515-9121
www.moonlightcreek.com

Jonah Thompson
Red Hand Studio
2019 North 50th Street, #4
Phoenix, AZ 85008
Phone: 602-275-6496

Larry "Matoska" Perry
White Bear Flutes-n-Stuff
512 West 1st Ave
Mesa, AZ 85210
Phone: 480-615-6737
www.whitebearflute.com

Pat Haran
1001 East Griswold Road, Lot #11
Phoenix, AZ 85020
Phone: 602-944-7717
haran14@home.com

California

Guillermo Martinez
Quetzacoatl
3801 Park View Lane, #14A
Irvine, CA 92612
Phone: 949-653-9989

Steffan Heydon
Two Towers Flutes
1705 San Ramon Rd.
Atascadero, CA 93422
Phone: 805-461-9405
www.twotowers.com

Wally Johnson
Ogis Flutes
P.O. Box 9717
Berkeley, CA 94709
Phone: 510-527-7673
Ogisflutes@AOL.COM

Ed "Sky" Walkingstik
Walkingstik-Man-Alone
P.O. Box 209
Canyon, CA 94616-0209
Phone: 916-334-8308
skyflute@AOL.COM

Stan Coslow
Wind Spirit Flutes
P.O. Box 8363
Woodland, CA 95776
Phone: 707-648-1009
www.windspiritflutes.com

Lew Paxton Price
P.O. Box 88
Garden Valley, CA 95633
Phone: 916-333-9470

Stephen and Vicki DeRuby
Love Flutes
P.O. Box 9307
San Diego, CA 92169-0307
Phone: 1-800-4-FLUTES
www.nativeloveflutes.com

Rick Bell
PVC Flute Kits
530 Prospect Avenue
South Pasadena, CA 91030
Phone: 626-403-5973
71574.470@compuserve.com

Bill Neal "Elk Whistle"
White Path Music
PMB 225, 305 N. Second Ave.
Upland, CA 91786-6028
Phone: 909-949-9792
www.whitepathmusic.com

Geoffrey Ellis
Earth Tone Flutes
P.O. Box 2507
McKinleyville, CA 95519
Phone: 707-839-9343
www.earthtoneflutes.com

Marvin Yazzie
Native American Flutes
24182 Madole Drive
Moreno Valley, CA 92557
Phone: 909-924-0926
www.yazzieflutes.com

Igor E. Sedor
Echo Quest
4385 West 138th Street, #E
Hawthorne, CA 90250
Phone: 310-644-8478

Bill Gould
AHoKEN
550 Industrial Way, Suite B
Fallbrook, CA 92028
Phone: 760-723-7144
www.AHOKEN.com

Phil Wick
Marmot Whistle Works
15752 Del Prado Drive
Hacienda Heights, CA 91745
Phone: 626-330-7749

Dr. Oliver W. Jones, Jr.
Wild Horse Mountain Flutes
8635 Cliffridge Avenue
La Jolla, CA 92037
Phone: 858-453-0201
www.wildhorsemtnflutes.com

Ron Eakins
Wildlife Carvings & Flutes
14845 Moccasin Street
La Puente, CA 91744
Phone: 626-333-3702
E-mail: carvalot@gte.net

Mark Brajevich
Ckenmark Designs
26100 Newport Road, A-12
Menefee, CA 92584
Phone: 909-679-2131
www.ckenmark.com

Mark Devine
Spiritsong Crafts & Trading
2776 Helen Street, A
Redding, CA 96002
Phone: 530-226-9784
E-mail: SpirtSongCrafts@AOL.COM

Darwin Forster
North American Flutes
6124 Wasson Lane
Sacramento, CA 95841
Phone: 916-332-2369
www.darwinflutes.com

Ted Smith
4129 Fruita Court
Sacramento, CA 95838
Phone: 916-923-2412
E-mail: tsmith8971@AOL.COM

W. Keith Park Deborah Wynsen
Wajo Woodland Creations
30751 Paseo El Arco
San Juan Capistrano, CA 92675
Phone: 949-481-1457
www.wajocreations.com

Colorado

Larry Spieler
'Chris Ti Coom' Flutes
13514 Wyandot Street
Westminster, CO 80234
Phone: 1-800-617-7879
www.christicoom.com

Raymond RedFeather
Heartwood Flutes
P.O. Box 297
LaVeta, CO 81055
Phone: 719-742-5781
www.heartwoodflutes.com

Tiquose Rivera
Firesky Flutes
7019 Burnt Mill Road
Beulah, CO 81023
Phone: 719-495-3109
E-mail: tiquose@fone.net

Jan Pickard
Compass Rose-PVC Flutes
P.O. Box 1562
Broomfield, CO 80038-1562
Phone: 393-949-8159
E-mail: compassroseevents@yahoo.com

Jim Taylor
292 Washington Avenue
Nunn, CO 80648
Phone: 970-897-2303
www.pawnee.com/flutes

Connecticut

Malcolm C. Shute, Jr.
Foxhead Wood Flutes
43 Westland Avenue
West Hartford, CT 06107
Phone: 860-561-3140
E-mail: macshute2@AOL.COM

Jim Adams
Proud Tradition Art Works
329 South Windham Road
Willimantic, CT 06226
Phone: 860-456-8648
www.cedarsongflutes.com

Florida

Sonny Nevaquaya
Nevaquaya Flutes
6340 NW 34th Strett
Hollywood, FL 33024
Phone: 954-322-6196

Billy Whitefox
American Indian Creations
1110 West 10th Court
Panama City, FL 32401
Phone: 850-784-1169
E-mail: LCRT@earthlink.net

Michael Graham Allen
Coyote Oldman Music
34 North Brevard Avenue
Cocoa Beach, FL 32931
Phone: 321-868-4005
www.coyoteoldman.com

Georgia

Lee Entrekin
Dreamwind Flutes
1427 High Point Place, NE
Atlanta, GA 30306-3200
Phone: 404-876-3911
E-mail: harpo@mindspring.com

Johnny Chattin
220 Warwick Street
Dahlonega, GA 30533
Phone: 706-864-5081
E-mail: tilel@alltel.net

Hawaii

Troy DeRoche
Song Stick Native American Flutes
P.O. Box 247
Hawi, HI 96719-0247
www.songstick.com

Iowa

Gary L. Parker
Tall Bear Flutes
106 North Elm Street
Glenwood, IA 51534
Phone: 712-527-1831
E-mail: gparker45@earthlink.net

Idaho

Joel Shaber
1006 Ironside Drive
Boise, ID 83706
Phone: 208-344-7514
JLShaber@AOL.COM

Illinois

Don Eagle Turtle
Eagle Turtle Flutes
13285 Country Hwy 12
Venedy, IL 62214
Phone: 618-824-6465
E-mail: woodshop@egyptian.net

Massachusetts

Barry D. Higgins
White Crow Flutes
111 Birch Street
Greenfield, MA 01301-1440
Phone: 413-774-5223
www.whitecrowflutes.com

Rick Roberts
Starseed Creations
P.O. Box 145
Whitinsville, MA 01588
Phone: 508-234-4126
www.starseedcreations.com

Maine

Tim Spotted Wolf
Turtle Island Music Company
RR 3, Box 2158
Bridgton, ME 04009
Phone: 207-647-4449
www.loveflutes.com

Hawk Henries
Hawk Henries Flutes
RR1, Box 171
East Sullivan, ME 04607
Phone: 207-422-2054
E-mail: henriesclan@hotmail.com

Eric Keppel
Earthsounds Music Company
31 Old Country Road
Winterport, ME 04496
Phone: 207-223-5288
www.earthsounds.com

Ken Green
White Owl Creations
PO Box 37 - 29 Old Route One
Searsport, ME 04974
Phone: 207-548-6751
E-mail: whiteowlflutes@prexar.com

Michigan

Lee Christiansen
Forest Song Flutes
617 Country Line Road W., #31
Manistee, MI 49660
Phone: 231-723-4392

Missouri

Jerry and Lisa Fretwell
Fretwell Flutes
Rt. 1, Box 73R
Everton, MO 65646
Phone: 417-535-6032
www.fretwellflutes.com

Jim and Toy Lane
JTL Flutes
411 Osceola Road
Fordland, MO 65652
Phone: 471-634-4071
E-mail: jimtoy@prodigy.net

Jeff King
Four Winds walking
Rt. 1, Box 51
Preston, MO 65732
Phone: 417-722-4558
www.fourwindswalking.com

Montana

Ken Light
Amon Olorin Flutes
492 Lemlama Lane
Arlee, MT 59821
Phone: 406-726-3353
www.aoflutes.com

Pete Formaz
Lone Eagle Flutes
P.O. Box 368
East Helena, MT 59635
Phone: 406-227-8317
E-mail: formaz@uswest.net

Chris Gochis
Hollowed Branch Flutes
116 North Foothills
Ronan, MT 59864
Phone: 406-676-4991
www.ronan.net/~gochis

Dave Fields
Wolf Spirit Flutes
11810 Chumrau Loop
Missoula, MT 59802
Phone: 406-258-6911
E-mail: lakotawolf@montana.com

Nebraska

Colyn Petersen
Woodland Voices Flutes
2202 South 11th Street
Omaha, NE 68108
Phone: 402-932-6894
www.woodlandvoices.com

New Hampshire

Gerry Ouellette
Raven Song Flutes
P.O. Box 955
Plymouth, NH 03264
Phone: 1-800-924-7414
www.aaaravensongflutes.com

New York

Roy Peters
Storyteller Flutes
5530 Sand Hill Road
Verona, NY 13478
Phone: 315-361-8372
www.storytellerflutes.com

North Carolina

Tom Minton
774 Old Toll Circle
Black Mountain, NC 28711
Phone: 828-669-5357

Jack B. Thomas
Silver Song Flutes
112 West Ketchie Street
China Grove, NC 28023
Phone: 704-857-3626
jacthomas@vnet.net

David Hall
Thunderbird Flutes
107 Volk Drive
Castle Hayne, NC 28429
Phone: 910-675-8850
www.thunderbirdflutes.com

Peter Motika
Total Freedom Flutes
9390 Walnut Creek Road
Marshall, NC 28753
Phone: 828-656-2323
www.petermotika.com

Geri LittleJohn
Woodsong Flutes
4134 Batcave Road
Old Fort, NC 28762

Hawk Hurst
2511 Bald Fork Road
Todd, NC 28684
Phone: 336-385-1402
E-mail: info@HawkHurstFlutes.com

Craig Arey
Present Moment Flutes
1926 Mountain Rd
Walnut Cove, NC 27052
Phone: 336-994-2493
E-mail: Areytree@cs.com

Lee Johnson
Kamama Spirit Flutes
www.kamamaspirit.com

Ohio

Mike Smallridge
Searching Bear Flutes
3792 Herriff Road
Ravenna, OH 44266
Phone: 330-296-7413
www.searchingbearflutes.com

Billy Faluski
Woodpecker Creations
1330 Dallas Street
Valley City, OH 44280
Phone: 330-958-0623
E-mail: crowbeak@yahoo.com

Oklahoma

Terry Frazier
Frazier's Sculpture
4216 Lamar Drive
Del City, OK 73115
Phone: 405-677-9404
E-mail: lightn16@AOL.COM

Oregon

Jeff Calavan
Laughing Mallard Company
90944 Leashore Drive
Vida, OR 97488
Phone: 1-888-88-FLUTE
www.customflutes.com

Gary Kuhl
Spirit Bird Flutes
26746 Powell Road
Eugene, OR 97405
Phone: 541-344-7917
E-mail: gskuhl@televar.com

Scott E. Loomis
Wind's Song Flutes
804 Covered Bridge Road
Rogue River, OR 97537
Phone: 541-582-0325
www.loomisflute.com

Ward Stroud
Following Generations Music
P.O. Box 787
Sisters, OR 97759
Phone: 541-504-0381
www.stroudflutes.com

Charles Littleleaf
Ancient Vision Flutes
P.O. Box 1225
Warm Sprints, OR 97761
Phone: 541-553-1662
www.nativeindianflutes.com

Ed Hrebec
Spirit of the Woods Flutes
2360 June Street
Hood River, OR 97031
Phone: 1-800-236-0406
www.spiritofthewoodsflutes.com

Jim and Robin McDonald
Eagle Song Flutes
P.O. Box 65 - 1095 South Hwy. 101
Rockaway Beach, OR 97136
Phone: 1-503-355-8300
www.nativeflutes.com

South Carolina

John D. Davis
The Chauga River Whittler
293 Davis Drive
Westminster, SC 29693-0319
Phone: 864-647-5243
chaugawhittler@earthlink.net

Bill Bristow
832 Hickory Grove Road
Bennettsville, SC 29512
Phone: 843-479-5041
E-mail: Bullmastiffdog@webtv.net

Tennesee

Danny Bigay and Kay LittleJohn
Mountain Spirit Flutes
490 Viking Mountain Road
Greeneville, TN 37743
Phone: 423-638-5750
www.mountainspiritflutes.com

Texas

Sleeping Bear
Earth Rhythms
16807 Village Oak Loop
Austin, TX 78717
Phone: 512-689-1116
www.bhw.com/earthrhythms

Butch and Laura Hall
Native American Flutes
P.O. Box 333
Weatherford, TX 76086-0333
Phone: 817-596-8155
www.butchhallflutes.com

William Gutierrez
Native American Flutes
4900 Pecan Hill
Mckinney, TX 75070
Phone: 972-540-6333
www.williamgutierrez.com

Terry A. Austin
Kokopelli Flutes
3128 Northeast Drive
Wichita Falls, TX 76305
Phone: 940-716-0901
www.kokopelliflutes.com

Utah

Richard Burdick
Native Heart
90 East 200 South
Orangeville, UT 84537
Phone: 435-748-2913
www.eaze.com/nativeheart/

Gordon Johnson
Wasatch Winds
P.O. Box 772
Morgan, UT 84050
E-mail: wasatchwinds@juno.com

Virginia

Leonard McGann
Lone Crow Flutes
2534 Difficult Creek Road
Bedford, VA 24523
Phone: 540-297-6077
www.lonecrowflutes.com

Carl Running Deer
RD Enterprises
P.O. Box 241
Berryville, VA 22611-0241
Phone: 810-592-4141
www.Running-Deer.com

Vermont

Kai Mayberger
White River Drum Works
P.O. Box 151
Bridgewater, VT 05034
Phone: 802-672-3055
www.whiteravendrums.com

Zacciah Blackburn
Sunreed Instruments
P.O. Box 389
220 Hidden Glen Road
Ascutney, VT 05030
Phone: 802-674-9585
www.sunreed.com

Washington

Dennis Pardee
Bear Paw Flutes
P.O. Box 783
Mukilteo, WA 98275
Phone: 425-355-1075
www.bearpawflutes.com

Tom and Matt Stewart
Stellar Musical Products
E. 2030 Phillips Lake Loop
Shelton, WA 98584
Phone: 1-888-427-8850
www.stellarflutes.com

Brad Sanders
Walking Wind Flutes
P.O. Box 2661
Westport, WA 98595
Phone: 360-268-2517
E-mail: Avalon@olynet.com

Wisconsin

Tom Gustin
The Flutemaker
500 Sherman Avenue
Stevens Point, WI 54481
Phone: 715-343-0665
E-mail: trgustin@coredcs.com

Conrad Glodowski
White Deer Indian Traders
1834 Red Pine Lane
Stevens Points, WI 54481
Phone: 715-344-9217
E-mail: cjgduke@coredcs.com

Rick Sampson
Sampson Woodland Flutes
W22747 Fox Coulee Lane
Galesville, WI 54630
Phone: 608-539-2039
www.sampsonwoodlandflutes.com

Louis Webster
106 Soth Platten
Green Bay, WI 54303
Phone: 920-497-1227
E-mail: thelittlebigband@yahoo.com

Australia

Tony and Deb Richards
Spiritwinds Flutes
63 Kewarra Street
Kewarra Beach, QLD 4879
Australia
www.spiritwinds.com.au

Canada

Alain Lauzon
Bezed Flutes
P.O. Box 1360
Alexandria, Ontario KOC-1A0
Canada
Phone: 613-525-4871
www.bezed.com

Spring Shine
Cedar Spirit Flutes
#5 Sunny Day Way
Argenta, BC, Canada
Phone: 250-366-0081
E-mail: webmaster@native-american-flutes.com

Appendix H

Early Windway Design of the Native American Flute

George Catlin was a Pennsylvania attorney whose apparent passion was not the law. Instead, he was intensely interested in painting. Being self-taught, Catlin favored portraits and documentation of the Plains Indians. Between 1832 and 1839, Catlin ventured out among the Plains Indians. During this time, he painted many portraits of the Indians that he encountered, as well as collecting items which the Indians used in their everyday life. In addition to sketching these everyday items, Catlin wrote many detailed notes and letters of his observations and experiences. These were first published in 1844.

In 1832, the American Fur Company launched their steamboat, called the Yellowstone, which was the first boat of its kind to make it up the Missouri River from St. Louis to Fort Union at the mouth of the Yellowstone River. This was a distance of 2,000 miles.

Catlin was on board when the Yellowstone left St. Louis on its maiden voyage. When the steamboat and its passengers reached Fort Pierre at the mouth of the Teton River on the upper Missouri river, Catlin wrote six letters. In these letters, he described the location as being "the heart of the country belonging to the numerous tribe of Sioux or Dahcotas" (Catlin, 1973).

While packing to leave this location, Catlin made drawings of objects that he collected on his journey. Of the dozen objects drawn, one of particular interest is a six-hole flute with an external windway clearly showing the block. There seems to be significant evidence that Catlin obtained this flute from the Sioux. However, there is no definitive documentation as to the flute's specific cultural origin or from whom this instrument was obtained. A line drawing of this flute is below:

Catlin states about this flute:

> "There is yet another wind instrument which I have added to my collection. From its appearance, it seems to have been borrowed, in part, from the civilized world. This is what is often on the frontier called a 'deer-skin flute,' a Winnebago courting flute - 'tsal-eet-quash-to.' It is perforated with holes for the fingers, sometimes for six, at others for three and four, having so many notes with their octaves. These notes are very irregularly graduated, showing clearly that they have very little taste or ear for melody. These instruments are blown in the end, and the sound produced is on the principle of the whistle.
>
> In the vicinity of the upper Mississippi, I often and familiarly heard this instrument, called the Winnebago courting flute. I was credibly informed by traders and others in those regions that the young men of that tribe meet with single success, oftentimes, in wooing their sweethearts with its simple notes which they blow for hours together, and from day to day, from the bank of some stream - some favorite rock or log on which they are seated, near to the wigwam which contains the object of their tender passion.

> Until her soul is touched, and she responds by some welcome signal, that she is ready to repay the young Orpheus for his pains, with the gift of her hand and her heart. How true these representations may have been made, I cannot say, but there certainly must have been some ground for the present cognomen by which it is known in that country." (Catlin, 1973)

Catlin first exhibited his paintings and artifacts in New York in 1837. In late 1839, he sailed with his exhibit to England where he remained for some 31 years before returning to the United States. By 1852, Catlin was on the verge of financial ruin. A wealthy American, Joseph Harrison, Jr., paid off Catlin's debts and took possession of his gallery which included all the paintings and collected artifacts. In 1879, Mrs. Joseph Harrison, Jr., donated the Catlin collection to the Smithsonian.

In a book published in 2002 by W.W. Norton and Company, there is a color photo of a Native American flute with the following description: "Flageolet, Pawnee, circa 1830s, Department of Anthropology, Smithsonian Institution, Gift of Mrs. Joseph Harrison, Jr." (Catlin, 2002). An examination of this color photograph and Catlin's original 1832 line drawing indicates to me that the two may very well be the same instrument. If so, I am skeptical of the Pawnee attribution. In addition, it appears that it was not until 1834 that Catlin apparently ventured into Pawnee territory, in the accompaniment of an expedition of the First Regiment of Mounted Dragoons out of Fort Gibson [close to Tulsa, Oklahoma] (Catlin, 1973). This is in contradiction to the fact that the line drawing was made by Catlin in 1832. Also, in the other writings of Catlin that I have examined, there is no mention of his acquisition of any other Native American flute - just the flute of which he made the line drawing.

ERRATUM – Flute Builders

Because of an error in the merging of databases errors occurred within the Flute Builders Listing. I apologize for any inconvenience that this may cause.

Please Remove the following which were included with errors or in error

Arkansas

Nev Autrey
Ash Flat, AR

Arizona

Terry Pendergrass
Mesa, AZ

Jonah Thompson
Phoenix, AZ

California

Ed "Sky" Walkingstik
Canyon, CA

Stan Coslow
Woodland, CA

Rick Bell
South Pasadena, CA

North Carolina

Tom Minton
Black Mountain, NC

Please Add the following which were omitted in error:

Michigan

Mikann Thompson
Wood Frog Crafts
8641 Brooks Rd
Brown City, MI 48416
810-346-2249
www.mach1audio.com/flute

Texas

Russell Wolf
Wolf Song Flues
1945 Helen Ln
Lewisville, TX 75067
972- 221-5879
wolf@airmail.net

Please Correct the following listings to read:

California

Guillermo Martinez
28691 Modjeska Canyon Road
Modjeska, CA 92626
714-649-3244
Quetflutes@earthlink.net

Australia

Tony Richards
Spirit Winds
61-7-4034-3966
tdr@spiritwinds.com.au
www.spiritwinds.com.au

NOTES

NOTES

WWW.MELBAY.COM

Made in the USA
Lexington, KY
03 May 2017